Caught in Garden of Mechanical Souls

Alice Beauverd

Published by The naughty witch's bookshelf, 2024.

CAUGHT IN GARDEN OF MECHANICAL SOULS

First edition. July 4, 2024.

Copyright © 2024 Alice Beauverd.

ISBN: 979-8230218302

Written by Alice Beauverd.

Caught in Garden of Mechanical Souls

Prologue

Iris's fingers flew over the keyboard, the sound of clattering keys filling the spacious room. The sun streamed in through the large windows, casting a warm glow over the modern, minimalist furniture. The walls were adorned with artwork, a collection of contemporary pieces that Iris had accumulated over the years. The room was a reflection of her: thoughtful, analytical, and put together.

"Come on, Elias, hurry up," she called out, not looking away from the computer screen. "I want to get started on this quest."

Elias, Iris's boyfriend of five years, sat on the couch behind her, tapping away on his laptop. "Just a few more seconds," he replied, his voice low and measured.

This room doubled as an epicenter for gaming adventures. On the screen, Iris's avatar appeared, a male figure with dark hair, yellow eyes, and a tall and slender body. He stood in the virtual world of 'Garden of Mechanical Souls' a TPS set in a robot infested world.

"Finally," Iris muttered, her fingers moving over the keyboard. "Elias, where are you? I don't see you in the game yet."

Elias's avatar appeared beside hers, a muscular figure with short brown hair, brown eyes, and a coat that fluttered in the virtual breeze.

"I'm here," he said, his voice now coming from the speakers."I have to admit, I'm always impressed by how quickly you can get online."

"Practice makes perfect," she replied with a smile, adjusting her posture. "Alright, let's get the others online and start the quest."

From the comfort of his own room, in his flat, Ian sat hunched over, his gaming computer's purring beside him. He was a short man with blond hair and blue eyes, a self-proclaimed geek and otaku. His avatar, a white-haired female with large breasts, pigtails, and a miniskirt, appeared on the screen, his character was the opposite of him in every way.

But that was the beauty of gaming; it allowed you to be anyone or anything you wanted.

"I'm in," he said quietly, his eyes glued to the screen. Ian had always been a bit of a shut-in, but he came alive in the virtual world.

He had a tendency to get too engrossed in his games, often forgetting about real-world commitments. Iris and Elias were used to it by now, often sending him gentle reminders about things like eating and sleeping.

Meanwhile, in a different house, Duncan, a confident and athletic man in his late twenties, finished up his preparations and connected to the game. He was the support, able to do recon and sniping. His avatar, a tall female with short green hair and green eyes appeared next to Ian's. She wore a hunting camouflage suit and held a KSVK 12.7 sniper rifle. Duncan had always been confident in his abilities, both in real life and in the game.

"Hey Duncan, thanks for joining," Iris's voice said through the speakers.

"No problem, I wouldn't miss this quest for anything," he replied, his eyes scanning the virtual landscape.

In another part of town, Astrid, a shy and introverted woman in her mid-twenties, with blonde hair, light blue eyes, and a little extra weight that she struggled with in the real world.,connected to the game. Her avatar appeared in the game as a woman with long blond hair, blue eyes, and a slender body. She wore a bodysuit and boots, she is the fastest among the group.

"Astrid's here," she said softly as her character appeared on the screen.

Iris smiled. "Great! We can begin the quest now."

The friends gathered together, their avatars standing together in the virtual world, ready to take on the challenges that lay ahead.

Iris, as the leader of the group, stood at the front, her avatar's yellow eyes scanning the area for any potential threats. In his hands, he held a Dan Wesson M1911 ACP pistol, its sleek design and matte black finish giving it a sense of elegance and deadliness. It was a weapon that suited her style, simple yet effective. But that wasn't all she had at her disposal. On her avatar's back, he carried a FN P90, a compact and high-powered submachine gun.

Elias stood next to her, in real life and in the game, his character's garb billowed majestically like a

cloak behind him. His weapons, a ruger SR-556 and a Ithaca 37, hung casually. The Ruger SR-556, an AR-15 style rifle, was not only reliable but proved its worth in many battles. While the Ithaca 37, a classic pump action shotgun often used for breaching.

CAUGHT IN GARDEN OF MECHANICAL SOULS

He donned an enormous military-style backpack that was filled to the brim with everything he might possibly require as a protector and guardian. This sturdy, well-equipped backpack served as both a symbol of his dedication to duty and a testament to his readiness to face whatever challenges lay ahead. He also has a big military backpack contenting all he may need for his role a a defender. His battle-worn uniform was adorned with patches and decorations.

To Iris's left stood Ian, his character's long white hair whipping about in the virtual breeze. He carried an M1 Garand Rifle, a classic weapon that held a special significance for him. It was a nod to his appreciation for history. A Astra model 900 and a bayonet strapped to each of his side completed his look. While the M1 Garand was powerful, Ian's true strength lay in his skills as a healer. He could heal allies using sexual acts, a strange particularity to the game, but something that the friends had come to accept and even rely on. With his hands and body, Ian could bring back their fallen comrades, making sure that they could continue the quest.

Duncan's avatar, the tall and green-haired sniper, stood off to the side, She carried upon her back a formidable KSVK 12.7 sniper rifle. Its large caliber and high power made it the perfect weapon for long-range combat. Her secondary weapons, a colt king cobra and a knife, complete the picture of her preparedness. She was dressed in a hunting camo suit, ready to blend into any environment and become one with the shadows.

And finally, standing off to the right was Astrid's character, with her long blond hair and blue eyes. She was dressed in a bodysuit with boots, perfect for fast-paced combat. Her mechanical sword glinted as the sun hit it, The sword was a work of art, crafted with precision and care. It was made of a dark, sleek metal, with intricate designs etched into the blade. The hilt was wrapped in leather, fitting comfortably in Astrid's hand, and the guard was shaped like a pair of wings, giving the weapon an almost ethereal quality. But what truly set the sword apart was its ability to transform. With a simple twist of the hilt, Astrid could change the sword's form, adapting it to any situation. The blade could elongate or shorten, the guard could expand or contract, and the handle could even split into two smaller swords. It was a versatile weapon, perfectly suited to Astrid's quick and agile fighting style. She also has a FN FNP at her hip, and grenades strapped to her belt. Astrid may have been shy and introverted in real life, but in this world, she thrived as an attacker, able to take down enemies with her fast and precise movements.

With the team now complete, Iris couldn't help but steal a glance at each of her friends and allies in this virtual world. They had been playing together for years, and she couldn't imagine a better group to embark on this new quest.

Iris, the analytical leader; Elias, the quiet and thoughtful defender; Ian, the quirky and otaku healer; Duncan, the experienced and confident support; Astrid, the shy and fast-moving attacker. They were a team, united by their shared love of gaming and their desire to explore the vast world of 'Garden of Mechanical Souls'.

As they began to venture out into the robot-infested world, Elias couldn't help but let out a chuckle. "Ian, you really need to do something about your character's appearance," he said, shaking his head.

"What's wrong with it?" Ian asked, defensive. "She's a healer, she needs to be cute!"

Elias rolled his eyes, "Ian, that's not the point. We've got a pretty cohesive aesthetic going on here, and your character is throwing it off. Yours looks like a walking anime convention. And besides, you shouldn't objectify her like that."

Ian let out a laugh, "If I have to stare at her all day, I want her to be cute! Besides, it's just a game."

Duncan cut in, "Actually, Ian, your avatar's appearance can affect the way you play. If you present yourself as a certain type of character, it can subconsciously influence your decision making and behavior in the game."

"Really?" Ian asked, his brows furrowing.

"Yeah," Astrid chimed in from her end. "It's a psychological thing, I think. But I say, if you like how your character looks, then go for it! It's about having fun after all."

Iris chuckled at the banter between her friends, but then she looked at her own avatar, a male figure with dark hair and yellow eyes. She had never given much thought to how her avatar appeared, but as she took in the details of his strong jawline and broad shoulders, she couldn't help but feeling a sense of pride. Her character was anything but cute, he was powerful and commanding.

The group continued their banter as they ventured further. Elias and Ian's friendly bickering was a constant background noise, like a familiar radio station. Astrid was quiet, but the occasional sound of her character's mechanical sword slicing through robots could be heard. Duncan provided commentary, pointing out interesting features in the landscape or offering advice on how to take down certain enemies.

He was always the first to spot a hidden chest or a clue to their next quest. Iris couldn't help but let out a smile as she listened to him, his experience and confidence shone through

in his every action, making him the perfect support. She felt grateful to have him on her team.

"Iris, are you listening?" Elias' voice jolted her out of her thoughts.

"Huh? Sorry, I was just thinking about something."

He chuckled, "Well, if we're going to finish this quest, we need to focus on the task at hand. And right now, it looks like we have a group of robots heading our way."

She frowned, taking in their surroundings. The area was littered with the remains of fallen robots, their metal bodies scattered about like a child's broken toys. In the distance, she could see a group of them approaching, their red eyes glowing ominously in the twilight.

"Alright, everyone, let's get into position," Iris ordered, her voice firm and steady. She quickly began to assess the situation, taking in the layout of the area and identifying potential weak points in the enemy's formation. She pointed towards a pile of rubble on their left flank, indicating where she wanted Elias to fortify their position. "Elias, build a fortification there, and Duncan, can you provide cover from that vantage point?" she directed, gesturing towards the rubble and the tall structures nearby.

As they scrambled to fulfill their roles, Iris couldn't help but feel a thrill run through her. There was something exhilarating about leading her friends into battle, about making split-second decisions that could mean the difference between victory and defeat. Iris had always been a cautious and analytical person in her everyday life, but in this virtual world, she found a freedom that she never knew existed. She was no longer just a 30-something-year-old woman with red hair and green eyes; she was a leader, a decision-maker, a powerful force to be reckoned with.

She watched with satisfaction as Elias began to build a fortification out of debris, his muscular avatar deftly shaping the rubble into a makeshift wall.

Duncan, not far behind, climbed up a tall structure and took aim with his sniper rifle, scanning the area for any signs of danger. Meanwhile, Iris turned to Ian. "Alright, Ian, I need you to go in cover with Elias."

Ian nodded. He quickly moved into position, his character's M1 Garand rifle at the ready.

"Astrid," Iris said, her voice clear and commanding. "I want you to try and take the enemy from behind."

Astrid nodded, her avatar's mechanical sword glinting in the virtual sun. "Right." she said, her voice barely above a whisper.

CAUGHT IN GARDEN OF MECHANICAL SOULS

The group waited in tense silence as the robots drew closer, their metallic footsteps echoing ominously in the air. Iris watched as Astrid crept off to the side, her character's movements swift and silent. She moved like a shadow, blending into the background as she made her way towards the enemy's flank.

Elias finished building the fortification just as the first wave of robots came into view. They were massive, towering over the players like metal giants. They had red eyes that glowed like hot coals, and sharp claws that could tear through steel. Iris's heart pounded in her chest as she watched the robots approach. This was it, the moment they had been waiting for. She took a deep breath and whispered, "Alright, everyone, let's do this."

Duncan, positioned on top of a tall structure, took aim with his KSVK 12.7 sniper rifle. He squeezed the trigger, and the shot rang out, echoing through the virtual world. The bullet hit its mark, taking out one of the robots and sending it sprawling to the ground.

"Nice shot!" Iris called out, her voice filled with excitement.

The other robots, seemingly enraged by the death of their comrade, began to move more rapidly towards them. Their metallic footsteps became louder and faster as they approached. Iris couldn't help but feel a shiver run down her spine. She knew that this was just a game, but the realism of it all was uncanny.

"Elias, hold your position," Iris ordered as she took cover behind the fortification he had built.

The bullets from the robot's guns ricocheted off the makeshift wall, sending sparks flying in every direction. Iris held her position, trusting in Elias's defenses. She raised her pistol, taking aim at a particularly large robot as it approached. She squeezed the trigger, the gun kicking back in her avatar's hand as the shot rang out. The bullet found its mark, flying straight into the robot's head. But the victory was short-lived, as the machine didn't fall. Instead, it emitted a low hum, and its eyes glowed brighter, before launching itself towards the fortification.

Iris quickly retreated behind the fortification, gesturing for Elias and Ian to do the same. The robot crashed into the wall.

Elias, quick to react, grabbed his Ruger SR-556 and began firing at the machine. Ian, not far behind, pulled out his M1 Garand rifle and joined in on the assault. The bullets flew through the air, striking the robot's metal exterior with a loud clang. But the machine seemed unfazed by the damage, continuing its relentless assault on the fortification.

"We need to take it down before it destroys our defenses," Iris shouted over the sound of gunfire. She took aim with her pistol, firing off shot after shot in an attempt to disable the machine.

But the robot was relentless, breaking through their defenses with a shocking force. Iris could hear the sound of debris crumbling around her as the robot continued its assault.

Out of the corner of her eye, she saw Astrid moving in for the kill. The blonde's avatar danced around the robot, dodging and weaving as it swung its arms wildly. With a swift movement, Astrid plunged her mechanical sword into the robot's back, causing it to stumble forward. Iris saw her chance and seized it.

She leapt up from her hiding spot and ran towards the robot, her pistol raised. "Elias! Now!" she shouted, the sound of gunfire growing louder behind her. Elias understood and began to lay down a barrage of covering fire.

Iris could feel her heart pounding in her chest as she closed the distance between herself and the robot. She closed her eyes, took a deep breath, and squeezed the trigger.

The bullet flew through the air, striking the robot's head with a loud clang. The machine froze for a brief moment, before collapsing to the ground with a deafening thud. Iris let out a sigh of relief as she surveyed the damage. The fortification was in shambles, but they had managed to take down the robot.

But their victory was short-lived as they suddenly heard a series of high-pitched beeps coming from all around them. Iris frowned, her eyes scanning the area for any signs of danger. And that's when she saw them - smaller robots, no bigger than a football, equipped with knife, scuttling towards them from every direction.

"What the hell?" Elias muttered, his voice filled with disbelief. "Where did those things come from?"

Iris shook her head, her mind racing as she tried to come up with a plan. "I don't know, but we need to take them down before they overwhelm us," she said, her voice firm and steady.

She raised her pistol, taking aim at one of the smaller robots as it approached.

The bullet found its mark, flying straight into the robot's head and reducing it to a pile of scrap metal.

She could see Elias and Ian exchanging worried glances, their hands tight on their weapons.

The small robots moved quickly, darting in and out of cover with surprising agility. Their small size made them difficult targets.

Iris, Elias, and Ian struggled to hit them, their shots flying wide. But Duncan remained calm, his eyes focused on the swarm of small robots. His weapon, the KSVK 12.7 sniper rifle, was more suited against bigger, stronger opponents. But Duncan knew that it could still be effective against smaller enemies like these.

He exhaled slowly, his breath steadying as he squeezed the trigger. The shot rang out, echoing through the virtual world. One of the smaller robots exploded in a shower of sparks and metal fragments.

Astrid had thrown a grenade at the group, taking out several of them with a satisfying boom. Astrid let out a relieved sigh, her avatar's sword still clutched tightly in her hand.

Iris couldn't help but smile as she watched Astrid, the blonde woman's confidence growing with each successful move. She knew that Astrid struggled with self-doubt in the real world, but in this virtual realm, she transformed into a fierce and powerful warrior.

As they focused their efforts on taking down the swarm of small robots, Iris couldn't help but notice that Ian seemed to be struggling more than the others.

She watched as he fired his M1 Garand rifle, the shots ringing out in quick succession. But his accuracy was lacking, and many of his bullets simply whizzed past the small robots, barely even grazing them.

"Ian, are you alright?" Iris called out, concern etched on her face. "You seem to be having trouble hitting them."

"I'm fine," Ian replied, a hint of frustration in his voice. "It's just these little bastards are so fast, it's hard to get a clear shot."

Elias couldn't help but chuckle at his friend's frustration, "Maybe you should try using a different weapon, Ian." Elias responded, his voice steady and

reassuring as he took aim with his ithaca 37, taking down a small robot.

Ian thought for a moment before shaking his head. "Nah, I love this weapon and I plan to keep using it! I'll just have to get better at using it against these fast little buggers."

But then, as if on cue, one of the

small robots darted out from behind cover and made a beeline for Ian. Without hesitation, Ian raised his M1 Garand rifle and fired off a shot. But the bullet grazed the robot's metal exterior, barely doing any damage. Ian cursed under his breath as he quickly ejected the empty magazine from his M1 Garand rifle, the characteristic "ping" echoing through the virtual world. The little robot let out a high-pitched beep as it continued to move towards Ian, its blade glinting menacingly in the sunlight.

CAUGHT IN GARDEN OF MECHANICAL SOULS

Iris watched in horror as the machine drew closer to Ian, ready to strike at any moment. But before it could land the killing blow, Elias leapt into action. With a roar, he stepped in front of Ian, shielding him with his own body. The robot's blade hit Elias 's avatar with a loud clang, causing him to stumble backwards. But he regained his footing quickly, lifting his Ithaca 37 and firing off a shot. The bullet hit the robot directly, causing it to explode in a shower of sparks and metal fragments.

Elias let out a sigh of relief as he lowered his weapon, a small smile playing at the corners of his lips.

But before he could say anything, Ian's avatar had already stepped forward, his hands glowing with a faint blue light. "Elias, I'm going to heal you," Ian said, as his character place her hands on Elias's avatar's chest.

The light from Ian's character's hands grew brighter, and the air around them seemed to crackle with energy. And then, unexpectedly, their characters' faces moved closer together, and they shared a passionate kiss. It was an intense moment, as Ian's avatar's lips met Elias's with a fiery passion.

Iris couldn't help but watch with wide eyes, her face flushed as she witnessed the intimacy between her two friend's avatar. The sight of their characters wrapped up in each other's arms, their hands exploring each other's bodies, was incredibly arousing.

Ian's avatar, with her large chest pressed against Elias', moved her hips in a slow, sensual rhythm, grinding against him.

As they broke apart, Elias couldn't help but criticize Ian's choice for his character's healing ability. "Ian, I know you love the idea of being able to heal your allies with sexual acts, but don't you think it's a little cheesy? And not to mention, unrealistic."

"But it's so much more fun this way!" Ian protested, pouting."Besides, it's a game! It's supposed to be unrealistic! And let's be real, I'm pretty sure you enjoyed the view,"

Iris couldn't help but laugh at her friends' antics, grateful for the reprieve in the heat of battle. "Alright, enough of that. We still have work to do," she reminded them, gesturing towards the remaining small robots that were still roaming around their vicinity.

Astrid's character continued to run while cutting down the small robots with her mechanical sword. Her avatar was swift and agile, a perfect match for her role as an attacker. She darted around the machines, striking them down one by one, her movements fluid and precise. With each strike, sparks flew into the air, creating a mesmerizing display of light against the darkening sky.

Elias couldn't help but watch in awe as Astrid moved with grace and power, her character's sword slicing through metal with ease.

But the reprieve was short-lived as Iris suddenly called out, "Guys, look out!"

In an instant, the air around them grew heavy, and a low hum echoed through the virtual world. Iris pointed towards a nearby building, where a massive scorpion-like robot was slowly emerging from behind the debris. The machine's sharp pincers snapped menacingly as it surveyed its surroundings.

"What the hell is that thing?" Duncan exclaimed, his voice filled with disbelief.

"It's our quest's objective," Iris replied, her voice grim. "We need to take it down."

The scorpion robot let out a loud roar as it charged towards them, its metallic legs clanking against the ground with every step. Iris couldn't help but feel a shiver of fear run down her spine as she watched the machine draw closer, the way it moved was uncanny, making her heart race as it bore down on them.

The scorpion-like robot was massive, towering over them like a dark omen. Its red eyes glowed with an otherworldly energy, piercing through the twilight like twin stars. Iris knew what she had to do, it was time for her to lead her team to victory and take down the machine.

"Alright, quick! Form up and follow my lead!" Iris shouted, her words slicing through the air like a whip. She quickly assessed the situation, looking for any weaknesses in the machine's armor that she could exploit.

"Duncan, take a shot at its head," she ordered.

Duncan nodded, raising his KSVK 12.7 sniper rifle to his shoulder and taking aim. He fired, and the bullet soared through the air, striking the scorpion robot's head with a loud clang. But to their surprise, it dealt little damage. The machine let out a loud roar, its pincers snapping wildly as it continued to advance towards them.

"Astrid, now!" Irisshouted, and without hesitation, Astrid sprang into action.

Her avatar moved with lightning-fast reflexes, darting towards the scorpion robot like a bolt of lightning. She held her mechanical sword with both hands, the blade glinting menacingly in the twilight. With a fierce battle cry, Astrid charged forward, her character's movements swift and agile as she closed the distance between herself and the machine.

The scorpion robot turned to face her, its pincers snapping dangerously close to Astrid's avatar. But she was too quick for it, darting to the side and striking out with her sword. Sparks flew as the blade bit into the machine's armor, but it barely seemed to notice. Astrid let out a sound of frustration but persisted in her efforts, striking again and again. The machine was relentless, pincers snapping at her as she danced around it. But the scorpion was just too overwhelming, its sheer size making it nearly impossible to outmaneuver.

Elias, with his ruger SR-556, was laying down cover fire, trying to pin the machine down and keep it from getting too close to Astrid. The bullets pinged harmlessly against the robot's thick armor plating, but it was enough to buy them some time. The scorpion robot roared, its pincers snapping wildly as it tried to find an opening. Ian and Iris kept shouting at the machine, each trying to get a clear shot.

Astrid's avatar darted around the scorpion robot, trying to find a weak spot. Elias was doing his best to provide cover fire, but the bullets from his Ruger SR-556 were barely making a dent in the machine's armor.

Iris scanned the area, her mind racing as she searched for a weak point. And then, it hit her - the scorpion robot's weak spot had to be its tail.

"Duncan, aim for its tail!" she shouted, gesturing towards the scorpion robot's long appendage.

Duncan immediately adjusted his aim and fired. The bullet struck its mark, hitting the base of the scorpion robot's tail. And just as Iris predicted, the machine let out a pained roar, the first sign of damage that they had dealt to it.

But the scorpion robot was not so easily defeated. With lightning-fast speed, it swung its tail around, revealing the deadly stinger at its tip.

As if sensing their strategy, the machine twisted its body around, lashing out with its tail.

The Scorpion pierced astride with his stinger, a terrifying sight to behold.

Iris' heart skipped a beat as she watched the sharp point of the tail come hurtling towards them, faster than she could react.

It struck Astrid's avatar with a loud thwack, sending her flying through the air.

She crashed to the ground with a sickening thud, her character's sword clattering to the ground beside her.

Ian rushed to her side to heal her.

But before he could reach her, Astrid's character push herself up onto one elbow. "Ian, I'm fine," she said, her voice shaky but determined. "I can keep fighting."

"Are you sure?" Ian asked, concern etched on his face. He couldn't shake the feeling that she was hurt worse than she was letting on.

"Yes," Astrid replied, her voice stronger now. "I want to keep fighting."

And with that, she pushed herself back up to her feet, her character's sword clutched tightly in her hand. She stood there for a moment, swaying slightly as she regained her balance.

But there was no time to waste. Iris knew that they needed to take down the scorpion robot quickly, before it could do any more damage.

"Alright," Iris said, her voice firm and steady. "We know the scorpion robot's tail is its weak spot. Let's focus our attack there."

The group nodded in agreement, and they renewed their assault on the machine. Duncan aimed for the tail, while Elias continued to provide cover fire.

Iris and Ian exchanged a quick glance before launching a coordinated attack on the scorpion robot's tail.

Iris charged forward, her avatar's strong legs propelling her towards the machine with surprising speed. She ducked and weaved around its massive legs, avoiding the sharp claws that swooped down towards her like blades. As she approached the tail, she saw her opportunity and took it, striking out with her Dan Wesson M1911 ACP pistol. The bullets found their target, lodging themselves in the scorpion robot's tail with a satisfying *thunk*.

Elias saw his opening and seized it. His character's muscles rippled as he charged towards the machine, his massive frame making him look almost superhuman. With a determined look on his face, he reached for his shovel, slamming it into the weak spot with all his might.

The scorpion robot let out an ear-piercing roar as it stumbled backwards, its balance thrown off by the attacks.

Iris couldn't help but cheer as she saw the damage they had dealt to the machine, but she knew that they still had a long way to go before they could take it down. She turned her attention back to the battle, scanning the area for any signs of danger.

The remaining small robots were still lurking around the edges of the battlefield, trying to flank them and catch them off guard. But Iris and her team were too focused on the scorpion robot to pay them much attention. They knew that if they could take down the big machine, the smaller ones would be no match for them.

But as they continued their assault on the scorpion robot, they started to realize just how difficult a task it was. Despite their relentless attack, the machine barely seemed to notice. Its armor plating was thick and sturdy, and the bullets from their guns barely left a dent in its surface.

But Iris and her team weren't the type to back down from a challenge. With renewed determination, they continued their assault on the machine. Ian had moved into position next to Iris, his avatar's M1 Garand rifle at the ready.

Together, they began firing on the machine's tail, coordinating their attacks for maximum impact.

Astrid, sensing an opportunity, lunged forward and lend a blow with her mechanical sword. The blade sliced through the air, catching the scorpion robot's tail mid-swing.

Sparks flew as the metal met resistance, but Astrid's character seemed unmoved. She twisted her blade, wrenching it free with a loud rip. The robot's tail was wounded, a small gash stretching along its surface.

But the scorpion robot was far from defeated. With a roar, it spun around, its tail whipping dangerously through the air. Iris dove to the side, narrowly avoiding a potentially fatal blow from the machine's lethal stinger.

Elias, not far behind, quickly took advantage of the scorpion robot's momentary loss of balance. He sprinted forward, closing the distance between him and the machine in just a few quick strides. With a fierce battle cry, he brought his Ithaca 37 up and fired at point-blank range directly into the scorpion robot's exposed tail. The force of the blast sent the machine reeling, and Iris saw her chance.

She leapt forward, her avatar's pistol raised, and fired off a series of shots at the scorpion robot's weak spot. The bullets hit their mark, causing the machine to stumble backwards.

But it was not defeated yet. With a roar, the scorpion robot spun around, its pincer whipping through the air towards Iris. She reacted instinctively, throwing herself to the side just as the pincer came hurtling towards her. But it was too fast, and she knew she wouldn't be able to dodge it entirely.

That's when Elias stepped in.His avatar's muscular form lunged forward, intercepting the scorpion robot's pincer with his own arm. The impact caused Elias to stumble, but he managed to hold his ground. The scorpion robot roared in frustration, its tail thrashing through the air, preparing to strike Elias.

But before it could hit, Duncan's shot rang out, hitting the scorpion robot's tail and interrupting its attack. Iris and Elias took the opportunity to fall back, their characters retreating to a safe distance.

As they did, Astrid's character pull out a grenade from her belt. With a fierce determination in her eyes, Astrid pulled the pin and tossed the grenade at the scorpion robot.

It landed at its feet with a thud. The grenade exploded with a deafening boom, sending shards of metal flying through the air. Iris squeezed her eyes shut, bracing for the impact. But when she opened them again, she was surprised to see the scorpion robot still standing. Its armor had taken a hit, but it seemed far from destroyed.

"Keep firing!" Iris shouted to her team. "We need to finish this thing off!"

They redoubled their efforts, their shots ringing out in a steady chorus. The scorpion robot roared and thrashed, its movements growing wilder as its weaknesses were exploited.

Iris could feel the tension in her muscles as she continued pulling the trigger of her Dan Wesson M1911 ACP pistol. Each shot landed with precision, tearing through the machine's armor and striking sensitive components.

Astrid, driven by determination, swung her mechanical sword in a sweeping arc that took off chunks of the robot's exoskeleton.

With a triumphant cry, she plunged her sword into the massive robot's weak spot, its tail. The scorpion robot let out a piercing wail, its arms twitching before going still. The tension in the air seemed to dissipate as the machine finally fell silent, its metal frame collapsing to the ground with a resounding crash. Iris let out a sigh of relief, lowering her weapon as she surveyed the damage.

But then, her gaze landed on Astrid, who had been standing nearby. The woman was swaying on her feet, her avatar's hand clutching at her chest.

"Astrid?" Iris asked, concern creeping into her voice. "Are you okay?"

Astrid didn't respond, instead letting out a pained gasp as she collapsed to the ground. Iris rushed to her side, horrified to see that the woman's health points were rapidly decreasing.She had been stung by the scorpion robot, and the venom was coursing through her veins, threatening to kill her.

"Ian, I need you," Iris said, her voice urgent.

Without hesitation, Ian rushed to Astrid's side, ready to heal her with his unique ability. But just as he was about to touch her, the remaining small robots turned their attention towards him and Astrid.

"Watch out!" Iris shouted, as she and Elias stepped in front of their fallen comrades. The small robots swarmed around them, their blades glinting ominously in the dim light.

Duncan quickly reload his rifle with expert precision. Iris and Elias fought back fiercely, their weapons blazing as they tried to fend off the relentless attack. But the small robots were numerous and determined, and it was clear that they would need backup soon.

Ian knew he had to act fast. He had to heal Astrid before the venom could spread any further. But with the small robots closing in on them, it was going to be a challenge.

Their characters began to writhe together in a passionate embrace.

Ian's avatar gripped Astrid's shoulder, pulling them closer as their noses brushed together. Their lips crashed together, tongues dueling and dancing in a delicious preview of what was to come.

Ian's avatar hands roamed over Astrid's body, feeling the curves and contours of her form through the fabric of her clothing.

Their characters' hips ground together, the friction between them sending waves of pleasure coursing through their bodies. Ian's avatar broke away from the kiss, her lips trailing down Astrid's neck as she nibbled and sucked on her sensitive flesh. Astrid's moans grew louder, her body arching and writhing beneath Ian's touch.

Elias and Iris fought back-to-back, back-to-back, holding the line against the relentless horde of small robots. Elias' Ruger SR-556 roared as he unloaded round after round into the machines, while Iris used her dexterity and agility to dodge and weave between them, striking with precision and lethal force.

Ian's avatar's hand snaked under Astrid's clothes, cupping her breast and teasing her nipple through the fabric of her bra. Astrid gasped, arching her back as she felt the pleasure intensify.

Ian's avatar rolled her nipple between his fingers, sending shivers down her spine. He squeezed and kneaded her breasts with growing urgency, as their lips met again in a deep kiss. Their breaths intermingled, hot and heavy, as their tongues danced together.

Ian's avatar's other hand slid down Astrid's body, cupping her sex through the fabric of her clothes. She writhed under his touch, moaning as she massaged her through the layers of material.

Ian's character quickly undressed Astrid's, removing every stitch of clothing from her trembling body. The sound of gunfire was distant now, drowned out by the sound of their own heavy breathing. Ian kissed Astrid again, his hands never leaving her body as they roamed over her curves.

Ian's avatar's fingers deftly slid under Astrid's clothes, finding her wet and ready. He teased her until she was begging for more, and then she slipped a finger inside of her. Astrid's character gasped, her hips bucking against her hand as he began to thrust in and out of her. Ian's avatar continued to caress her breasts, teasing her nipples between his fingers as they kissed.

Duncan, Iris, and Elias were still locked in battle with the small robots, but Ian's focus was solely on Astrid. He could feel the tension in her body as she fought to stay conscious, the venom from the scorpion robot's sting slowly spread through her veins.

"Hold on, Astrid," Ian whispered. "I'm going to make you feel better."

With that, his avatar quickly pulled off her own clothes, leaving her in just her bra and panties. She straddled Astrid's prone form, her eyes blazing with desire. Ian's avatar leaned down and took one of Astrid's nipples into her mouth, flicking it with her tongue and sucking hard.

CAUGHT IN GARDEN OF MECHANICAL SOULS

Astrid's back arched off the ground, a gasp escaping her lips. Her hands clutched at Ian's avatar's hair as she moaned in pleasure. Ian's avatar knew what she was doing – healing Astrid with her body, giving her the sexual energy and release she needed to fight off the scorpion robot's venom. She was using every trick in the book, from nibbling on her earlobe to tracing her ribs with her tongue, making sure to touch all of Astrid's body with reverence and desire. Her avatar's hand explored every curve and angle of Astrid's body, her fingers tracing intricate patterns on her skin.

Astrid's character responded with a moan, her hands reaching up to grip Ian's avatar's shoulders. Ian's avatar continued to touch and tease her, her fingers never staying in one place for long. They moved down to Astrid's inner thighs, spreading them gently apart.

Ian's avatar moved her face closer, inhaling deeply and letting out a low growl at the scent of Astrid's arousal. She couldn't help but let out a moan as she felt her breath on her sensitive skin.

Without warning, Ian's avatar plunged her tongue deep into Astrid's wetness, tasting her sweetness and drawing another loud moan from her lips. She lapped at her, exploring her as she writhed beneath her.

Her tongue snaked out, tracing the outline of Astrid's clit before sucking it into her mouth. Astrid moaned louder, her back arching off the ground as she ground herself against Ian's face.

Ian's avatar was relentless, and she didn't stop until Astrid was shivering and gasping, on the brink of orgasm. With one final flick of her tongue, Astrid cried out, her body trembling as waves of pleasure washed over her.

As Ian's avatar sat up, she knew that Astrid was going to be okay. The venom from the scorpion robot's sting was receding, and Astrid's character was already regaining her strength. Ian's avatar helped her up, and the two of them shared a tender kiss.

Astrid smiled up at him, feeling the warmth spread through her body, banishing the last traces of the venom.

Just as they turned to rejoin the others, a group of small robots head straight for them. Iris quickly took charge, her P90 at the ready and with a fierce determination, she charged towards the machines.

She fired off a series of shots, each one hitting its mark with deadly precision. The robots fell one by one, their metal bodies clattering to the ground.

Elias and Duncan joined in, unloading their weapons on the remaining machines. Together, they fought off the robots, their teamwork and skill overpowering the mechanical foes.

Once they had defeated the last of the machines, they took a moment to catch their breaths, looking around at each other with a mixture of relief and excitement.

They had survived a challenging battle, and they had done it together.

Iris couldn't help but smile as she looked at her friends, her fellow adventurers. They were a diverse and unlikely group, brought together by their love of gaming and their mutual desire to experience something new.

Just then, something strange happened in the real world. It was subtle at first, a faint rumbling beneath their feet that they might have dismissed as nothing.

But then, just as they were about to relax, the room around them began to fade. The walls, the furniture, the bright sunlight streaming in through the windows, all of it blurred and vanished, leaving nothing but a featureless white expanse in its place.

Iris' first instinct was to panic. She reached out for Elias, calling his name, but her voice seemed to fade into the void. She could see him looking around in confusion, but she couldn't get to him.

CAUGHT IN GARDEN OF MECHANICAL SOULS

Meanwhile, in Duncan's home the same thing happened. The room around him blurred and vanished, leaving nothing but the same white expanse.

Ian's noticed that his computer screen had gone blank. When he looked up, he saw the same white expanse that had swallowed up his friends.

And in Astrid's bedroom, she too was met with the same sight. The four walls that had contained her small, cluttered sanctuary were suddenly gone, leaving only a swirling void behind.

Iris, Elias, Ian, Duncan, and Astrid found themselves floating in the vast expanse, surrounded by nothing but a sea of white. The last thing they remembered was their epic battle against the scorpion robot in their game, but that had faded into the background, replaced by this strange and confusing reality.

As they tried to make sense of their surroundings, their vision began to blur, and a deep exhaustion overcame them. One by one, they succumbed to the darkness, their bodies drifting away in the featureless void.

Ian was the first to fall, his mind and body unable to cope with the sudden shift in reality. he slipped away quietly, his consciousness fading into a deep sleep. Elias was next, his eyes fluttering closed as he let out a sigh of relief. Iris followed soon after, his body heavy with exhaustion. Duncan fought to stay awake, but even his strength was no match for the strange power at work here. And finally, Astrid closed her eyes, slipping away into the darkness as her mind gave in to the overwhelming fatigue.

Chapter 1: Ian / Healer

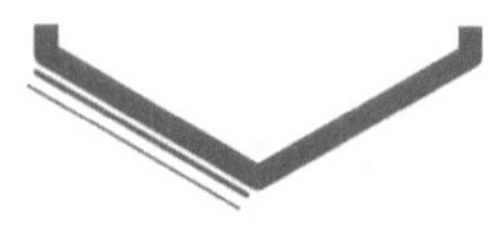

As Ian regained consciousness, he slowly opened his eyes to find himself standing in a vast garden filled with metallic automatons. The intricate design of the garden, with its towering structures and verdant foliage, was a stark contrast against the cold metal it housed.

Ian could hardly believe his eyes. Was this all a dream? Had he managed to somehow enter the game world while he was sleeping? It seemed impossible, but as he looked down at his hands, he saw that they were no longer his own. Instead, he was seeing the delicate fingers of his female avatar, her pale skin contrasting sharply with the lush vegetation around her.

And then, as he looked down, he saw them - two perfectly round, firm, and perky breasts, encased in a tight-fitting blouse that struggled to contain them. Ian couldn't believe it. Was this really happening? Was he now seeing the world from the perspective of his female avatar?

Ian couldn't believe it, but the evidence was impossible to deny. He looked down at his body again, taking in the curves and contours of his new form with a mixture of shock and awe. He had always been a little self-conscious about his own body, but now he found himself in a form that was the exact opposite of what he was used to. His hips flared out, drawing the eye to the miniskirt that barely covered them. His legs were long and lithe, and his feet were encased in delicate-looking heels that he wasn't sure he could walk in. His hair was a cascade of long, flowing white strands that fell in neat pigtails on either side of his face. He reached up to touch his face, feeling the softness of his skin and the curves of his cheekbones.

But as Ian took in the sight of his new body, he couldn't help but feel a sense of panic setting in. He had no idea how he had ended up here, or what had happened to his friends. Had they experienced the same transformation as he had ? Or had they been left behind in the real world ?

As the reality of his situation sunk in, Ian couldn't help but feel a sense of fear and uncertainty. He had never felt so vulnerable before, not in his real life and certainly not in the game world. But there was no denying it - he was now a woman, and he had no idea how to navigate this new reality.

Suddenly, Ian's thoughts were interrupted by a message that popped up in front of him. It was from Iris, requesting that he meet her back at their temporary base camp. He glanced around, trying to get his bearings, but it was difficult to tell where he was in the maze-like garden.

The metallic automatons that populated the area seemed to be on some sort of pre-determined path, and he didn't want to get too close to them.

Ian decided to take out his map to check his location, but as he unfolded it, he realized that it was not the familiar game map he was used to. Instead, it looked like an old-fashioned parchment, complete with ink drawings and strange symbols.

He studied it carefully, trying to make sense of the lines and curves. It appeared that he was in the heart of the garden, and that he would then need to traverse the forest of cogs in order to reach Iris's location. Ian glanced nervously at the map, trying to memorize the path to the forest of cogs.

Ian couldn't help but feel a sense of unease. He had never felt so vulnerable before, and the thought of facing off against any enemy, be they human or machine, was enough to make his knees knock together.

But even in the midst of his fear, Ian couldn't deny the thrill that ran through his veins.

He had always been a shut-in, content to spend his days holed up in his room with his video games and anime. But now, he was in the middle of a real-life adventure, and not just any adventure, but one that took place in the game world he had come to love and know so well.

As Ian started walking, he stumbled to his new body gravity and the heels he was wearing. It was a strange feeling, being in a female body, and the added difficulty of walking in heels made it even more challenging. He had to take small, deliberate steps to avoid tripping and falling. He couldn't help but feel embarrassed, knowing that if anyone were to see him, they would surely laugh at his clumsy attempts to navigate the garden.

But as he continued on his way, Ian's thoughts were interrupted by a sudden realization. He nearly forgot about his rifle. He quickly turned around and made his way back to where he had woken up.

As he approached the spot, he saw the M1 Garand lying on the ground, just as he had left it. He picked it up, feeling its weight in his hands, with a sense of relief.

Ian took a moment to admire the sleek design of the rifle, its wooden stock and metal barrel gleaming in the sunlight. He had always been a bit of a gun enthusiast, and the M1 Garand was one of his favorites.

Ian took a deep breath and raised the rifle to his shoulder, aiming at a nearby tree. He closed one eye, focusing on the trunk, and slowly squeezed the trigger.

The shot rang out, echoing through the garden, and the bullet hit its mark with a satisfying thud. Ian couldn't help but grin as he lowered the rifle, feeling a sense of pride and accomplishment.

He had never used a gun before, but it seemed that the game's world had somehow granted him the knowledge and skill he needed to wield one with accuracy.

He continued to make his way through the garden, following the map's instructions as closely as he could. The metallic automatons that roamed the area paid him no mind, seemingly content to continue their programmed paths without deviation. Ian wondered what would happen if he were to get too close to them, or worse, if he were to attack them.

As he made his way carefully through the garden, trying to avoid the mechanical beasts that prowled the area, he accidentally tripped over a tree root and stumbled forward. His rifle, which he had been holding with a white-knuckle grip, slipped from his hand and clattered to the ground. His chest hit the ground with a thud, and he let out a gasp of pain. He could feel them throbbing with pain, and he knew that they were going to be sore for a while.

After catching his breath, Ian picked himself up and dusted off his clothes. He then reached down and picked

up his rifle, checking it for any damage. To his relief, it appeared to be undamaged.

Ian took a deep breath, his heart racing as he looked around nervously. He couldn't help but feel a sense of vulnerability as he saw the towering metallic automatons patrolling the garden. He was grateful for the fact that they appeared to be unaware of his presence, but he knew that it was only a matter of time before one of them noticed him. And then what? Would he be able to defend himself against these machines with his M1 Garand? He wasn't sure.

Ian's thoughts were interrupted by the sound of a twig snapping nearby.

He spun around, the M1 Garand raised and ready, but there was nothing there. He scanned the area, his heart pounding in his chest. Had one of the automatons noticed him?

Just as he was about to let out a sigh of relief, he heard it again - the unmistakable sound of a footstep in the underbrush. This time, he didn't hesitate. He bolted, moving as fast as his legs would carry him.

He knew that he couldn't outrun a machine, but maybe he could outmaneuver it.

Ian dashed through the winding paths of the garden, the automatons giving chase. Their metal bodies whirred and clicked as they moved, a frightening sound that echoed in his ears. His heart raced as he ran, his mind racing with thoughts of what would happen if he was caught.

As he sprinted past a dense thicket of trees, he spotted a narrow path that veered off to the left. He took a risk and darted down it, hoping that it would lead him to safety. The path was narrow and winding, twisting and turning in ways that made it difficult for him to keep his footing. But Ian didn't let that stop him. He pressed on, his legs aching as he pushed himself to run faster.

He could hear the metallic automatons clanking and whirring in the distance, but they seemed to be getting further and further away. Ian let out a sigh of relief, leaning against a tree to catch his breath. He couldn't believe what had just happened. He had never been in a real-life situation like that before, and the adrenaline was still coursing through his veins.

As he looked down at himself, he was reminded of his new, female form. He couldn't help but feel a sense of disorientation as he took in the curves and contours of his new body. He had always been a geek and a otaku, and the thought of being in a female form was both exhilarating and terrifying. He felt a twinge of excitement in his chest as he ran his fingers over the smooth skin of his arms, but he couldn't shake off the feeling of vulnerability. He couldn't afford to be distracted by his new form or the sensations it elicited.

CAUGHT IN GARDEN OF MECHANICAL SOULS

He had always been a shut-in, content with living vicariously through his characters in the game. But now, he was thrust into a world where he had to rely on his wits and instincts to survive.

As Ian caught his breath, he couldn't help but feel a sense of awe at the beauty of the garden. The lush greenery and towering metallic structures were a sight to behold, and Ian marveled at the level of detail in the game. His eyes were drawn to the metallic flowers that adorned the branches of the garden's trees.

He then heard the sound of water trickling nearby. He followed the sound until he came upon a small, crystal-clear pond. The sight of the calm water was soothing, and Ian felt his muscles start to relax.

He leaned down and cupped his hands, taking a sip of the cool water. It was refreshing, and he couldn't help but feel grateful for this small respite from his harrowing escape.

As he gazed into the water, he saw his own reflection staring back at him, or rather, her.

His new, female form was still a shock to his system, and he couldn't help but feel a sense of unease as he took in the unfamiliar features that stared back at him. Her long white hair flowed in soft waves around her shoulders, shimmering like spun silk in the sunlight. Her blue eyes were wide and expressive, framed by thick lashes that made them seem even more striking. She had a delicate nose and full, pink lips that curved into a shy smile as she looked back at him. Ian couldn't believe what he was seeing. This was his avatar, the one that he had spent countless hours designing and tweaking to fit his ideal image of a female protagonist in his mind. She was beautiful. And yet, at the same time, she was also undeniably himself.

As Ian looked at his reflection, transfixed by what he saw. The sight of his own face, now transformed into that of a beautiful woman, evoked within him an array of feelings. There was undeniably a sense of exhilaration and gratitude coursing through his veins. He felt fortunate for having been granted this unique experience – the chance to inhabit a female avatar in the digital realm, allowing him to fully immerse himself in her world and embrace every aspect of her existence. However, amidst these euphoric sentiments, there lingered a nagging undercurrent of unease. It wasn't just the physical transformation that unsettled him; rather, it was the profound shift in perception that accompanied it. As he gazed upon his altered visage, Ian couldn't help but acknowledge the vulnerabilities inherent in his new persona. Despite the novelty and excitement, he couldn't escape the lingering awareness of how easily his virtual femininity could be exploited or misconstrued. While he reveled in the opportunities afforded by his gender swap, he also grappled with the heightened sensitivity that came along with it. The wind that tickled his skin elicited sensations he had never before experienced, leaving him overcome by an unfamiliar yet pleasurable ache. Even the slightest movement felt intimate – every step he took sent jolts of pleasure coursing through his body, threatening to overwhelm him.

As he took in his newfound sensations, Ian couldn't help but feel a sense of shame. He had never thought of himself as a pervert, but now, he was having such thoughts that he couldn't shake off. His mind wandered to dark places, and he couldn't help but feel a sense of guilt and disgust.

He knew he had to keep moving if he wanted to find his teammates, but the weight of his new body made every step a struggle. He couldn't help but feel exposed in his short skirt and tight blouse, and he found himself constantly tugging at his clothes to cover up. It was a strange feeling, being in a form that was so different from his own, and he couldn't shake the feeling of vulnerability that came with it. The thought of facing any danger in this form made his stomach turn.

But Ian also couldn't deny the thrill that coursed through his veins as he moved, the feeling of his hips swaying with each step and the sensation of his luscious locks bouncing around him. He had always been fascinated by the idea of experiencing life from a female perspective, but he never thought it would actually happen.

He shook his head, trying to clear his thoughts. Now was not the time to be thinking about such things.

Ian looked down at the map once more, checking his bearings. It seemed the "Forest of Cogs" was not too far now, but he would need to be careful as the path would take him through a dense thicket of trees, where it would be easy to become disoriented or lost.

As he followed the path towards the forest of cogs , he began to notice more details about the

game world.

The way the leaves on the trees shimmered as if they were made of glass, the softness of the moss under his feet, and the gentle hum of the mechanical creatures that inhabited this world. It all felt so real, so tangible. Even the air felt different, with a sweet, almost metallic scent that he found strangely intoxicating. Ian couldn't believe that he was actually here, experiencing this world with all of his senses.

As he walked, he couldn't help but feel a sense of awe and wonder. He had always been fascinated by the game world, but to actually be here, in the flesh (or at least, his female avatar's flesh) was truly something else. He felt like a child on Christmas morning, bursting with excitement and anticipation for what was to come.

But along with the excitement and wonder, there was also a sense of unease and fear. Ian couldn't shake off the thought of what would happen if he were to die in the game. Would he simply respawn at the last save point, or would his consciousness be forever lost? The thought was terrifying.

As he navigated the dense thicket of trees, Ian couldn't help but feel a growing sense of unease. The trees were getting thicker and the underbrush more dense, making it difficult to move forward. He could hear the distant sound of gears turning and pistons hissing, signaling the presence of the automatons.

Finally, after what seemed like hours of walking, he saw the entrance to the forest of cogs looming ahead.

The trees were tall and twisted, their branches adorned with metallic cogs that glinted in the sunlight. It was as if someone had taken a piece of machinery and somehow grafted it onto living trees. Ian couldn't help but marvel at the sight, even as he felt a sense of unease creeping up his spine.

As Ian approached the entrance, he noticed the cogs hanging from the branches, like fruits waiting to be plucked. He reached up and touched one, feeling the cold metal against his fingers. It was an odd sensation, and he couldn't help but feel a sense of unease.

With a deep breath, Ian stepped forward into the forest of cogs, the scent of oil and metal tickling his nose. The sound of gears and pistons grew louder with each step, and he could feel the thrum of their vibrations against the soles of his feet. The thought of facing off against these mechanical beasts made his hands tremble. He had never been one for physical exertion or bravery. But here he was, in a female form, embarking on an adventure unlike any other.

Suddenly, a rustling in the underbrush caught his attention. He spun around, raising the M1 Garand to his shoulder, his heart pounding in his chest. But it was only a small, fearful-looking creature with metal limbs and a red light where its eyes should have been. It looked up at him, seeming to beg for mercy, and for a moment, Ian hesitated.

He had always been a kind person, even in the game world, and he didn't want to hurt this innocent creature if he could help it.

He lowered his weapon and slowly approached the strange being. It cowered as he drew closer, but then timidly reached out a metal paw towards him.

"Hey there, little guy. It's okay," Ian said softly, as he knelt down beside it. He was surprised at the kindness in his own voice, and how gently he handled the small creature. It nuzzled against his leg, and he couldn't help but chuckle. "You're so cute," he said, stroking its metal head. He felt a sense of warmth towards this innocent creature, and a sense of relief that it hadn't turned out to be an enemy.

But as he was stroking its metal head, it suddenly let out a strange beep, and before Ian knew it, he found himself surrounded by robots in the form of wolves.

They were sleek and silver, with glowing red eyes and sharp metal teeth. Ian couldn't believe what he was seeing - these were the infamous Mechanical Wolves of the game world, known for their deadly speed and strength. Their metallic fur gleamed in the dim light of the forest.

Ian's heart raced as he stood up, gripping his M1 Garand tightly.

The mechanical wolves snarled, their teeth glinting in the dim light. Ian knew he couldn't outrun them - they were faster and stronger than him, and there was no way he could escape.

The wolves circled around him, their sharp teeth bared and their claws clicking against the metal ground.

Ian took a deep breath, trying to steady his nerves as he raised the rifle to his shoulder. He knew that he couldn't afford to hesitate or show any sign of weakness.

He closed one eye, focusing on the lead wolf as he slowly squeezed the trigger. The rifle kicked against his shoulder, and the sound of the shot echoed throughout the forest.

Chapter 2: Iris and Elias

Iris couldn't help but feel a surge of anxiety as she looked down at her new form. Her heart was racing, and she felt like she couldn't catch her breath. She had always been a cautious and analytical person, but in this moment, she felt anything but.

"I-I don't understand," she stammered, her voice barely above a whisper. "How did this happen? Why am I in this body?" she asked, her voice trembling. She looked up at Elias, hoping for an answer, but he just shrugged.

"I have no idea, Iris. All I know is that I woke up in this world as my avatar. And from the looks of it, so did you."

Iris took a deep breath and looked down at her new body again. She had always been comfortable in her own skin, but now, she couldn't help feeling self-conscious. She didn't know how to navigate the world as this new masculine version of herself. .She reached down, her fingers brushing against the unfamiliar sensation. She couldn't believe what she was feeling. She looked up at Elias, her eyes wide with shock. She was a woman, through and through, and this new form felt wrong, foreign to her.

"Elias, I-I have a penis," she stammered, her voice barely above a whisper.

The words hung heavy in the air, a reminder of the bizarre circumstances that had brought them to this alternate reality.

Elias put a reassuring hand on Iris' shoulder, feeling the tension in her muscles. He had always admired her ability to remain calm and collected in any situation, but now she was clearly struggling to come to terms with this new reality.

"It's okay, Iris. We'll figure this out together," he told her, his voice gentle and reassuring.

Iris took a deep breath and nodded, her fingers still tracing the outline of her new form.

She knew that she couldn't afford to dwell on this for too long; they needed to focus on finding a way out of this alternate reality.

Elias looked around, trying to take in their surroundings. They were standing in the middle of a vast plain, the ground covered in broken metal of different sizes. In the distance, he could see the ruins of what looked like an old laboratory, the building half-buried in the earth.

Iris, on the other hand, was still

trying to come to terms with her new body. She couldn't believe what had happened to her, and she couldn't shake off the feeling of disorientation that came with it She looked up at Elias, her eyes pleading for an explanation.

But Elias just shrugged his shoulders and gave her a reassuring smile. "I don't know how or why we're here, Iris, but we need to focus on finding a way out. We can't change our appearance, but we can use our abilities to our advantage.

We should get to the temporary base camp, the old laboratory, and regroup with the others." Elias said, trying to keep his voice steady.

Iris nodded, taking a deep breath. "You're right. Let's move out."

They set off towards the old laboratory, their footsteps echoing through the empty landscape. Iris couldn't shake off the feeling of unease that had settled in her stomach. She couldn't help but feel like they were being watched, even though there was nothing around for miles.

As they walked, Iris remembered that as a leader, she as a ability to send messages to her allies even if they were far away. She quickly pulled out her communication device and sent a message asking them to meet her at the temporary base. She hoped that they would receive it soon, and that they were safe.

As they walked, Iris couldn't help but stealthily observe Elias from the corner of her eye. His muscular build was more pronounced in this form, his shoulders broader and his legs stronger.

Elias was aware of Iris' frequent glances, but he didn't say anything. He understood that she was trying to come to terms with her new form, and to be honest, so was he. He couldn't quite comprehend how they had ended up in this alternate reality, but he knew that they needed to stay together if they wanted to survive.

They continued their trek towards the old laboratory, the ground crunching beneath their feet.

Elias had his rifle at the ready, constantly scanning their surroundings for any potential threats.

They walked in silence for what felt like hours, their thoughts consumed by their new reality. Iris couldn't help but feel frustrated and helpless in her new body. She was a woman, dammit! And now she was stuck in this strange world as a man. She let out a sigh and adjusted her avatar's clothing, trying to find comfort in the alien form.But no matter what she did, she couldn't shake off the feeling of wrongness that coursed through her veins. She looked down at her rough, calloused hands. She couldn't help but miss the softness and delicate touch of her own hands. She was a stranger in her own body.

Elias, on the other hand, seemed to take everything in stride. He walked confidently, his eyes scanning the surroundings for any signs of danger. The tall and big body of his avatar suited him well, and he seemed to move with a sense of purpose. Iris couldn't help but feel a pang of jealousy towards him. He seemed to have accepted his fate with an uncanny ease while she was still trying to comprehend her new reality. Iris couldn't help but feel a sense of resentment towards him. She tried to shake off the feeling, knowing that they needed to work together to survive.

Suddenly, a loud whirring sound filled the air. Iris and Elias spun around, their weapons at the ready. Their eyes widened in shock as they saw a group of robotic centaurs charging towards them. Their metallic bodies gleaming in the sunlight. They had the upper body of a man while the lower half was that of a horse, made of intricate gears and cogs. Their metallic hooves clanked loudly against the ground as they closed in, their eyes glowing with an eerie light. Elias quickly took position, his fingers dancing over the trigger of his gun as he sized up the enemy. Iris followed suit, letting out a deep breath as she aimed her pistol at the oncoming mechanical beasts.

She could feel her heart hammering in her chest, her hands slightly trembling as she squeezed the trigger. The gunshots rang through the air, deafening in their intensity. The mechanical centaurs snarled and reared, their robotic limbs slicing through the air as they attempted to dodge the hail of bullets. Elias' Ruger SR-556 and Iris' FN P90 proved to be formidable weapons against their foes, the barrage of bullets ripping through the metallic bodies of the centaurs and leaving them lifeless on the ground. The centaurs are durable and can withstand a reasonable amount of damage, but the relentless attack proved too much for the mechanical beasts.

After a few minutes of intense combat, the last centaur falls to the ground, defeated. Elias and Iris let out a sigh of relief, their bodies drenched in sweat as they stare at the fallen robots. The adrenaline of the fight starts to wear off, leaving them as exhausted and as overwhelmed as ever. Iris couldn't believe what just happened. They were in the middle of an alternate reality, and now they were fighting robotic centaurs. It all felt like a surreal nightmare.

Elias takes a moment to catch his breath, reloading his Ruger SR-556 as he surveys the area for any remaining threats.

"Are you okay?" Elias asks, his voice barely above a whisper as he glances over at Iris. She nods, her eyes not leaving the scene before her.

"I'm fine," she replies, her voice shaky but determined. She takes a deep breath, trying to calm her racing heart.

Elias nods, his eyes still scanning their surroundings. "We should keep moving," he says, his voice steady and reassuring. Iris agrees, and they continue their trek towards the old laboratory. The sun beats down on them, casting long shadows on the ground. She couldn't help but feel grateful for Elias' presence, for his steadiness and his unwavering determination to find a way out.

As they walk, they finally reach the entrance of the old laboratory. The door creaks open, revealing a dimly lit space filled with broken machines and discarded equipment. Elias and Iris cautiously make their way up the metal staircase, weapons at the ready. The air is thick with dust, and the sound of their footsteps echoes through the empty halls.

As they reach the second floor, they see a room that serve as their temporary base camp. It's small but easy to defend, with windows overlooking the rest of the laboratory. Iris quickly moves to secure the perimeter, checking each corner and crevice for any signs of danger. Elias follows suit, setting up traps and barricades to protect them from any potential threats. They work in silence, the tension between them palpable. Iris can feel Elias' eyes on her, and she can't help but feel self-conscious in this new body. She constantly adjusts her clothing, trying to find a sense of normalcy.

As they set up, Iris can't help but feel a sudden surge of attraction towards Elias. She observes his muscular build as he moves around the room, working efficiently and skillfully to secure their base. His rugged masculinity and strong presence ignites a spark within her that she can't ignore. She yearns to embrace him, to feel his arms around her. But as she approaches him, she notices a shift in his demeanor. Elias stiffens, and she can see a hint of discomfort in his eyes. She stops mid-step, trying to make sense of the sudden change.

"Iris, I can't hug you back," Elias says, his voice low and pained. "I can't pretend that everything is normal when it's not. You're in a male body, and I don't know how to reconcile that with my feelings for you."

Iris took a step back, hurt and confused. She had been feeling so many emotions since they had woken up in this strange world, and she had hoped that she could find comfort in Elias's arms. But now, she was left feeling rejected and alone. "I understand," she said quietly, her voice barely above a whisper. "I didn't think about how this would affect you. I'm sorry."

Elias shook his head. "No, don't apologize. It's not your fault. I just need some time to process everything that's happened. And I need to figure out how to deal with these feelings I have for you when you're in a man body."

Iris nodded, understanding what Elias was going through. She couldn't imagine how difficult it must be for him to see her like this. Iris was still trying to come to terms with her own feelings about her new form, and now she had to worry about Elias too. She couldn't help but resent him for not being able to accept her in this new body. She knew that it wasn't fair to blame him for his feelings, but she couldn't help the way she felt. She wanted him to be able to see past her physical appearance and still love her for who she was inside.

But even as these thoughts swirled through her mind, she knew that she couldn't let them consume her. They had more pressing matters to attend to, like finding a way out of this alternate reality and figuring out who or what had brought them here in the first place.

As she turned her attention back to the task at hand, she couldn't help but notice that Elias seemed to be avoiding her gaze. Iris couldn't blame him - she knew that her new form was just as confusing for him as it was for her. But she couldn't help but feel a pang of sadness at the thought of not being able to find comfort in his arms.

Meanwhile, Elias couldn't shake off the feeling of unease that had settled in his stomach. He had always been attracted to Iris, but now that she was in this new body, he didn't know how to reconcile those feelings. He couldn't bring himself to touch her, not when she looked so different.

Elias couldn't help but feel guilty for his lack of affection towards Iris. He knew that she was still the same person on the inside, but he couldn't shake off the feeling that something had changed between them. Iris, on the other hand, was trying her best to hide her own feelings of disappointment and hurt. She didn't want Elias to feel uncomfortable around her, but she couldn't help but feel like she had lost a part of herself. She looked down at her new body, the unfamiliar muscles and curves. She couldn't reconcile this stranger's body with her own identity. Iris took a deep breath, trying to push away her negative thoughts. She couldn't let herself get consumed by her feelings of fear and sadness. She needed to be a leader, not just for herself and Elias, but for their entire group.

They continued to set up their base camp, working in silence as they tried to ignore the awkward tension between them. Elias's mind was consumed with confusion and guilt, while Iris was fighting to keep her own emotions in check. Despite their internal struggles, they both knew that they couldn't let their personal feelings interfere with their survival.

As they worked, Iris's mind couldn't help but drift back to the message she had sent out earlier. She wondered if her friends had received it, and if they were on their way to meet her. She hoped that they were safe, and that they weren't facing any of the dangers that she and Elias had just encountered. Iris glanced over at Elias, feeling a pang of sadness in her chest. She knew that he was still struggling with her new form, and she didn't want to add any more stress to an already tense situation.

As they finished setting up the base camp, Iris couldn't shake off the feeling of unease that had settled in her stomach. She kept looking at her new body, her hands absentmindedly straying to the area where her new penis was. She couldn't help but feel self-conscious about it, and she couldn't help but feel a sense of disconnect from her own body.

Elias, on the other hand, seemed to be avoiding looking at her altogether. Iris couldn't blame him, she thought, as she watched him from the corner of her eye. He was probably just as uncomfortable with this new situation as she was. But still, it hurt to see him act like she was suddenly a stranger to him.

As they settled into their temporary base, Iris found herself constantly fidgeting with her clothes, trying to find a way to hide the bulge that she couldn't ignore. She felt like she was constantly on display, and it was only amplifying the discomfort she already felt.

Elias, on the other hand, had taken up position at the window, scanning the landscape for any signs of enemies. He had barely said a word since they had entered the base camp, leaving Iris to sit in silence with her thoughts.

As Iris fidgeted with her clothes, trying to make her new penis less noticeable, she felt a sudden surge of blood flow to her groin. She gasped in surprise, her hand instinctively going to cover the growing bulge in her pants. "Elias," she said softly, her voice barely above a whisper. "I-I need your help."

Elias turned away from the window, his eyes widening in surprise as he saw the look of panic on Iris's face. He quickly crossed the room, his hands reaching out to help her.

"What's wrong?" he asked, his voice filled with concern.

"I-I got an erection," Iris stammered, her face turning red with embarrassment. "I don't know what to do."Iris whispered, her voice shaking with frustration and embarrassment.

Elias's eyes widened in surprise, but he quickly regained his composure. "It's okay, Iris," he said, his voice gentle. "This is all just a part of your new form. It's going to take some getting used to," Elias told her, his voice soothing. Iris nodded, taking a deep breath as she tried to calm down. But as she closed her eyes, she couldn't help but feel a surge of excitement coursing through her veins.

"I can't help it, Elias," she whispered, her voice trembling with desire. "I feel like I'm losing control."

Elias looked at her, his eyes filled with concern. "Just try to relax and think of something else. Maybe imagine that you're back in your own body, or think about something that calms you down."

But Iris couldn't help it. The more she thought about it, the more excited she became. She felt a warmth spreading through her body, settling between her legs. She let out a soft gasp as she felt her arousal growing, her new penis swelling and twitching. She couldn't help but reach down and touch herself, her fingers tracing the outline of her shaft. She was a woman, but she had a man's body, and she couldn't ignore the strange new sensations that came with it. Elias, unable to watch, turned back to the window, his heart pounding in his chest.

Iris's touch was sending waves of pleasure coursing through her body, and she couldn't help but moan softly. She had never felt anything like this before, and she couldn't help but be drawn in by the raw, primal desire that was coursing through her veins.

Elias, on the other hand, was doing his best to ignore what was happening just a few feet away from him. He had never seen Iris like this before, and he didn't know how to react. He felt a strange guilt, and he couldn't help but wonder if he was betraying her by not joining in.

Iris, lost in her own sensations, barely noticed Elias's change of position. Her fingers were working in a frantic rhythm as she pleasured herself, her breath hitching with each passing second. She let out a low moan, her hips bucking against her hand as she reached her climax.

She felt a surge of pleasure flood through her veins, igniting a fire deep within her core. She gasped for breath, her fingers still wrapped around her aching shaft as she rode out the waves of pleasure.

She couldn't believe what had just happened. She had just experienced an orgasm as a man, and it had been unlike anything she had ever felt before.

As the waves of pleasure subsided, Iris couldn't help but feel curious about the strange, sticky fluid that had leaked from her new penis. She had never experienced ejaculation before, and she couldn't help but wonder what it tasted like.

Without hesitation, she brought her fingers to her mouth and tentatively licked the sticky fluid. It was salty and slightly bitter, but there was something strangely satisfying about the taste. It was a reminder that she was no longer a woman, but a man.

Elias, still standing at the window, couldn't help but turn around at the sound of Iris's gasp.

His eyes widened as he saw her licking her fingers, her cheeks flushed with pleasure.

"Iris," he whispered, his voice filled with disbelief. "What are you doing?"

Iris looked up at him, her eyes shining with desire and curiosity. "I just wanted to see what it tasted like," she said, her voice husky and low.

Elias swallowed hard, trying to keep his own arousal at bay. He knew that he couldn't give in to his own desires, not until he could come to terms with Iris's new form.

But even as he stood there, watching her explore her new body, he couldn't help but feel a growing sense of arousal. The way she moved, the way she touched herself, it was all so different, yet so mesmerizingly familiar.

Elias felt his own desires stirring within him, but he pushed them away, trying to focus on the task at hand.

"Iris, we need to be careful," he said, his voice strained and tight. "We don't know what's going to happen to us here."

Iris nodded, pulling her hand away from her body. She knew that Elias was right, but it was difficult to focus on anything other than the strange new sensations coursing through her veins. Iris had always been a sexual person, but she had never experienced desire like this before. It was overwhelming and intoxicating, and she couldn't shake it off.

Elias, on the other hand, was doing his best to remain strong for both of them. He knew that Iris was struggling with her new form, and he wanted to support her in any way he could. But seeing her touch herself like that had been difficult, to say the least.

He shifted uncomfortably in his seat, trying to discreetly adjust his own growing arousal.

Iris, too, felt herself getting lost in the moment. She couldn't believe what had just happened - the way her body had responded to her own touch, the way it had made her feel powerful and alive. But she also knew that they couldn't let this consume them. They had a mission to complete, and they couldn't afford to get distracted.

She took a deep breath, trying to calm herself down. This was all so overwhelming, and she needed to keep a clear head if they were going to survive in this strange new world. "You're right, Elias," she said, her voice steady. "We can't let our guard down. We need to figure out what's going on and find a way to get back home."

Elias nodded, turning back to the window. "I'll keep watch," he said. "You should get some rest."

Iris nodded, stretching out on the makeshift bed they had created. The adrenaline from the fight and the shock of her new body had left her feeling drained. She closed her eyes, trying to clear her mind and focus on their plan.

Elias stood vigilant by the window, his eyes scanning their surroundings. Despite his earlier reservations, he couldn't help but feel a sense of protectiveness towards Iris. He couldn't shake off the feeling that he needed to keep her safe.

As he watched her sleep, he couldn't help but think about their past. They had been lovers for years, their relationship growing stronger with each passing day. But this new development had thrown a wrench in their love life, leaving Elias feeling conflicted.

Meanwhile, Iris was oblivious to Elias's inner turmoil. She was lost in a world of chaos and uncertainty, and she needed him more than ever. She trusted him implicitly, and she knew that he would keep her safe from harm.

But even as she slept, the gears in her mind were turning. She was still trying to come to terms with her new identity. Iris knew that she was still the same person inside, but her new male body felt foreign to her. She couldn't ignore the strange new sensations that came with it.

But despite the challenges she was facing, Iris refused to let it define her. She was determined to overcome these obstacles and find a way back home. She couldn't just give up and let herself be consumed by fear and doubt. She needed to be strong for herself and for Elias.

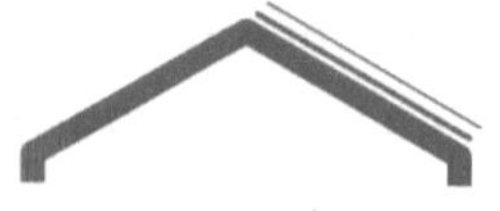

Chapter 3: Duncan / support

Duncan's eyes slowly fluttered open as the cool breeze gently tickled his face. He took a deep breath, inhaling the metallic scent that permeated the air. His fingers twitched as he tried to stretch, feeling the unfamiliar ache in his joints.

He glanced down at his hands, noticing the subtle differences in his fingers - their length, the softness of his palms, and the absence of a wedding ring.

It was then that it hit him - he was no longer in his own body. Panic set in as he frantically searched for a mirror, needing to see the truth for himself. Upon seeing his reflection in the broken window of a nearby building, he recoiled. Gone were the short brown hairs, hazel eyes, and muscular physique he was accustomed to. In its place was a tall, slender woman with short green hair, green eyes, and a body that was both foreign and familiar at the same time.

Panic set in as he tried to make sense of what was happening. He looked down at his chest, feeling the weight of his new breasts through the fabric of his shirt. He could feel the curves of his hips and the swell of his bottom. His body was now that of a woman, much to his surprise. It was then that memories of his character creation in the game flooded back. He had chosen a female avatar for a change, but little did he know that he would end up in this female form as well.

Duncan struggled with this new reality, attempting to reconcile his masculine personality with this new, feminine body. He felt a strange combination of confusion, disgust, and intrigue towards the new form that he was now inhabiting. He ran his fingers through his short green hair, feeling the texture difference from his usual hair. He slowly got up, wobbling slightly as he adjusted to the unfamiliar movements of his new body.

He couldn't help but feel a sense of unease in this unfamiliar body. His movements were different, and the weight of the KSVK 12.7 sniper rifle slung over his shoulder felt strange. Duncan's fingers traced the contours of the colt king cobra handgun sheathed at his hip, and the weight of the knife tucked into his boot felt alien. The tailored hunting camo suit he now wore hugged her curves and moved fluidly with his body.

He shifted his weight from one foot to the other, trying to find his balance. His hips swayed gently as he walked, and he couldn't help but feel self-conscious about it. He was used to a more rugged and masculine gait. This new body felt so vulnerable and exposed, and it made him feel on edge.

With every step he took, he felt the weight of his new form. His feet hit the ground differently, and his stride was shorter than he was used to. His hips moved in a way that felt alien to him, and he found himself constantly adjusting to this new way of walking.

Duncan scoped out his surroundings, taking note of the tall, looming building that seemed to stretch up to the sky's end. He saw the various signs of decay - broken windows, shattered pillars, and mounds of rubble scattered around the place. The whole area seemed eerily still, and he felt a chill run down his spine as he took in his surroundings. The city seemed to be in a perpetual state of twilight, with the sun never seeming to rise above the horizon.

The air was thick with fog, and the sound of distant machinery echoed through the empty streets. Duncan felt a sense of unease as he navigated the desolate landscape. He heard a faint beeping noise coming from his wristwatch. He glanced down at the screen, seeing a message from Iris asking him to rendezvous at their temporary base. Duncan's heart leapt with relief - at least he knew that she was safe.

Duncan sighed, knowing that he had to make a decision. He looked up at the towering buildings around him, the narrow streets weaving in and out of sight. He could try his luck in the labyrinth of streets, but he knew that his sniper rifle would be useless in such tight quarters. Alternatively, he could venture into the old metro system, but the stronger robots that inhabited those tunnels made it a daunting prospect.

After a moment of contemplation, Duncan decided to take his chances in the streets. He slung the KSVK 12.7 sniper rifle over his shoulder, feeling its weight against his back. He checked the clip on the colt king cobra handgun, making sure it was fully loaded. He adjusted the knife in his boot, feeling its comforting presence. He took a deep breath, trying to steady his nerves as he stepped out into the foggy streets.

The city was eerily quiet, and Duncan couldn't shake off the feeling of being watched. He hugged the shadows as he moved through the narrow alleys, trying to avoid detection. The streets were deserted, save for the occasional patrols of robotic guards. Duncan's senses were on high alert as he tracked their movements, trying to find a way around. He knew that if he made a wrong move, he would be caught and possibly killed.

But amidst the mind-numbing fear and the anxiety that gnawed at his gut, there was a small spark of excitement that coursed through his veins. It was a thrill he hadn't experienced before in his life, and it made him feel alive.

The thought of it didn't make sense at first. How could he possibly find pleasure in such a dangerous situation?

He felt a stirring deep within him, something he hadn't felt since before the transformation.

He gritted his teeth, trying to shake off the feeling. This wasn't the time for such thoughts, not when his life depended on staying sharp and focused.

Duncan's fingers clenched around the grip of his colt king cobra, and he took a deep, steadying breath. He couldn't let his mind wander, not when danger lurked around every corner.

But as he moved through the city, dodging patrols and avoiding traps, he couldn't shake the feeling that something was missing. He felt a strange emptiness deep within his core, a gnawing hunger that he couldn't quite put his finger on.

It wasn't until he stumbled upon a dimly lit alleyway that it hit him. The emptiness, the hunger, it was all because of the absence of something so integral to his masculinity. He couldn't help but think about the feel of his old body's penis, the weight and girth, the way it had felt in his hand, in someone else's. The thought made him ache with desire and he leaned against the cold brick wall for support.

His hand unconsciously drifted down to the new area between his legs, the space where his penis used to be. It was still sensitive, still aroused, but it wasn't the same. It wasn't his. He let out a frustrated groan, banging his head back against the wall.

The constant feeling of arousal was driving him crazy. He couldn't think straight, couldn't focus on anything other than the throbbing need between his legs.

But as he stood there, in the dark alleyway, he couldn't help but let his mind wander.

He closed his eyes, and in his mind's eye, he saw his new body, the lithe and slender figure he now possessed, looking at his old body, the muscular form he was used to.

He reached down, running his fingers over the new curves of his body. It was strange, foreign, yet there was something undeniably arousing about it. He closed his eyes, imagining it was his old body touching him, exploring every curve of this new form.

His hand moved lower, to the area between his legs where his penis used to be. He could still feel the arousal, the desire coursing through him. He imagined it was his old self, taking control, pleasuring this new body in ways he never thought possible.

The thought was intoxicating, overwhelming. He leaned back against the wall, letting the fantasy take over.

His mind raced with dirty thoughts, his imagination running wild. He thought of his old self, pleasuring this new body. He thought of dominating it, making it submit to his every whim. The thought made him moan, his hips bucking as he imagined it, hot and heavy and rough.

"Oh, fuck," he whispered, biting his lower lip as he worked his free hand inside his pants. He had always been a dominant lover, taking control and reveling in every moan and whimper of pleasure he could pull from his partner. He thought of his old self, the confidence and the masculine energy that he possessed.

He moaned softly as he imagined his old self, taking him from behind, thrusting hard and fast. He felt himself getting closer, his fingers moving faster and faster.

The thought of his old body, so strong and powerful, was almost too much to bear. He bit his lower lip, feeling the pleasure build up inside him. He imagined his old self, whispering dirty things into his ear, telling him how good he felt, how much he loved every curve of his new form. He could hear the heavy breathing of his own masculine persona in his mind, urging him to take control, to dominate.

In his imagination, his old self took charge. He pictured his old body grabbing is new form by the hips and thrusting deep and hard, causing a loud gasp to escape his lips. As he fingered himself, he couldn't help but feel like it was his old penis that was inside his vagina. The thought of it made him even more aroused, causing him to moan and buck his hips against his own hand. He imagined the feeling of being dominated and taken control of by his old self, the masculine energy that he was so used to. The fantasy was so intense that he could almost feel the weight of his old body on top of him, thrusting and pumping fiercely.

He could hear the wet and sticky sounds of sex, the sound of skin slapping against skin. He could feel the warmth of his old masculine form, filling him up, dominating him completely. He gasped, feeling himself on the brink of an intense orgasm. He imagined his old orgasm, powerful and forceful, filling him up completely until it spilled out of him. He whimpered, biting his lower lip as the intense pleasure coursed through him.

He couldn't hold back any longer. He let out a low moan as he came, the pleasure washing over him in waves. He leaned back against the wall, panting and breathless. He couldn't believe what had just happened. He had just pleasured himself, imagining his old body taking control

Duncan slowly opened his eyes, panting heavily as he came back to reality. He looked down at his hand, sticky with his own fluids, and couldn't help but feel a sense of disgust and confusion.

It felt wrong, twisted. He had always identified as straight, and the thought of being intimate with a man, even if that man was himself, was something he couldn't wrap his head around. But the desire, the intense need to feel something, to feel connected, was too much to ignore.

Duncan's fingers trembled as he wiped his hand clean on his pants, trying to collect himself. He took a deep breath, trying to calm down and regain his composure.

What the hell was he doing? Duncan couldn't believe what had just happened. He had almost forgotten where he was, lost in the intense pleasure that had coursed through his body. But now, as he stood there in the alleyway, he couldn't shake off the feeling of shame and disgust that had taken over him.

He looked down at himself with disgust, at the fluids that still clung to his fingers. It was wrong, he thought. It was twisted and perverse.

But even as the thought crossed Duncan's mind, he couldn't help but feel a stirring in his loins. He tried to shake off the feeling, to push it away, but it was no use. How could he possibly feel such a strong urge to be penetrate? It didn't make any sense to him. And yet, the desire throbbed inside of him, a constant ache that begged for satisfaction.

He realized that the thoughts and desires racing through his mind were not simply a product of hormones or anatomy. He saw that the craving to be penetrated was actually a desire for vulnerability and connection, a need to be filled and claimed. Duncan felt ashamed of these feelings and tried to suppress them. But the more he tried, the more they persisted, and the more he hated himself for it. He despised his new body, and the way it made him feel, the way it made him think.

Duncan's thoughts were interrupted by the sound of a loud bang. He quickly snapped out of his trance and drew his colt king cobra, ready for combat.

He peered around the corner of the alleyway and saw a group of robots closing in on him. They were humanoid in shape and made of a metallic alloy. Each one was armed with a rifle, and they were all aiming at him.

Duncan cursed under his breath. He had stopped paying attention to his surroundings, and now he was paying the price.

He quickly took cover behind a nearby dumpster, using it as a makeshift shield. The robots opened fire, their bullets pinging off the metal surface and whizzing past his head.

Duncan took a deep breath and steadied himself. He could feel the sweat beading on his forehead as he peeked around the dumpster, taking aim at the lead robot. He squeezed the trigger of his colt king cobra, hitting the robot right between the eyes.

It crumpled to the ground with a loud crash.

The other robots quickly moved to take its place, firing their rifles at Duncan with reckless abandon. He could hear the bullets whizzing past his head as he dove behind a nearby wall, trying to catch his breath.

He knew that he had to stay focused and use his recon skills to make it out of this situation alive. He visualized the alleyway in his mind, creating a mental map of the obstacles and vantage points. He knew that if he could use the buildings and dumpsters as cover, he could take out the robots one by one.

He peeked around the corner of the wall and fired a few shots. He watched as one of the robots stumbled backwards, its metallic body smoking and sparking.

Duncan reloaded his colt king cobra with shaking hands, trying to steady his nerves. He peeked out from behind the wall, assessing the situation.

He had managed to take out two of the robots, but there were still three left, each one more determined to take him down.

Duncan gritted his teeth, readying himself for the fight. He had always been confident in his abilities, but there was something different about this fight. He couldn't shake off the feeling of vulnerability that coursed through his veins, a constant reminder of the new body he now possessed.

He took a deep breath, trying to steady his nerves.

Even amidst the chaos of the fight, he couldn't shake off the lingering desires that had plagued him earlier. The thought of being penetrated, of submitting to someone else's pleasure, was still there, and it made his muscles tense with anticipation.

Duncan knew that he had to push these thoughts away, had to focus on the fight at hand. But even as he took aim and fired his gun, he couldn't help but imagine the feeling of being filled up, of being claimed by someone else.

He gritted his teeth, trying to suppress the thoughts. It felt like a sick joke, a cruel trick. He was a man, or at least he had been. He had always identified as a man, had always been attracted to women. And now, here he was, in a woman's body, with a constant ache between his legs.

But the desires persisted, even as the robots closed in on him. He could feel his breathing become more erratic as the thoughts of submitting to someone else's pleasure became more

prevalent. He could picture another man, strong and confident, pinning him against the brick wall of the alleyway, taking control of the situation. He imagined that man's lips on his, his tongue exploring his mouth as he crushed their bodies together. The thought of it made him moan, the pressure between his legs building up again.

Duncan's mind continued to wander as the fight raged on around him. He could see himself on his knees, submitting completely to the other man. He could feel the man's hard cock in his mouth, taste his salty skin and musky scent. The thought of it made him dizzy with lust, and he stumbled backwards, nearly dropping his gun.

The robots took advantage of this momentary lapse of concentration, and one of them fired a shot that whizzed past his ear.

Duncan snapped back to reality, realizing he had let his guard down. But the image of the man from his fantasy remained in his mind, and he couldn't shake it off. It was as if his body was betraying him, forcing him to confront desires that he had never before considered.

The fight raged on, and Duncan found himself struggling to keep up. He was used to being the hunter, not the hunted. But his mind seemed to be in a constant state of distraction, the tempting thoughts of the man from his fantasy so vivid that it felt like he was actually here with him.

He knew that he had to get a grip on himself, had to push these thoughts away and focus on the fight. But as the bullets whizzed past his head and the sound of metal scraping against concrete filled his ears, it proved to be a nearly impossible task.

His body tensed with anticipation and fear, sweat dripping down his brow as the robots continued to press their attack. Each time one of their bullets grazed his skin, a jolt of pleasure shot through him, culminating in a throbbing ache between his legs.

The robots seemed to be growing more aggressive with each passing second, and Duncan knew he had to find a way to gain the upper hand. He took a deep breath, focusing his mind on the task at hand.

He needed to gather his wits and fight back with a clear head. He moved quickly and quietly, using the terrain to his advantage as he skirted around the remaining robots, making his way deeper into the alleyway.

As he moved, he couldn't shake off the thoughts of vulnerability and submission that had plagued him earlier. It was as if they had taken root in his mind, germinating and growing stronger with each passing moment.

He couldn't escape the intense cravings, the desire to be filled up and claimed by someone else. It felt wrong, twisted even. But it was there, and he couldn't deny it.

Duncan could feel the weight of these illicit desires as he ducked and weaved around obstacles, fired off round after round at the pursuing robots.

With every step he took, he tried to ignore the throbbing between his legs and focus on the task at hand.

The hunter's instinct within him, normally so clear and unwavering, was clouded by a haze of desire that he couldn't shake.

He grunted in frustration. This was not the time to be distracted by such things, not when his life was on the line. But even as he reprimanded himself, his mind returned to the fantasy. He could hear the man's harsh voice in his ear as he whispered, "You belong to me now." And he could feel the man's strong arms wrap around him, pulling him close as he surrendered to the pleasure that coursed through his body, the feeling of being completely dominated and vulnerable. The thought of it made his skin tingle, and he felt a hot flush rise to his cheeks.

Meanwhile, the robots were still in hot pursuit. Duncan knew that he had to get a grip on his wayward thoughts if he wanted to survive this encounter. With renewed determination, he took cover behind a decrepit wall and raised his colt king cobra, waiting for the right moment to strike. The fog had grown denser, obscuring his vision and making it difficult to get a clear shot. But he knew that he had to stay focused and trust in his instincts.

As the robots approached, Duncan took a deep breath, centering himself. He waited for the perfect moment and then, with a swift motion, he emerged from his cover and fired. His bullets found their mark, taking down two of the robots in quick succession.

But the third one retaliated with a barrage of bullets that forced Duncan to take cover. He cursed under his breath as he reloaded, the sounds of the robots' mechanical footsteps echoing through the deserted alleyway.

Duncan knew he couldn't keep this up for much longer. His mind was still reeling from the intense desires he had experienced just moments ago, and he struggled to focus. But his training took over, and he managed to take down the last robot in a flurry of movement and bullet fire.

As the robot crumpled to the ground, Duncan let out a ragged breath, leaning against the wall for support. He was shaking with a mix of adrenaline and something else he couldn't quite identify. He looked down at his hands, still gripping the colt king cobra handgun, and noticed that they were trembling, and couldn't help but feel a sense of disgust. He was a man. But now, in this new body, he felt so unsure of himself, and the constant arousal was driving him crazy.

Duncan shook his head, trying to clear his thoughts. He needed to focus on the mission, not the confusing feelings that were bubbling up inside of him. With a determined look on his face, he made his way through the ruined metropolis, constantly on the lookout for any danger that might come his way.

As he approached the edge of the city, he came to a fork in the road. One path led through a the forest of cogs, the other through the molten gorge.

Duncan knew that this was a crucial decision. The path through the forest of cogs would be treacherous, but so was the path through the molten gorge.

He took a deep breath and weighed his options carefully.

Finally, he made up his mind and start walking.

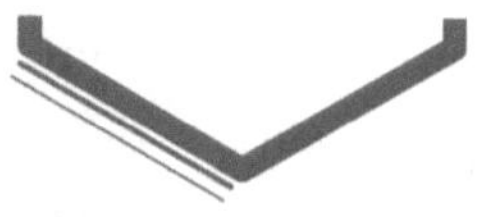

Chapter 4: Astrid / attacker

Astrid woke up in the game world, her avatar lying in a lush green bush, her heart racing as she tried to figure out what had just happened.

She looked around, taking in the vast garden filled with metallic automatons. She couldn't believe she was here, that this was real.

She got up and dusted herself off, taking a deep breath to steady her nerves. As she did, she couldn't help but steal a glance at her new form. Astrid's avatar was everything she had ever wanted to be - strong, lithe, and agile.

She ran her fingers through her long, golden hair and admired her own reflection in the nearby puddle. Her eyes, once a timid shade of blue, now sparkled with excitement and determination. She felt invincible in this new body.

As she gazed at her own reflection, Astrid couldn't help but feel a sense of pride and power that had long been absent from her life. She felt a surge of energy and confidence as she stood tall, ready to take on whatever the game world had to offer. she couldn't help but remember her real-life body. Astrid had always been self-conscious about her weight, but now, in this game, she felt perfectly comfortable in her own skin. It was as if she had finally found the confidence she had always been lacking.

Astrid moved gracefully through the garden, her every motion fluid and precise unlike her real life. She marveled at the way her avatar's body moved, how easily she glided through the air, how quickly she could run and jump. She couldn't believe this was her now. She felt like she could do anything.

Astrid began to explore the garden, taking in the sights and sounds of this new world. She admired the metallic automatons, their gears and cogs whirring and turning in perfect harmony. She marveled at the way they moved, with a grace and precision that belied their mechanical nature.

As she wandered through the garden, she suddenly heard the sound of her earpiece buzzing. She tapped it, and a voice filled her ear.

"Hey, Astrid. It's Iris. Meet me at the temporary base as soon as you can."

She followed the map to the temporary base, feeling a thrill as she moved with ease and speed. She couldn't help but compare this to her real life, where she often felt sluggish and slow, hindered by her self-perceived limitations.

The wind whipped through her hair, and she couldn't help but grin as she sprinted across the field. It was exhilarating, this newfound freedom, and she felt powerful and capable.

But then she saw them, a group of robots standing ominously in the distance. She slowed down, curiosity piqued. She couldn't help but feel an overwhelming urge to test her new abilities, to see what she was truly capable of.

She crept closer, her mechanical sword gripped tightly in her hand. She was ready for anything, heart pounding with excitement. As she approached the group, they turned to face her, their cold, metallic eyes meeting hers.

Without hesitation, Astrid charged at them, her sword flashing through the air. The robots moved quickly, but she was faster. She darted around them, striking from every angle.

The clash of metal against metal filled the air as she fought, each blow stronger than the last. Her heart raced with excitement, adrenaline coursing through her veins as she danced around the robots. She reveled in the feeling of power and control, something she had never experienced before. It was as if she had been born for this moment, made to fight and conquer. Each strike was precise, a well-rehearsed dance that flowed naturally from her fingertips.

As the battle raged on, she found herself lost in the rhythm of the fight. It was an intoxicating feeling, like nothing she had ever experienced before. Astrid was a woman who had always struggled with her body image, her weight and her lack of confidence had held her back in real life. But as she fought, her body moving with a grace and precision she never knew she possessed, she felt free. She felt alive.

And for the first time in her life, Astrid felt sexy. She couldn't help but feel a surge of pleasure with each strike of her sword. The way the metal sliced through the air, the feeling of power and domination, and the adrenaline coursing through her veins ignited something primal deep within her.

She couldn't help but let out a low moan. The sound echoed through the garden, adding to the chaotic sounds of the fight. The robots turned their attention to her, their eyes glowing with a new hunger. She reveled in the power she held over them, the way her body moved with such grace and confidence. And as she fought, she could feel her body responding to the adrenaline, the pleasure building up between her legs.

She let out a moan as she plunged her sword into one of the robots, feeling the warm metal give way beneath her blade. It was such an intense sensation, the feeling of power and control, that it was hard not to get lost in it.

She closed her eyes and let herself surrender to the feeling, letting it overtake her.

She couldn't believe what was happening to her body. She had never experienced anything like this before, but she couldn't deny how good it felt. She could feel herself becoming more and more aroused with each passing moment, her desire building up to a crescendo.

As she fought, she became more and more lost in the feeling. She moaned again, letting the sound fill the air. It was a low, primal sound that seemed to come from somewhere deep inside of her. It was a sound that she had never made before, and it took her by surprise. It was as if the intensity of the fight had awakened something inside of her, something primal and unhinged. It was a sound of pure animalistic pleasure.

She let out a loud groan as she thrust her sword into one of the robots with a satisfying crunch. She couldn't help it. The feeling of power, the adrenaline, and the sheer eroticism of the situation had taken over her body. She was completely consumed by it.

She could feel herself becoming wet, a warmth spreading between her legs as she fought with a renewed vigor. Each strike was fueled by the pleasure coursing through her body.

The sounds of the fight faded into the background as the pleasure took over. She let out another moan as she swung her sword with renewed vigor, her hips thrusting back and forth as she fought. She felt like a wild animal, fierce and uninhibited.

The sensation was so intense that it was almost too much to bear. Astrid's heart raced, her breath coming in short, shallow gasps as she fought the robots. She could feel herself getting closer to the edge, her body shaking with pleasure.

It was as if she was making love to the enemy, each thrust of her sword sending waves of pleasure coursing through her body.

She was on the brink of ecstasy, her clit throbbing with every strike of her weapon. She couldn't hold back any longer, her orgasm building up with the same intensity as the fight.

She threw her head back and let out a loud, primal scream as she came, the pleasure coursing through her body and fueling her strikes.

The orgasm seemed to last forever, her entire body trembling with pleasure as she fought.

As she slowly came down from her high, she realized that the fight had ended. The robots lay scattered on the ground, their cold metallic bodies twisted and broken. She looked at them, her gaze lingering on the damage she had inflicted.

She felt a sense of pride and satisfaction surge through her body, replacing the post-climax haze. She had never felt so alive, so powerful, and so free.

She took a deep breath, letting the feeling of victory wash over her, grounding her in the present moment. She felt a weight lifted off her shoulders, like she had just shed her old skin and emerged as a new, stronger person. She smiled to herself, feeling a newfound sense of confidence and pride.

She had never experienced anything like this before - the rush of adrenaline, the thrill of the fight, and the overwhelming pleasure. It was a heady mixture, and one that she couldn't get enough of.

Astrid couldn't wait to feel that rush again, to experience that freedom and power.

As she made her way to the temporary base, she thought about the irony of the situation. In the game world, she had found a confidence and a sensuality that had always eluded her in real life.

The thought made her smile, and she quickened her pace as she headed towards Iris. She wondered if her friend had experienced anything similar - the way the game world had a heightened intensity, the way the most mundane actions were infused with an undercurrent of pleasure. She wondered if Iris had discovered the sensuality that was hidden beneath the surface of every battle, every victory. She couldn't wait to find out.

As she made her way to the temporary base, Astrid reflected on the events that had led her to this point. She had always loved video games, ever since she was a little girl. Her parents had indulged her passion, buying her the latest consoles and games for every birthday and holiday. But as she grew older, her interest in gaming had been dismissed by her peers. It was a childish thing, they told her. Something for boys, not for young women on the brink of adulthood.

She had been told time and time again that she needed to grow up and focus on more "important" things. But she had never been able to shake her love of gaming, her need to lose herself in another world.

It was what had led her to this moment, to this new world that had opened up before her.

Chapter 5: Surrounded

Ian watched as the one of the robot wolf fell to the ground, its body convulsing in the throes of death.

His heart was racing, his hands shaking as he fumbled with his M1 Garand Rifle, trying to reload as quickly as possible.

He could feel his ears ringing from the loud gunshots, the smell of smoke and burning metal filling the air.

He was in trouble.

Out of the corner of his eye, he saw a blur of movement. He turned just in time to see another robot wolf charging towards him, its steel jaws open wide. Ian didn't have time to react, and the impact of the robot wolf sent him flying to the ground.

His head spun from the force of the collision, and he felt a sharp pain shoot down his spine.

The robot wolf let out a metallic howl as it prepared to finish him off. Ian's mind raced as he struggled to get back on his feet. His legs felt like jelly, and he could barely lift his arms to defend himself.

The robot wolf lunged forward, its jaws snapping shut just in front of his face. Ian rolled to the side, narrowly avoiding the deadly bite. He could feel the cold metal of the robot wolf's jaws brushing against his ear, and he shuddered in fear and disgust.

He knew that he couldn't keep this up for much longer. His body was weak, his mind exhausted. But more than that, he was frightened. Terrified of the thought of being torn apart by these monstrous machines.

CAUGHT IN GARDEN OF MECHANICAL SOULS

Ian had always been the quiet, unassuming type. He liked his games and his books, and he had never been one to take risks. But now, here he was, fighting for his life against an army of robotic beasts. It was like something straight out of one of his favorite anime, but the reality was far more terrifying.

As the robot wolf lunged at him once again, Ian barely managed to parry its jaws with his rifle. He could feel the cold metallic teeth gnashing against the wood and metal of his gun. His breath hitched in fear, his arms shaking as he tried to keep the robot wolf at bay.

As he pushed back against the wolf, Ian's fingers brushed against the cold metal of the Astra Model 900, still tucked securely in his holster.

With a surge of adrenaline, he pulled the weapon free, aiming it at the wolf's head. He squeezed the trigger, and the gun roared to life, the bullet tearing through the metal wolf's skull with a sickening crunch.

The wolf collapsed to the ground, its body twitching and sputtering as it powered down.

But even as Ian let out a sigh of relief, he knew that this was far from over.

There were still several robots wolves around him, their red eyes glowing ominously in the dim light.

As if on cue, one of the robots lunged forward, its metal jaws clamping down on Ian's left leg. He let out a scream of pain, his vision going white with agony. He could feel the metal teeth biting deep into his flesh, the pain excruciating and unbearable.

He dropped his Astra Model 900 as he fell to the ground, his hands scrabbling at the dirt as he tried to pull himself away from the robot's deadly grip. But the machine's hold was too strong, and Ian could feel himself being dragged.

In desperation, Ian reached for his bayonet, which he had tucked into his belt. With all the force he could muster, he thrust it into the robot's chest, driving it deep into its metallic body.

The wolf sputtered and fell still, its grip loosening around Ian's leg.

But the pain was unlike anything Ian had ever felt before. It was a deep, searing agony that pulsed through his entire body. He could feel the warmth of his own blood pooling around him as he desperately tried to crawl away from the mechanical beasts. He feel himself going into shock, his mind reeling with fear and desperation.

As if sensing vulnerability, another robot wolf lunged at him, its cold metallic teeth snapping shut dangerously close to his face. Ian let out a whimper, his vision swimming as he swung the bayonet wildly in front of him.

He could feel himself losing consciousness, the pain in his leg becoming a distant throb as his mind began to shut down. He didn't want to die here, not like this.

Suddenly, he heard the sound of gunfire ringing through the air. The bullets whizzed past him, striking the robots with deadly precision. Ian watched in amazement

as one robot wolf after another fell to the ground, the metal of their bodies buckling under the force of the shots.

He looked and see a figure emerging from the fog, a tall, athletic woman with short green hair, dressed in a hunting camo suit.

"Ian, move!" The woman shouted as he continued to rain bullets down on the robots. Ian didn't need to be told twice. He crawled away from the fallen robot wolf, his legs shaking with pain and exhaustion.

He glanced up at the woman, who was standing confidently with a KSVK 12.7 sniper rifle tucked into her shoulder. The gun swung in a practiced arc as she scanned the area, taking down any rogue robots that dared to venture too close to the fallen Ian.

As the last of the robots fell, the woman turned to him, a concerned look on her face. "Ian, are you okay?"

But Ian wasn't listening. His mind was racing, his thoughts a jumbled mess of pain and confusion.

"Duncan" He finally managed to croak out, his voice barely above a whisper.

Duncan knelt down beside him, her eyes filled with concern. "Yes, it's me, Ian. Don't worry, I've got you."

Ian's mind was still reeling from the pain, but he managed to focus on Duncan's question. "What?" He croaked, his voice barely above a whisper.

Duncan leaned in closer, her eyes filled with concern. "Ian, can you still use your character's abilities now that you're in the game? You know, the healing ability."

Ian's mind raced as he tried to process the question. He had never considered the possibility of using his character's abilities in the real world. But then again, this wasn't the real world. This was a game.

"I don't know," he finally managed to say, his voice barely above a whisper. "I've yet to tried it."

Duncan nodded, her eyes filled with determination. "Well, now's the time to try. You need to heal your leg, Ian. You're losing too much blood."

Ian looked down at his leg, which was still bleeding profusely. He knew that she was right. If he didn't do something soon, he was going to lose consciousness and bleed out.

Taking a deep breath, he closed his eyes and focused on the sensations of his body.

He could feel the heat radiating from the wound, the warmth of his own blood as it soaked through his rights. With a flick of his thoughts, he imagined the feeling of a warm, soothing sensation spreading over his leg.

At first, nothing happened. He could still feel the pain and the heat of the wound. But then, slowly, he could feel a warmth spreading from his groin, up through his body, to his leg. It was a strange sensation, one that he had never experienced before. But he knew that something was happening.

He could feel the warmth spreading from his groin, and with it, a tingling sensation that started in his pelvis and radiated outward.

With a deep breath, he closed his eyes and let himself go, allowing the pleasure to wash over him.

As he began to touch himself, he could feel the warmth in his leg growing more intense, the tingling sensation spreading throughout his entire body.He could feel his heart racing, his breath coming in short, shallow gasps as he explored his body.

His fingers traced a path up his inner thigh, the sensation of his own touch making him shiver with anticipation. He let out a low moan as he reached the apex of his thighs, his fingers brushing against the fabric of his underwear.

He could feel the warmth spreading from his leg, up through his body, to his groin. He let out a low moan as he slipped his hand beneath the fabric, feeling the heat of his own body.

He could feel the softness of his skin, the firmness of his chest. He let out a sigh of pleasure as he began to explore, his fingers tracing the contours of his own body.

He could feel the warmth of his own hand, the heat of his body radiating through his skin. He could feel the hardness of his nipples, the sensation sending a jolt of pleasure through his body. He let out a low moan as he continued to touch himself, his fingers tracing patterns on his chest, his nipples. The sensation was intense, almost overwhelming, but he didn't want to stop.

As he continued to touch himself, he could feel the heat in his leg growing more intense, the tingling sensation spreading throughout his entire body.

He could feel the warm, slick wetness of his own arousal as he continued to touch himself, his fingers exploring his new body.

He could feel his heart racing, his blood boiling with desire as he let out a low moan, his hips bucking up to meet his own touch.

Duncan watched as Ian writhed with pleasure, his eyes squeezed shut as he touched himself. Duncan couldn't deny the feeling of unease that washed over him as he watched. As he watched Ian touch himself, Duncan couldn't help but feel a strange sense of detachment.

The truth was, Duncan didn't find Ian's new female body attractive anymore. It wasn't that Ian's character wasn't beautiful, because she was. Her long white hair, blue eyes, and big breasts were all things that Duncan would have found attractive before. But now, in his new female body, Duncan found himself feeling nothing.

It was a strange and unsettling realization for Duncan. He had always identified as a straight man, and now, here he was, in a female body, unable to feel any attraction towards women. Instead, he found himself unable to stop thinking about men. It was as if his new body had somehow changed his sexual orientation.

Ian's fingers continued to dance over his body, tracing patterns and teasing his sensitive flesh. He could feel his heart pounding, his breath quickening as he let out a low moan. His fingers were slick with his own arousal, and he couldn't help but feel a sense of pleasure and release as he touched himself. It was a strange and surreal experience, being in a new body, experiencing new sensations. He couldn't help but feel a sense of wonder and delight as he explored his own body. He let out another moan as he slipped his fingers between his thighs, feeling the warmth and wetness of his own arousal.

As he touched himself, he could feel the heat in his leg growing more intense, the tingling sensation spreading throughout his entire body. He could feel his body trembling, his breath coming in short, shallow gasps as he neared climax.

He let out a long, low moan as he came, the pleasure shooting through his body like a bolt of lightning. His legs shook, his whole body convulsing with pleasure as the orgasm washed over him in waves.

As he lay there, panting and spent, Ian couldn't help but feel a sense of relief. The pain in his leg was gone, replaced by a warm, sated feeling that spread throughout his body.

Ian opened his eyes and looked up at Duncan, who was still watching him with a concerned expression on his face.

"Did it work?" Duncan asked, his voice filled with concern.

Ian sat up, wincing as he put weight on his once injured leg. To his surprise, the pain was completely gone. He looked down at his leg , expecting to see blood and gore, but instead, he saw only smooth, unblemished skin. The only trace remaining of the gruesome wound was torn fabric of his tight-highs.

Ian couldn't believe what had just happened. But as he looked down at his now unscathed leg, there was no denying that it was true.

Ian's heart was still racing from the recent events, and he couldn't help the feeling of awe and disbelief that washed over him. The pain was gone, replaced by a warm, sated sensation that still lingered in his body.

Duncan watched as Ian slowly got to his feet, his eyes wide with wonder. "Well, that's certainly one way to heal a wound," Duncan remarked, a smirk playing at the corners of his lips.

Ian couldn't help but feel his cheeks grow hot as he realized what he had just done in front of Duncan. It was strange and surreal, but at the same time, it was also incredibly erotic. He couldn't help but feel a spark of desire as he locked eyes with Duncan, and for a moment, he thought Duncan might lean in for a kiss.

But instead, Duncan cleared his throat and looked away, breaking the tension between them. "We should probably get moving. We're not out of danger yet." Duncan's voice cut through the tension, bringing Ian back to reality.

Ian blushed, his cheeks turning a deep shade of red as he realized that Duncan had caught him staring. He quickly looked away, not wanting to embarrass himself any further, readjusting the M1 Garand Rifle on his shoulder. He could feel the weight of the gun, the solidity of it grounding him in the game world.

Duncan had noticed the way Ian was looking at him, as if he wanted to be kissed.

But to Duncan's incomprehension, he couldn't seem to find women's bodies attractive anymore. Instead, his mind was filled with thoughts of men, their bodies and the desire to be close to them.

As Duncan handed Ian a water bottle, their fingers brushed against each other, sending a jolt of electricity through Ian bodies. Ian quickly pulled away, his cheeks flushed with embarrassment. He couldn't quite understand why he was feeling this way towards Duncan, but he couldn't deny the attraction he felt for him.

Duncan, on the other hand, was feeling equally as confused. He had always identified as straight, but now, in this game world, he couldn't stop thinking about men. It was as if his new female body had somehow changed his sexual orientation. He couldn't help but feel confusion towards his newfound feelings.

"We should start moving," Ian urged, breaking the silence between them as he picked up the Astra Model 900, which had fallen to the ground during the fight. He checked the gun, ensuring it was fully loaded before holstering it once again.

Duncan nodded in agreement, her eyes scanning their surroundings as she moved towards the front. "We still have a ways to go before we reach the temporary base. Let's stay on high alert and avoid any unnecessary risks."

As the two of them made their way through

the forest of cogs, the silence between them was heavy with unspoken words. They moved with a quiet, cautious grace, their senses on high alert for any signs of danger.

Ian couldn't help but steal occasional glances at Duncan, taking in the way the other woman moved with fluid, athletic grace. He couldn't deny the attraction he felt towards her, even if he didn't fully understand it. As he watched the way Duncan moved with grace and confidence, he couldn't help but feel himself drawn to him.

Duncan, on the other hand, was oblivious to Ian's admiring gaze. He was lost in his own thoughts, trying to make sense of her newfound attraction to men.

It was as if his new female body had awakened a dormant part of him, and he couldn't deny the allure of the male form. But at the same time, it was also confusing and scary. And now he was questioning his own identity.

Meanwhile, Ian was still getting used to his new female body. He ran his hands over his long white hair, marveling at its softness. His new body was a sight to behold; small and slender kinda like his original self, but with curves in all the right places. His breasts were large and heavy, and he couldn't help but feel self-conscious about them.

As they walked, Ian found himself becoming more aware of the way his hips swayed with each step, the way his breasts bounced slightly with each movement. It was a strange and unfamiliar sensation, one that caused him to blush furiously and bite his lower lip in embarrassment. He couldn't help but feel vulnerable and exposed in this new body, but he found that he liked it.

He had always been a little self-conscious about his height and looks, but now, he felt confident in this new female body. He couldn't help but feel a spark of excitement as he moved.

Duncan, on the other hand, was still struggling with the changes in his body. He couldn't help but feel a sense of unease as he looked down at himself. His mind was still trying to process the fact that he was now in a female body. It was a strange and unfamiliar sensation, one that he couldn't get used to.

As they continued their journey, Ian found himself growing more and more aware of the sensations of his new body. He could feel the softness of his own skin, the firm curve of his breasts, and the pleasurable sensation as he brushed against himself. It was a strange and unfamiliar feeling, but at the same time, it was also incredibly erotic. Ian couldn't help but feel a spark of desire as he grazed his own body, the new sensations that came with his new form were intense and exhilarating.

The events that had taken place had left Ian feeling a little overwhelmed, but at the same time, there was a sense of wonderment as he took in the beauty of the game world around him. It had a surreal quality to it, one that was both exhilarating and slightly unsettling.

Ian had never felt anything like this before, and he couldn't help but feel a sense of excitement as he moved. He could feel the tingling sensation of his body's new sensations, his skin flushing with heat.

Ian couldn't help but feel a spark of excitement as he exited the forest of cogs. The forest had been dangerous and unpredictable, but it was also a place of discovery and wonder.

Duncan, on the other hand, was relieved to finally leave the forest behind. He couldn't help but feel a sense of relief as they stepped out into the open, bright sunshine. The forest had been a place of danger and uncertainty, and he was glad to finally be free of it.

Chapter 6: Regroup

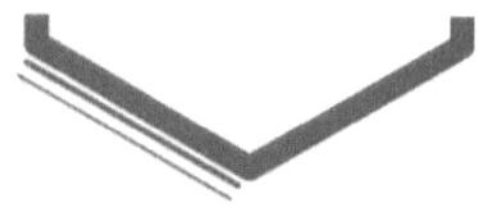

Iris and Elias had been patiently awaiting at the temporary base camp, inside the ruined laboratory. They knew they would eventually arrive, but time seemed to drag on forever as they waited. Iris felt a responsibility to ensure everyone's safety. She tried to shake off the feeling of unease that had been lingering in her chest.

Elias had been resting against a nearby wall. His brows were furrowed with worry, his dark eyes scanning the horizon as if he expected something to come charging out of the forest.

Iris, on the other hand, had been busy with her own thoughts. She was worried about Astrid, Ian and Duncan. Her mind was racing with questions about what had happened to them.

Iris glanced over at Elias, who was still looking out into the distance. She couldn't shake off the feeling of unease. She felt a strong urge to reach out and comfort him, but she held back, unsure of how he would react.

Just then, a loud noise caught their attention. Iris and Elias turned to see Astrid

emerge from behind a hill, her mechanical sword glinting in the sunlight. She looked triumphant, her eyes shining with a fierce determination.

Her sleek, blonde hair flowed behind her as she moved, her legs eating up the distance between her and the temporary base with ease.

CAUGHT IN GARDEN OF MECHANICAL SOULS

The robots in her path didn't stand a chance. She moved with a grace and agility that was almost inhuman, her mechanical sword slicing through metal and circuits with ease.

With each kill, she let out a triumphant cry, her eyes shining with a fierce determination.

As Astrid approached the temporary base, Iris and Elias couldn't help but stare in amazement. They had never seen anything like it before. Astrid's movements were fluid and precise, each swing of her sword slicing through the robots as if they were made of paper.

"Astrid!" Iris called out, waving her arms to get her attention.

Astrid turned towards them, a wide smile spreading across her face. "Iris! Elias! I made it!"

She ran towards them, her mechanical sword still raised high. As she reached the temporary base, she dropped to her knees, panting.

"I'm so glad you're safe," Iris said, helping Astrid to her feet. "We were worried sick about you."

"I'm fine, Iris," Astrid reassured her, brushing off her concerns. "I've made it this far on my own, haven't I? I can handle myself."

Elias nodded in agreement. "You certainly can, Astrid."

Astrid grinned, her eyes shining with a fierce determination. "I'll say. These robots didn't stand a chance. I've never felt so alive before." Astrid's voice was filled with excitement, and Iris couldn't help but feel a spark of admiration for the younger woman.

But as much as Iris wanted to bask in the feeling of relief and accomplishment, she couldn't shake off the nagging feeling of unease that had been lingering in her chest. She couldn't help but wonder what had happened to Ian and Duncan. She knew that they were all going through a lot, and she couldn't help but feel a sense of responsibility for their safety.

Astrid, still panting from the fight, looked up at Iris. "Iris, can I ask you something?" she said, her voice barely above a whisper.

Iris looked down at Astrid, her brows furrowed with concern. "Of course, Astrid. What is it?"

Astrid hesitated for a moment before speaking. "I was wondering... how do you feel about your new body? I mean, I know it must be strange for you, being in a man's body and all."

Iris looked down at herself, taking in the sight of her new form. She had to admit, it was strange. She ran her hands over her own chest, feeling the firmness of the muscles that had replaced the softness of her breasts.

Astrid's gaze dropped to Iris's own chest, and Iris couldn't help but feel a flush of embarrassment at the attention. She looked away, trying to focus on anything else but the sight of Astrid's form.

"I'm sorry," Astrid said, her voice soft. "I didn't mean to stare."

Iris shook her head, trying to dismiss the feeling. "No, it's fine," she said, her voice barely above a whisper. "I just... I'm not used to this yet." Iris admitted, still in a bit of shock from the sudden change in her body. She couldn't help but feel a little excited at the sight of Astrid flushed and panting from the earlier fight.

Astrid nodded, understanding the complexity of the situation. "I know it's strange, but you're handling it so well. I couldn't imagine being in your shoes." She smiled warmly at Iris, taking her hand in a comforting gesture.

Iris couldn't help but feel a jolt of electricity at Astrid's touch, her heart racing in her chest. She quickly pulled away, trying to hide her embarrassment. "Thanks, Astrid. I appreciate it." She said, trying to keep her voice steady. She couldn't shake off the feeling of unease, but at the same time, she couldn't deny the spark of excitement that she felt. She couldn't help but feel drawn to Astrid, even if she didn't fully understand why.

Astrid noticed the change in Iris's demeanor, and a small smile spread across her lips. She had always found Iris's personality to be an attractive, and now, with her new male form, she couldn't help but feel a spark of desire. But at the same time, she couldn't deny the confusion and guilt that came with those feelings. She kept her gaze cast down, not daring to meet Iris's eyes.

"Iris, I need to tell you something," Astrid said, her voice barely above a whisper. She glanced back up at Iris, her eyes filled with uncertainty. "I think I might be... attracted to you."

Iris felt as if the wind had been knocked out of her. She blinked, unsure of how to respond. She had never considered the possibility of being attracted to women before, but now, she couldn't deny the spark of excitement that she felt. She couldn't help but feel a little flustered and unsure of how to proceed.

"I-I don't know what to say," Iris stammered, her mind racing with a mixture of confusion and excitement. She couldn't help but feel a spark of attraction towards Astrid, but at the same time, she couldn't shake off the feeling of guilt. She looked over at Elias, who was watching the exchange with a mixture of confusion and hurt on his face.

Elias couldn't believe what he was hearing. He had always known that Iris was a beautiful and desirable woman, but he had never considered the possibility of her being attracted to other women. He felt a pang of jealousy as he watched Astrid gaze at Iris, his heart heavy with the weight of his emotions.

He couldn't deny the feelings of hurt and confusion that had taken hold of him. He loved Iris, and he couldn't stand the thought of her being with someone else.

"Iris, can I talk to you for a moment?" Elias asked, his voice tense with emotion.

Iris looked up at him, a confused expression on her face. "Sure, what's up?"

Elias hesitated for a moment before speaking. "It's about Astrid," he said, his voice barely above a whisper. "I don't like the way she's looking at you."

Iris raised an eyebrow, her confusion deepening. "What do you mean? She's just being friendly."

Elias shook his head, his jaw clenched with frustration. "No, it's more than that. I can see it in her eyes. She wants you, and it's making me jealous."

Iris blinked, surprised by Elias' words. She had never seen him like this before, and she couldn't help but feel a little flustered by his sudden display of emotion. "Elias, it's not like that," Iris said, trying to reassure him. "Astrid and I are just friends. I would never do anything to hurt you."

Elias looked away, his jaw clenched. "I know that, Iris. But it's hard for me to see her looking at you like that."

Iris couldn't help but feel a pang of guilt as she looked at Elias. She knew how he felt, but at the same time, she couldn't deny the spark of attraction that she felt towards Astrid.

She took a deep breath, trying to steady herself. "Elias, I need you to understand something. I'm still the same person, even if I'm in a man's body. I need to feel loved and comforted, just like anyone else."

Elias sighed, running a hand through his hair. "I know, Iris. It's just... it's hard for me to see you like this. You're not the same person I fell in love with."

Iris's heart sank at his words. "What are you saying, Elias? That you don't love me anymore?"

"No, of course not," Elias quickly reassured her. "I still love you, Iris. But it's different now. I can't help but feel like I've lost the woman I fell in love with."

Iris felt tears prick at the corners of her eyes. "So, what are you saying? That we're over?"

"No, Iris. I'm not saying that," Elias said, his voice softening. "I'm just saying that this is all a lot to take in. I need some time to adjust to the changes. I can't be intimate with you while you're in a man's body. It just feels... wrong." Elias finished.

"I understand, Elias," Iris said, trying to keep her voice steady. She couldn't deny the hurt she felt at his words, but she knew that he was struggling to come to terms with the changes in her body. "I'll give you the space you need. But please know that I'm still the same person inside."

Elias nodded, and the two of them stood in silence for a moment. Iris couldn't help but feel a heavy weight in her chest as she watched him walk away. She knew that he needed time to come to terms with the changes, but it still hurt to know that he couldn't be intimate with her in her new form.

Astrid, who had been quietly watching the exchange, stepped forward. "Iris, I need to talk to you," she said, her voice soft.

Iris looked up at Astrid, a confused expression on her face. "What is it, Astrid?"

Astrid took a deep breath, gathering her courage. "I need to apologize to you. I know that it's my fault that you and Elias argued. I shouldn't have confessed my feelings to you like that. I didn't mean to hurt you or Elias." Astrid's eyes filled with regret. "I know that this must be difficult for both of you, and I didn't mean to make things worse. It's just that being in this new body has brought out feelings in me that I never knew were there. And seeing you in your new form, it's been hard for me to ignore the attraction I feel towards you."

Iris looked into Astrid's eyes, her heart racing. She couldn't deny the spark of attraction she felt towards Astrid, but she didn't want to hurt Elias. "I understand," Iris said, taking a deep breath. "I feel the same way, but I don't want to betray Elias. I need to find a way to make things right with him."

Astrid nodded, understanding Iris's position. "I know. I just wanted to apologize for what I did. I never meant to come between you two." Astrid said, her voice barely above a whisper.

Iris shook her head, understanding the turmoil that Astrid was going through. She couldn't deny the spark of attraction that she felt towards the other woman, but she knew that she couldn't act on it while she was with Elias. "It's not your fault, Astrid. I'm still figuring things out myself. I need to find a way to make things right with Elias."

Astrid nodded in agreement, understanding the complexity of the situation.

Meanwhile, Elias had stepped outside the lab to cool off, the tension between him and Iris weighing heavily on his mind. He couldn't shake off the feeling of unease. He had never felt so conflicted before, and he didn't know how to handle it. He wandered around the outskirts of the lab, trying to clear his head. He needed some time to think.

As he was walking, he noticed Ian and Duncan approaching from afar. He could see the look of exhaustion on their faces, but he couldn't deny the sense of relief that washed over him as he saw them coming. "Guys, over here!" Elias called out, waving his arms to get their attention.

Ian and Duncan picked up their pace as soon as they saw Elias. They were both relieved to have made it back in one piece. It had been a tough journey getting here, but they were determined to make it.

As they drew closer, Elias couldn't help but notice the way Ian's breasts jiggled as he walked. He tried to avert his gaze, but he couldn't deny the way his eyes were drawn to them.

Duncan, on the other hand, couldn't help but feel a sense of excitement as he took in the sight of Elias' masculine form. He couldn't deny the way his body reacted to the other man, and he couldn't help but feel a sense of disgust at the way his body reacted to Elias. It was as if he had lost control over his own desires, and he didn't know how to handle it.

As they approached Elias, Ian couldn't help but feel a sense of embarrassment at the way his breasts were bouncing with each step.

He crossed his arms over his chest, trying to hide them from Elias view.

He couldn't help but feel a sense of discomfort as Elias continued to stare at him.

"What's wrong, Ian?" Elias asked, noticing the other man's discomfort.

"I don't like the way you're looking at me," Ian replied, his voice barely above a whisper.

Elias's gaze snapped up to Ian's face, a look of confusion crossing his features. "What do you mean?" he asked.

"Like you're undressing me with your eyes," Ian said, his cheeks flushed with color. "It's disturbing."

Elias couldn't deny the way his gaze had been drawn to Ian's chest, but he couldn't understand why it would be seen as a problem. "I just can't help but notice the changes in your body. It's strange for me, seeing you like this, with breasts. and they're... well, they're quite large."

Ian couldn't help but feel a flush of embarrassment flood his cheeks. He didn't like being the center of attention, especially not when it came to his body. "Please just stop looking at me," he pleaded, lowering his gaze to the ground.

But as much as Ian tried to hide, Elias couldn't tear his gaze away.

Duncan, who had been quietly watching the exchange, couldn't help but feel a pang of jealousy. He couldn't understand why he was feeling this way towards Elias, but the sight of him staring at Ian's chest filled him with a sense of unease, but he couldn't deny the intense desire that was coursing through his veins. He had never felt this way before, and he didn't know how to handle it.

"Hey, cut it out, Elias," Duncan snapped, stepping between them. "Ian's not a piece of meat for you to ogle at. You should only have eyes for me." Duncan said, his voice laced with a hint of jealousy. Realizing what he just said, Duncan tried to cover it up. "I mean, you should only have eyes for Iris, as her boyfriend." Duncan finished awkwardly, trying to backtrack from his unintentional confession.

However, the words had already been spoken, and the tension in the air only grew thicker.

Elias turned to look at Duncan, a mixture of confusion and hurt etched on his face. "What did you just say?" he asked.

Duncan's face turned beet red as he stammered, trying to come up with an excuse for what he had just said. "I-I didn't mean it that way, Elias," he said, taking a step back. "I just meant that you should only be focusing on Iris right now. That's all." Duncan said, his voice barely a whisper, as he struggled to contain the turmoil of emotions that were coursing through his veins. He couldn't deny the way he felt towards Elias, but he couldn't help but feel a sense of guilt and confusion at the same time. He had always been straight, or so he thought. But now, in this alternate reality, he couldn't help but feel a spark of desire towards the man in front of him. He couldn't understand it, and he felt ashamed of himself for even thinking it. Duncan felt a stirring in his loins. He tried to ignore it. But the feeling persisted, and he couldn't shake it off.

Elias, for his part, couldn't help but feel a sense of embarrassment as Duncan stared at him with a look of desire. He had never seen his friend look at him like that before, and it made him feel uncomfortable. But he also couldn't shake off the feeling of unease that had taken hold of him. He couldn't deny the way his heart raced as he took in the sight of Duncan's new form, with her short green hair, her green eyes, and her well-built body. She looked like a confident, athletic woman, and there was no denying the way she looked at him. Elias couldn't deny the way his heart raced as he took in the sight of Duncan's new form. He tried to shake off the feeling, but it

was no use. He couldn't help but feel a spark of attraction towards her, despite the fact that she was his male friend.

He couldn't understand why he was feeling this way, but he couldn't deny it either. He felt a stirring in his loins as he watched her, and he couldn't help but feel a sense of guilt and confusion at the same time. He couldn't understand it, and he felt ashamed of himself for even thinking it.

Ian, sensing the strange mood, spoke up. "Hey, guys, I think we should all go inside with Iris and Astrid. It's not safe out here with all these robots around."

Duncan nodded, still looking at Elias with a mixture of desire and confusion. "Yeah, you're right. Let's go."

The three of them made their way back to the temporary base, where Iris and Astrid were waiting for them. As they approached, Iris couldn't help but feel a sense of relief at seeing them all safe and sound. "You guys made it," she said, a small smile spreading across her lips.

But her smile quickly faded as she took in the strange atmosphere between Duncan and Elias. "Is everything okay?" she asked, her gaze flicking between the two men.

Elias and Duncan exchanged a look, both of them looking uncomfortable.

"We're fine," Duncan said, breaking the silence. "Just a little... thrown off by the changes."

Iris nodded, understanding the turmoil that they were going through. But as she looked at Duncan, she couldn't help but notice the way his gaze lingered on her new form. She could see the desire in his eyes, and she couldn't deny the way her own body reacted to his gaze. She felt a flush of heat spread across her cheeks as she took in the sight of Duncan's new form. Duncan looked like a confident, athletic woman, and there was no denying the way he looked at her. She couldn't understand why she was feeling this way, but she couldn't deny it either.

"We need to discuss what to do next," Iris said, trying to break the tension in the room. "We need to make our way to the game's only city. It's the best place to go if we can find answers and get out of this alternate reality. I think we should stick together and make our way to the city as a group. It's too dangerous to travel alone, and we don't know what kind of dangers we'll encounter along the way." Iris looked around the room, making eye contact with each member of the group. "We need to stick together and have each other's backs. That's the only way we're going to make it through this."

Her words were met with nods of agreement from everyone in the room. Despite the tension and confusion, they all knew that working together was the only way they were going to get through this bizarre situation. And so, with a newfound sense of determination, they began to plan their journey to the city.

"What do you think the NPCs will be like in the city?" Ian asked, breaking the silence. "Will they still follow their programming or will they have free will now that the game is real?"

"I don't know, Ian," Iris said, shaking her head. "But I think it's safe to assume that they'll be different. They might have more complex behaviors and emotions, and they might not be as predictable as they were in the game."

"But what if they become hostile?" Ian asked, his voice trembling slightly.

"That's a valid concern, Ian," Iris responded, her voice steady and reassuring. "But I have a feeling that they might have their own personalities and desires, just like we do. We just need to approach them with caution and try to communicate with them as best we can." Iris looked around the room, making sure everyone was on the same page. "We also need to be mindful of our surroundings and keep an eye out for any potential threats."

Duncan nodded in agreement, his gaze lingering on Iris's form for a moment longer. He couldn't deny the way he felt, but he knew that he had to keep it under control. He couldn't let his feelings for Iris get in the way of their survival.

As the group discussed their plans, Astrid couldn't help but steal glances at Iris. Ian sat quietly in the corner, taking in the conversation around him. He couldn't help but feel overwhelmed by the strange turn of events. He had always been a shut-in, preferring the comfort of his own home to the chaos of the outside world. But now, he was thrust into a strange new reality, one where he had become a woman. He couldn't deny the way his new body made him feel, and he couldn't help but feel a sense of fascination with his new form.

But at the same time, he couldn't shake off the fear of the dangers that this new world posed. He had always been vulnerable in the real world, and now, in this game world, he was even more so. His new body was small and delicate, and it made him feel exposed. He couldn't deny the feeling of excitement that he felt, but he also couldn't shake off the fear that came with it. He was scared of what could happen to him in this new world, and he couldn't help but feel overwhelmed.

As the group continued to talk, Duncan's mind couldn't help but wander. He kept stealing glances at Elias, taking in the other man's muscular form. He couldn't deny the strange pull that he felt towards him, but he couldn't understand it either. But now, in this alternate reality, he found himself being drawn to Elias's masculine energy. Duncan's thoughts trailed off as he watched Elias talk animatedly with Iris, his gaze lingering on the other man's lips as he spoke.

Meanwhile, Astrid couldn't help but feel a pang of jealousy as she watched Iris and Elias interact. She couldn't deny the way her heart raced as she watched them, and she found herself struggling to control her growing desire for Iris. She had never felt this way before, and she couldn't understand why. But she couldn't deny the spark of attraction that had ignited between them, and she found herself drawn towards Iris like a moth to a flame.

As the group finished their discussion, they decided to set out towards the city at first light. For now, they needed to rest and gather their strength for the journey ahead.

Iris, however, couldn't shake off the thought of sharing a room with Elias. She wanted to be close to him, to feel his warmth next to her as they slept. She had always found comfort in his presence.

Iris approached Elias as he was setting up a makeshift bed for himself in a separate room. "Elias, can I sleep next to you tonight?" she asked, her voice soft and hesitant.

Elias turned to look at her, his expression unreadable. "I don't think that's a good idea, Iris," he said, his voice firm. "We need to maintain some distance between us."

Iris couldn't help but feel a pang of hurt at his words. She knew that he was still struggling to come to terms with her new form, but it still hurt to hear him say that. "But why not, Elias?" she asked, her voice trembling slightly. "I need to feel close to you." Iris's voice was barely above a whisper as she spoke, and Elias could see the longing in her eyes. "I understand how you feel, Iris. But I don't know if I can give you what you need right now. It's all so confusing, seeing you like this."

"I know, Elias. I'm sorry. I didn't choose this; it just happened. But I'm still me, Iris.I didn't change, just my appearance." Iris's voice was laced with sadness, her green eyes pleading with Elias to understand.

Elias sighed, running a hand through his short black hair. I know." He took a step closer to her. "I just need some time to adjust. Can you give me that?" Elias looked into Iris's eyes, and he could see the hurt and longing in her gaze. He knew that she needed him, and he didn't want to deny her that comfort. But at the same time, he couldn't shake off the feeling of unease that he felt at the thought of being intimate with her in her new form.

"Iris, I don't know if I can do that," Elias said, his voice soft.

"Then I'll sleep with Astrid ," Iris said, her voice firm.

Elias's eyes widened in surprise. "What?" he asked, taken aback.

"You heard me," Iris said, crossing her arms over her chest. "If you don't want to be intimate with me, then I'll find someone else who does. I'm not going to deny my own needs." "But Iris, you're my girlfriend. I love you," he said, his voice filled with emotion.

"And I love you, Elias. But I can't help the way I feel," Iris said, her voice softening. "I need to feel desired, and if you can't give me that, then I need to find someone who can."

Elias couldn't deny the hurt that he felt at her words. He knew that she was in pain, struggling with her own feelings. But the thought of her being intimate with someone else was unbearable.

"Iris, please," he begged, trying to find the right words to say. "Can't we just work through this together? I love you, and I want to be with you. But this is all so strange and new, and I don't know if I can handle it."

Iris looked into Elias's eyes, searching for understanding and empathy. She saw the turmoil and conflict in his gaze , but she couldn't help the way she felt. She needed to feel desired and loved, and if Elias couldn't give her that, then she needed to find it elsewhere. But she also didn't want to hurt him or damage their relationship. "Elias, I don't want to hurt you," she said softly. "I just need to find a way to cope with these new feelings and experiences. And I need to feel desired and loved, even if it's not from you."

Iris's words cut through Elias like a knife, and he couldn't deny the feeling of jealousy and hurt that washed over him. He knew that he loved her, but the thought of her being with someone else was too much to bear. He couldn't help the way he felt, and it was clear that Iris couldn't either.

As the two of them stood there, locked in a silent standoff, the tension between them was palpable. Elias could see the hurt and longing in Iris's eyes, but he couldn't shake off the feeling of unease that he felt at the thought of being intimate with her in her new

form. He knew that he loved her, but the thought of being with her in this new way was still too much for him to handle.

Iris, seeing the look on Elias's face, sighed in frustration. She couldn't force him to feel something that he didn't, and she couldn't keep waiting around for him to come to terms with her new form. She needed to take matters into her own hands.

"Elias, I'm going to go talk to Astrid," she said, turning to leave the room. "I need to figure some things out, and I don't want to keep waiting around for you to make a decision."

Elias's heart sank as he watched her walk away. He knew that he had hurt her, and he didn't want to lose her. But he also didn't know how to move forward. He didn't know how to bridge the gap that had formed between them. He didn't know how to reconcile his feelings for her with her new form. He didn't know how to show her that he loved her, even if she looked different.

Elias watched as Iris left the room, his heart heavy with dread. He knew that he had a lot of thinking to do. He knew that he needed to come to terms with his feelings and find a way to bridge the gap between them. He couldn't lose Iris; she was everything to him. He had to find a way to reconcile his feelings and move forward. But for now, he needed to clear his head and think.

Elias decided to sleep it off and speak to her in the morning. He lay down on his makeshift bed, staring up at the ceiling, lost in thought.

Meanwhile, Ian and Duncan were preparing for the night in another room. They had decided to bunk together, both of them feeling uneasy about sleeping alone.

"Hey, Duncan, are you okay?" Ian asked, his voice soft as he looked over at his friend.

Duncan sighed, looking up from his makeshift bed. "I don't know," he said, his voice laced with exhaustion. "This whole situation is just so overwhelming. I feel like I'm losing myself in this new body."

Ian looked down at his chest, where his new large breasts were housed. The sensation of having them was still strange and foreign to him, and he couldn't help but feel a sense of vulnerability and insecurity. "I know how you feel, Duncan," Ian said, his voice soft and understanding. "But we're all in this together. We'll figure it out and find a way to make it work."

Duncan nodded, feeling a sense of gratitude towards Ian.

As they settled into their makeshift beds, Duncan couldn't shake off the thoughts of Elias and Iris. He couldn't deny the desire that he felt for them, but he also couldn't understand why he was feeling this way. He had never been attracted to men before, and it was all so confusing and overwhelming.

He couldn't deny the way his thoughts kept drifting towards Elias. He had always admired Elias's strength and confidence, but now, he couldn't help but see him in a different light. He couldn't help but wonder what it would be like to touch him, to feel his skin under his fingers. He couldn't deny the way his thoughts kept drifting towards Elias's body, and the things he wanted to do to him.

As these thoughts swirled in his mind, Duncan couldn't help but feel a stirring in his loins. He couldn't shake off the arousal that was building within him, and he knew that he needed to release it.

He looked over at Ian, who was lying on his makeshift bed, fast asleep. Duncan couldn't help but feel a stirring of desire as he think about Elias. He couldn't deny the way his body reacted to him, and he knew that he needed to do something about it.

He glanced over at Ian one more time, making sure that he was still asleep. Then, with a trembling hand, he reached down and began to touch himself. He closed his eyes, imagining what it would be like to be touch by Elias, to be claim by him. He couldn't help the images that flooded his mind as he begin to touch himself with more urgency.

Duncan imagined Elias' lips on his, his hand on the back of his head holding him there as their tongues dance together in a passionate kiss. He couldn't help the moan that escaped his lips as he imagine being penetrated by the other man, having him deep inside him. His fingers moved faster and faster, matching the rhythm of his imagined thrusts. He could feel the orgasm building within him, the pleasure curling in his stomach and spreading throughout his body.

The thought of it was too much, and soon enough Duncan was panting heavily as his hand moved quickly. He couldn't help but imagine Elias on top of him, his muscles ripple as he thrust in and out of him. He imagined feeling him inside of him, filling him up, and Duncan couldn't help but whimper in pleasure. It was all so dirty and wrong, but it felt so good. His breathing grew heavy, and he moaned as he continued to touch himself. He fantasized about Elias's hands on his hips, holding him down as he took him deeper and harder. He thought about the way Elias's muscles would ripple and tense with every thrust, the other man's moans filling his ears.

But just as the orgasm was about to take over, Duncan heard a soft noise coming from Ian's direction. Duncan froze, his heart racing as he realized that Ian was awake and had likely heard him. He quickly pulled his hand away and turned to face Ian, his cheeks flushed with embarrassment.

"I-I'm sorry, I didn't mean to wake you up," Duncan stammered, his voice barely above a whisper.

Ian looked over at Duncan, a small smile playing at the corners of his lips. "It's okay, Duncan," he said, his voice soft and understanding. "I know how you feel. I've been struggling with my own feelings in this new body."

Duncan looked at Ian, a sense of relief washing over him. He knew that he could trust Ian, and he felt grateful for his understanding and acceptance.

"I just don't understand why I'm feeling this way," Duncan said, his voice filled with confusion and frustration. "It's all so overwhelming."

Ian nodded, understanding the turmoil that Duncan was going through. "It's okay to feel confused, Duncan," he said, his voice soft and reassuring. "This whole situation is strange and new for all of us. We're all still trying to figure out how we feel about ourselves and our new bodies."

Duncan nodded, taking in Ian's words of wisdom. But even as they spoke, he couldn't shake off the thoughts of Elias that kept flooding his mind. He couldn't deny the desire that he felt for him, and he knew that he needed to do something about it.

Duncan got up from his bed and decided to go for a walk to clear his head. As he walked, he couldn't shake off the thoughts of Elias that kept flooding his mind. He was still struggling to come to terms with his newfound attraction to men, and he didn't know how to navigate these feelings.

As Duncan turned a corner, he caught sight of Iris entering Astrid's room. Duncan continued to walk, lost in thought. He couldn't deny the attraction he felt for Elias, but he couldn't shake off the feeling of unease that came with it.

Meanwhile, in Astrid's room, Iris was expressing her frustrations to Astrid about Elias. "I just don't know what to do, Astrid," Iris said, her voice laced with frustration. "Elias is being so stubborn and distant. I just want him to understand and accept me for who I am."

Astrid looked over at Iris, her expression sympathetic. "I understand, Iris," Astrid said, her voice soft and understanding. "It's not easy, but you have to give him time. He'll come around eventually."

But as Astrid looked at Iris, she couldn't shake off the thoughts that had been running through her mind. Astrid couldn't deny the spark of attraction that had ignited between them, and she found herself taking advantage of the situation.

"Come here, Iris," Astrid said, her voice soft and inviting. "Let me give you a hug."

Iris hesitated for a moment, but then she relented and stepped into Astrid's embrace.As Astrid's arms wrapped around her, she couldn't help but feel a sense of warmth and comfort. She closed her eyes and took a deep breath, letting out a sigh of relief. It had been a long and stressful day, and she was grateful for the chance to relax and unwind.

Astrid held her tightly, allowing her comfort and warmth to envelop Iris. Iris couldn't deny the way she felt in Astrid's arms, and she found her body responding to the other woman's touch.It was unfamiliar and strange, but she couldn't deny the arousal that was building within her. She couldn't help but feel a spark of attraction and excitement.

Astrid, feeling Iris's body respond to her touch, couldn't help but feel a sense of satisfaction and desire. She knew that Iris was still getting used to her new male form, but she couldn't deny the way she felt about her. She had always been somehow attracted to Iris, even as girls, but now she couldn't shake off the growing desire that was building within her.

Iris pulled away, her face flushed with embarrassment.

"I'm sorry, Astrid," Iris said, her voice trembling slightly. "I didn't mean for that to happen."

Astrid looked at Iris, a small smile playing at the corners of her lips.

"Don't worry about it, Iris," she said, her voice soft and understanding. "I know it's all new for you, and it's okay to feel confused and overwhelmed. But I'm here for you, and I'll support you no matter what."

Iris couldn't help but feel a surge of gratitude towards Astrid. She had always been there for her, and she couldn't imagine going through this strange new world without her. She glanced over at Astrid, taking in the other woman's slender form and delicate features.

Iris couldn't deny the way her heart raced as she looked at her, and she couldn't shake off the feeling of excitement that washed over her. She had always been close to Astrid, but now, in her new male body, she couldn't help but feel a spark of attraction that was unfamiliar and strange.

Astrid, sensing the change in Iris's demeanor, couldn't help but feel a surge of excitement and desire. She stepped closer to Iris, her body brushing up against her.

Iris couldn't help but gasp as Astrid pressed herself against her, the other woman's hands running over her chest. "Stop," Iris stammered, trying to push Astrid away. "I can't do this. I'm with Elias."

But Astrid didn't listen. She leaned in, her lips finding Iris's in a fierce kiss. Iris couldn't help but respond, her body betraying her as she kissed Astrid back.

"Iris, I want you," Astrid whispered, her hand slipping under Iris's waistband. "I can't deny it anymore.

Iris's heart raced as Astrid's hand explored her body. She knew it was wrong, but she couldn't deny the excitement that coursed through her veins. S

"But what about Elias?" Iris asked, her voice barely above a whisper.

"He doesn't have to know," Astrid said, nibbling on Iris's earlobe."We can have this moment, just the two of us."

Iris's mind raced as Astrid's hand explored her body. She knew she should push her away, but she couldn't deny the desire that surged through her veins. She had never been with a woman before, but there was something about Astrid that drew her in.

She couldn't deny the longing she felt in Astrid's arms, and she knew that she needed to explore this new desire. Iris was still hesitant, but the passion building between them was too strong to resist.

"Astrid, wait," Iris panted, trying to catch her breath. "I've never done this before. I don't know if I can...do this" Iris gasped as Astrid's hand moved down her body, slipping under her underwear. The other woman's

fingers wrapped around Iris's new penis, and she couldn't help but gasp as Astrid began to stroke her. It was a strange and unfamiliar sensation, but she couldn't deny the pleasure that coursed through her veins.

"You can, Iris," Astrid whispered, her lips finding Iris's again in a deep, passionate kiss.

"You can do anything you set your mind to."

Astrid's voice was soft, encouraging as she moved her hand up and down Iris's shaft.

Iris gasped as the other woman's fingers teased her, exploring the new sensations that came with her male form. She couldn't deny how much she was enjoying it, despite her initial hesitation.

Astrid's breathing became ragged as she continued to touch Iris. She couldn't believe this was happening, but she couldn't deny how much she wanted it. She pushed Iris back onto the bed, her hands never leaving Iris's body. She climbed on top of Iris, her lips finding their way to Iris's neck.

Iris couldn't help but moan as Astrid's lips and teeth left their mark on her skin. "Astrid," she gasped, arching against the other woman.

Astrid smiled wickedly before claiming Iris's lips in a fierce kiss once more. Her hand began to move faster, feeling the girth of Iris's dick grow against her palm.

As she stroked it, Iris moaned beneath her, her body arching towards Astrid's. Astrid could feel the wetness growing between her own legs, and she began to grind against Iris in anticipation.

Her body ached to be closer, to feel more of Iris's touch. She could feel the heat radiating from Iris's groin, the hardness between her legs. And she wanted it. She wanted all of it. She wanted to feel Iris's hardness inside her, filling her up and making her scream with pleasure. And she was determined to have it.

With a quick movement, Astrid pulled down Iris's pants, exposing the hard cock that jutted out from between her legs. Iris gasped at the sudden movement, but before she could protest, Astrid was already shedding her own clothes.

She stood before Iris, completely naked, her curves on display for the other woman to see. Her nipples were hard and erect, her breasts full and round. And between her legs, a patch of blonde curls hid her most intimate area. Astrid climbed on top of Iris, straddling her hips and rubbing her pussy against Iris's cock. Iris couldn't help but stare at Astrid's body, the curves and angles of her form illuminated by the soft light that filtered into the room.

Iris couldn't help but gasp as she felt Astrid's wetness against her. It was a new and unfamiliar sensation, but she couldn't deny how much she was enjoying it. She couldn't deny the arousal that surged through her veins as Astrid's pussy rubbed against her cock.

Astrid moaned her hips grinding harder against Iris's cock. She could feel the heat radiating from between her legs, and she knew that she needed more. She wanted Iris inside her, filling her up and making her scream with pleasure.

With a quick movement, Astrid reached down and guided Iris's cock to her entrance. She gasped as the tip of the cock pressed against her, the feeling almost too much to bear. But she didn't stop. She pushed down, feeling the girth of Iris's cock entering her slowly.

Iris couldn't believe what was happening.

She had never been with a woman before, and she couldn't deny the strange, yet exhilarating sensation of Astrid's wetness wrapping around her cock. It was different from anything she had ever experienced, and she couldn't help but feel a growing sense of pleasure as Astrid's pussy enveloped her fully.

Iris couldn't help but gasp as Astrid began to move, her hips rocking back and forth as she rode her cock.

The sensation was almost overwhelming, and Iris couldn't deny the arousal that surged through her veins.

She reached up, her fingers tangling in Astrid's hair as she pulled the other woman down for a deep, passionate kiss.

Their tongues danced together as Astrid rode her, the hot, wet feeling of Astrid's pussy driving Iris wild. She couldn't believe how much she was enjoying this, how much she craved the feeling of Astrid's pussy wrapped around her cock. It was so dirty, so wrong, but it felt so right.

Iris's fingers tightened in Astrid's hair as she thrust up to meet her, their bodies moving in time together. She could feel herself getting close, the pleasure building deep within her core.

"Iris, Iris," Astrid moaned, her voice hoarse as she rode harder and faster. "I'm so close, Iris. Don't stop." Astrid's voice was a hoarse whisper, her breath hot against Iris's neck. Her hips began to move of their own accord, meeting Astrid's thrust for thrust. The feeling of Astrid's wetness, the sensation of her muscles tightening around Iris's cock, all of it was overwhelming, and Iris couldn't help but let out a filthy moan. Astrid's pussy was so tight, gripping Iris's cock like a vice.

Iris couldn't believe how incredible it felt, the sensation of her cock buried deep inside Astrid's warm, wet pussy. She had never felt anything like it before, and she couldn't help but moan in pleasure.

She had never realized how different sex was as a man. It was a strange and unfamiliar feeling, but Iris couldn't deny how much she was enjoying it. She felt like a different person, a more confident and assertive version of herself. She couldn't help but feel a sense of power and control as she watched Astrid's body writhe in pleasure beneath her.

Iris's heart raced as she pounded into Astrid's pussy, the sound of skin slapping against skin filling the room.

Iris's hands moved down to cup Astrid's breasts, her fingers pinching and tweaking the other woman's nipples. Astrid moaned at the sensation, her pussy tightening around Iris's cock.

Iris couldn't help but feel a sense of satisfaction and dominance as she rolled Astrid's nipples between her thumb and forefinger. She had never felt so powerful and confident before, and she wanted to make Astrid feel good, to make her scream with pleasure.

With that thought in mind, Iris took a deep breath and pulled out of Astrid's pussy, making the other woman gasp.

"What are you doing?" Astrid asked, looking up at Iris with a mixture of confusion and desire.

Iris didn't answer. Instead, she grabbed Astrid's hips and pulled her up onto all fours. Astrid let out a surprised gasp as she found herself in this new position, but she didn't resist. She trusted Iris, and she knew that whatever Iris had in mind would be good. Iris couldn't help but stare at Astrid's ass. Iris reached out, her fingers tracing the curve of Astrid's ass before slipping between her legs, feeling the wetness that coated Astrid's pussy.

Astrid moaned as Iris touched her, the sensation of Iris's fingers on her pussy almost too much to bear. Iris couldn't help but feel a sense of satisfaction as Astrid moaned beneath her, her body responding to Iris's touch.

Iris positioned herself behind Astrid, her cock hard and ready. She teased Astrid for a moment, tracing the tip of her dick along

Astrid's entrance. Astrid whimpered, eager for Iris's penetration. And without warning, Iris thrust into Astrid, filling her up completely.

"Oh, god, Iris," Astrid moaned, her voice hoarse with pleasure. "Yes, yes, just like that."

Iris began to thrust in and out of Astrid, the rhythm of their lovemaking intensifying with every passing moment. Iris couldn't believe how different sex was as a man, how much more intense and visceral it felt. She could feel every millimeter of her cock as it slid in and out of Astrid's wet, tight pussy, feel the way Astrid's muscles clenched around it, trying to draw her deeper.

Iris reached forward and grabbed a fistful of Astrid's long blonde hair, tugging it back as she continued to thrust in and out of the other woman, her hips slapping against Astrid's ass.

Astrid couldn't help but moan and gasp with every brutal thrust, her pussy feeling like it was on fire. It was obvious that Iris was enjoying herself, reveling in the control she had over Astrid. Iris could feel her orgasm building deep within her core, each thrust pushing her closer and closer to the edge.

She could feel Astrid's pleasure mounting as well, the other woman's pussy tightening around Iris's cock with each thrust. Iris could feel Astrid's juices coating her dick, the wetness making each thrust easier and more intense.

"I'm going to come, Astrid," Iris gasped, sweat beading on her forehead as she thrust harder and faster into the other woman.

Astrid moaned in response, her own orgasm building. She could feel Iris's cock twitching inside her. Astrid felt her pussy tightening around Iris's cock, the slickness coating Iris's shaft as she thrust inside of her.

She was close, so close to coming. Her clit was swollen and sensitive, aching for attention. She reached down and began to rub it in swift circles as Iris fucked her harder, the sensation almost too much to bear.

Iris groaned, her hands gripping Astrid's hips as she fucked her from behind. The sight of Astrid's ass in the air, her pussy wrapped around Iris's cock was driving Iris wild. She couldn't believe how good it felt, how wet and tight Astrid's pussy was. She could feel her orgasm building, the pressure growing within her. She wanted to come, to fill Astrid up with her seed.

And so she gritted her teeth, determined to make the other woman orgasm first. She could feel Astrid's pussy tightening around her cock, the other woman's moans growing louder and more desperate.

"Iris, Iris, I'm gonna come!" Astrid cried out, her fingers working frantically at her clit.

Iris couldn't hold back any longer. With a shout of pleasure, she came inside Astrid, her cock twitching as it filled the other woman's pussy with hot, sticky cum.

At the same time, Astrid's orgasm overtook her, her body shaking and trembling as she came hard.

They both sprawled out on the bed, panting and trying to catch their breath.

"Damn, Iris," Astrid breathed, her body still shuddering with aftershocks of pleasure. "That was...that was intense."

Iris couldn't help but agree as she lay there, her mind still reeling from what had just happened. She had never experienced anything like it before, and she couldn't deny how much she had enjoyed it. But even as she lay there, basking in the afterglow of their lovemaking, she couldn't shake off the feeling of guilt that weighed heavily on her chest. She had betrayed Elias, the man she loved, and the consequences of her actions were now setting in. Iris couldn't shake off the feeling that she had done something wrong, that she had crossed a line that could never be uncrossed. Despite the intense pleasure that she had experienced, she couldn't help but feel a pang of regret as she looked over at Astrid.

Astrid, on the other hand, seemed to be basking in their shared intimacy. She laid there, her head resting on Iris's chest, her body sated and content.

Iris looked down at Astrid, her eyes soft with affection. She couldn't deny the connection she felt with the other woman, the way they fit together so perfectly. But the guilt still lingered, and she knew she needed to talk to Elias about what had happened. She needed to come clean about her actions and face the consequences, no matter how difficult they may be. As she lay there in the aftermath of their lovemaking, she couldn't help but feel a sense of dread wash over her. She knew that things would never be the same between her and Elias, but she also knew that she couldn't keep what had happened a secret. She owed it to him to be honest, even if it meant losing him forever.

As they lay in bed, wrapped in each other's arms, Iris couldn't help but feel a sense of guilt and sadness wash over her. She knew that she needed to talk to Elias about what had happened, but she also knew that it could wait until tomorrow. For now, she just wanted to relax in Astrid's arms and enjoy the afterglow of their lovemaking.

"Are you okay, Iris?" Astrid asked, her voice soft and concerned.

Iris looked up at Astrid and smiled weakly. "I will be," she said. "But I need some time to process everything that's happened. And I need to talk to Elias."

Astrid nodded in understanding. "I understand," she said. "And I'll be here for you, no matter what happens."

Iris felt a surge of gratitude towards Astrid. She didn't know what the future held for her and Elias, but she knew that she could always count on Astrid to be there for her. As they lay in bed, wrapped in each other's arms, Iris couldn't help but feel a sense of comfort and security. She closed her eyes and took a deep breath, letting it out slowly. She knew that she had a lot to think about, a lot to process.

But for now, she just wanted to enjoy this moment of peace and intimacy.

Iris listened as Astrid's soft breathing evened out, indicating that she had fallen asleep. As she looked at her, Iris couldn't help but feel a mix of emotions: the thrill of their shared experiences, the guilt of her betrayal towards Elias, and the fear of the unknown. She knew that things would be different from now on, no matter what her decision would be. Iris sighed, and closed her eyes, trying to find sleep.

Meanwhile, Duncan was pacing around. He couldn't shake off the feeling that had been growing inside him since he entered this world. He wanted to talk to Elias about it, but he was too afraid of what the other man might think.

Duncan finally decided to gather his courage and talk to Elias. He hesitated for a moment, but then knocked on the door.

"Elias, can I talk to you?" Duncan asked, his voice barely above a whisper.

Elias opened the door, wearing only a pair of pants. "Sure, Duncan, what's up?" he asked, his voice friendly and inviting.

But as Duncan stepped inside the room, he couldn't help but feel a flutter of excitement in his chest. Elias was standing in front of him, his broad shoulders and muscular arms on full display. Duncan couldn't deny the way his heart raced as he looked at Elias, his mind filled with thoughts that he couldn't quite understand.

"What's going on, Duncan?" Elias asked, turning to face him. His eyes widened in surprise as he took in Duncan's appearance. "Is everything okay?"

Duncan swallowed hard, trying to push down the growing arousal that threatened to overwhelm him. "Yeah, everything's fine," Duncan hesitated for a moment, biting his lower lip as he gathered his thoughts. "Uh, I just wanted to talk to you about something," he said, his voice barely above a whisper.

Elias raised an eyebrow, his expression curious. "Sure, come in," he said, stepping aside to allow Duncan entry.

Duncan hesitated for a moment, trying to find the right words. He had never been good at expressing his feelings, and now, in this strange new world, it felt like an impossible task.

"It's just...I haven't been feeling like myself lately," Duncan finally managed to say. "I mean, I was always attracted to women, but since we arrived in this world, I've been having these...thoughts. About men. About you."

Elias stared at him, his brow furrowed in confusion. "About me?"

Duncan nodded, feeling his cheeks heat up. "Yes, I know it's wrong, but I can't shake off these feelings. It's like this new body is changing me, making me desire things I never thought I would. And I don't know how to deal with it," Duncan said, his voice trembling slightly.

Elias stared at him, stunned by his confession. He had never thought of Duncan in that way before, and now he couldn't shake off the feeling of confusion and shock that had taken over him. "Duncan, I don't know what to say," Elias stammered, taking a step back.

Duncan looked at him, his eyes filled with fear and vulnerability. "I know it's wrong, and I don't expect you to feel the same way," he said, his voice barely above a whisper. "I just needed to tell someone, and I trust you."

Elias looked at Duncan, his expression unreadable. He couldn't deny the way his heart raced as he looked at the other man, his mind filled with thoughts that he couldn't quite understand. He had never thought of Duncan in that way before, but now that the other man had brought it up, he couldn't help but notice the way Duncan's eyes shone in the dim light, the curve of his lips, and the flush of his cheeks.

Elias took a deep breath, trying to push down the confusing thoughts that swirled within him. He couldn't help but view Duncan in a different light, and it was a struggle to reconcile his feelings.

"I understand, Duncan," Elias said, his voice gentle. "I promise I won't judge you for how you feel. But I can't deny that what you just told me has caught me off guard."

Duncan nodded, understanding the other man's reaction. "I know, and I'm sorry for that. I just couldn't keep it inside me anymore."Duncan's voice was quiet, barely above a whisper.

Elias looked at him, taking in his flushed face and the way he was avoiding eye contact as he awaited Elias's response. But instead of responding with shock or anger, Elias looked at Duncan with a newfound appreciation. In the low light of the room, the curves and angles of Duncan's face seemed softer, more feminine, and Elias couldn't deny the attraction he felt towards his friend.

"Duncan," Elias said, his voice husky. "You are beautiful."

Duncan's eyes widened in surprise, his heart pounding in his chest as he looked up at Elias. The other man's gaze was intense, his eyes dark with desire. Duncan felt a surge of excitement run through him, his body responding to Elias's words in a way that he couldn't quite understand. He had never felt this way about a man before, and yet, as he looked into Elias's eyes, he couldn't deny the powerful attraction that he felt towards him.

Duncan felt a flood of desire run through him, his body responding in a way that he couldn't control. He took a step closer to Elias, his heart pounding in his chest.

Elias watched as Duncan approached him, his pulse quickening as the other man drew near. He couldn't deny the arousal that surged through him, the way his body responded to Duncan's proximity.

As Duncan moved closer, Elias reached out, his hand gently brushing against Duncan's cheek. Duncan closed his eyes, a soft sigh escaping his lips as he leaned into the touch.

But just as their lips were about to meet, Elias pulled back, his eyes wide with

alarm.

"Wait, Duncan," Elias said, his voice strained. "We can't do this. I can't do this to Iris."

Duncan nodded, understanding where Elias was coming from. But at the same time, he couldn't shake off the feeling of disappointment that washed over him. He had been hoping for a different response.Duncan looked down, disappointment etched on his face.

Elias sighed, placing a comforting hand on Duncan's shoulder."I understand how you feel, Duncan, but we can't let our desires cloud our judgement." Elias said, trying to maintain his composure.

"But what if she is cheating on you with Astrid? I mean, I saw her going into her room." Duncan blurted out. "What if your relationship with Iris isn't as solid as you think it is? What if this is her way of exploring her own desires and needs, just like we are?" Duncan asked, looking up at Elias with a mixture of hope and fear.

Elias looked down at Duncan, his mind racing with thoughts and doubts. He couldn't deny the possibility that Iris might be exploring her own desires.

After all, this game had changed them all in unexpected ways. He had seen Duncan's newfound attraction to men, and Ian's vulnerability in his new female body. Even Astrid's behavior had become more aggressive and bold. The game had brought out different aspects of their personalities, and forced them to face desires and kinks that they had never even knew existed. Elias couldn't deny the urge to give in to his own desires. Despite everything, he couldn't shake off

the thought of Duncan, his body so close to his own.

He could sense Duncan's desire, and he couldn't deny the way it made him feel now that the other man had transformed into a woman, a beautiful and desirable woman who wanted him.

Duncan couldn't believe what he was doing, couldn't believe the thoughts that were going through his head. But he couldn't stop himself. he had to touch him, had to feel his hardness beneath his fingers.

Duncan reached out tentatively, his hand shaking as he wrapped his fingers around Elias's thick shaft. He heard him gasp at his touch, and he looked up at him through his eyelashes, his heart racing in his chest. He could see the desire in Elias eyes, the way he was looking at him like he wanted to devour him whole. And Duncan wanted him to, wanted him to take him and make him his own. He had never felt such a burning desire before, and it was all he could think about. The voice in his head warning him to stop, to think about what he was doing, was growing more and more distant, replaced by his overwhelming desire to feel Elias inside him.

"Please," Duncan whispered, his voice barely above a whisper. "Please, I need you."

Elias looked at Duncan, his eyes filled with a mix of desire and guilt. He knew what Duncan was asking for, and he wanted to give it to him. But at the same time, he couldn't shake off the feeling of guilt that weighed heavily on his chest. He had never cheated on Iris before, and the thought of doing so now made him feel sick to his stomach.

"Duncan, I don't know if this is a good idea," Elias said, his voice hesitant. He wanted to give in to the temptation, but he knew it was wrong. He couldn't betray Iris like that, no matter how strong the temptation was.

"Please, Elias," Duncan begged, his voice filled with desperation. "I need this. I need you. I know it's wrong, but I can't help how I feel."

Elias looked into Duncan's eyes and saw the desperation and desire in them. He knew that he couldn't deny Duncan what he wanted, not when he was looking at him like that. He took a deep breath, trying to silence the voice in his head that was screaming at him not to do this.

He knew the consequences of his actions, but the pull towards Duncan was too strong. He couldn't resist, not when the other man was looking at him with such longing and desire. He nodded his head, unable to find the words to reply. He then closed his eyes as he felt Duncan's hand on his shaft, moving up and down slowly, gently. Elias's resolve started to crumble as he let out a soft moan as he felt Duncan's fingers wrap around him, sliding up and down his length, twisting slightly. He felt himself growing harder, thicker, as Duncan touched him. He couldn't believe he was doing this, but at the same time, he couldn't resist. He wanted this, wanted Duncan.

Elias opened his eyes and looked down at Duncan, who was still staring up at him with a pleading expression. He reached down and tangled his fingers in Duncan's hair, almost roughly pulling his head back so that they were looking directly into each other's eyes. "I want you to be sure about this," Elias said in a low voice, his eyes filled with a mix of desire and regret. "Once we start, there's no going back."

Duncan nodded, his breath hitching in his throat.

As much as he found it wrong to be with a man, he couldn't resist the urge. He had tried to deny it, to push it down and ignore it, but it had only grown stronger. He had never felt such a burning desire before, and now he couldn't turn away.

"I'm sure," he whispered, his eyes filled with need.

Elias held Duncan's gaze for a beat longer before loosening his grip on his hair and leaning down to speak into his ear. "Say it then," he growled, his voice low and commanding.

Duncan's chest heaved as he struggled to catch his breath. "I want you," he finally managed to choke out, his voice barely above a whisper.

Elias's eyes darkened at the words, his self-control slipping away. "Say it again," he commanded, his hand still buried in Duncan's hair.

"I want you, Elias. I want you to fuck me," Duncan breathed, his voice shaky with desire.

Without another word, Elias yanked Duncan's hair, pulling him in for a brutal kiss. As their lips met, he couldn't help but feel a rush of excitement at the thought of taking Duncan, of making him his.

He pushed him down onto the bed, following him down and pinning him to the mattress as their lips crashed together. His hands roamed over Duncan's body, feeling the curves of his new, womanly form, loving the way she felt underneath his fingertips. Each thrust of his tongue was met with one from Duncan, their moans and gasps adding to the heat building between them.

He trailed his lips down Duncan's jawline and towards her neck, leaving a trail of burning kisses behind. He sucked and bit at the skin, watching as it turned pink and feeling the shiver that ran down Duncan's body. He moved lower, pulling at the collar of Duncan's shirt to reveal the soft, round curves of his breasts. His mouth watered as he took in the sight of Duncan's nipples, already hard and pointing towards him, begging to be touched and sucked.

Without hesitation, Elias wrapped his lips around one of the nipples and sucked hard, eliciting a moan of pleasure from Duncan. He rolled the nipple between his teeth, leaving marks on Duncan's pale skin.He then switched over to the other nipple, giving it equal attention. He continued to tease and torment Duncan's nipples with his mouth and fingers, loving the way he writhed and moaned underneath him.

"Elias," Duncan gasped, his back arching off the bed. "I need more. Please, I can't take it any longer."

With a feral grin, Elias moved down on his body, pulling Duncan pants down in one rough motion.

He was greeted by the sight of Duncan's simple white panties, soaked through with the evidence of his new vagina's arousal.

Elias couldn't help but growl at the sight, a primal satisfaction settling in his chest. He hooked his fingers under the waistband of the underwear and pulled them down, revealing Duncan's glistening pussy.

Elias let out a low growl as he took in the sight of Duncan's new vagina, the lips swollen and wet with desire. He spread Duncan legs wide, exposing his pussy to his gaze.

Duncan's breath hitched as he felt Elias's gaze on him, and he couldn't help but feel a sense of vulnerability wash over him. He had never felt so exposed, so open to another person before. But at the same time, he couldn't deny the thrill that coursed through him as Elias looked at him with such hunger in his eyes.

He felt himself growing even more aroused, his newly sensitive body responding to the attention like never before.

"Please," Duncan begged, knowing how dirty and shameful it was to beg for this but unable to stop himself. " I need to feel you inside me. I need to feel your cock filling me up and making me yours."

Elias hissed, his self-control snapping. He couldn't resist Duncan any longer, couldn't deny the desperate need to claim him. He reached down and grabbed his cock, giving it a few rough strokes before lining it up with Duncan's entrance. "You're mine now," he growled as he slowly pushed inside.

Duncan gasped at the feeling of Elias entering him, his body stretching to accommodate the thick shaft.

It was nothing like he had ever felt before, a strange mix of pleasure and pain that left him feeling helpless and vulnerable. He felt a thrill run through him as Elias filled him up, the feeling of fullness and possession making him feel completely and utterly claimed by the other man.

Elias gritted his teeth as he pushed deeper into Duncan, relishing the feeling of the tight, wet heat around him and he couldn't deny the thrill that surged through him as he claimed Duncan's body as his own.

Duncan, for his part, was completely lost in the sensation of being filled up by Elias. He couldn't believe how incredible it felt, how much he wanted this, even as he knew he should be disgusted by it. But as Elias began to move inside him, he couldn't help the moans and gasps that escaped his lips, his hips bucking up to meet the other man's thrusts.

"It feel amazing," Duncan groaned, his voice strained with pleasure. "I never knew it could feel like this.I should hate it, but I can't help but find it incredible," Duncan said, panting as Elias continued to thrust into him. "It's so wrong, but it feels so right. I don't know how to process these feelings, but I can't deny them either. I want you, Elias. I want you inside me, making me yours."

Elias's lips curved into a smirk at Duncan's words. "You think that feels good, just wait," he growled, grabbing Duncan's legs and hitching them over his shoulders.

Duncan gasped as he felt himself being stretched even further, his sensitive opening burning with the delicious feeling of being filled to the brim with Elias's cock. Elias grunted, sweat dripping down his forehead as he pushed deeper into Duncan's newfound pussy.

Duncan couldn't help himself, his new body quickly becoming sensitive to the raw power and dominance exuded by Elias. He felt himself being stretched to his limits, the feeling of fullness only intensified by the new angle created by Elias's position.

Elias, too, was lost in the moment, feeling his self-control slipping away as he took in the sight of Duncan's pleasure-contorted face. He couldn't help but feel a rush of arousal at the thought of completely possessing the other man, of filling him up and making him his own.

He reached down, roughly grabbing hold of Duncan's hard nipples and twisting them between his fingers. Duncan cried out, his back arching off the bed as the pleasure-pain sent a jolt of electricity straight to his core. Elias grunted, his own pleasure building as he watched Duncan's reactions.

"You like that?" he growled, twisting harder. "Answer me, Duncan."

"Yes," Duncan gasped, his hips bucking up in a futile attempt to get more friction. "I like it. I like it a lot." Duncan moaned out as Elias continued to thrust in and out of him. The pleasure was overwhelming, consuming his entire being. He had never felt anything like this before. It was as if every nerve in his body was on fire, and Elias was the one stoking the flames.

Duncan couldn't believe the things he was feeling, the things he was allowing to happen. But somehow, it just felt right. He had never felt such intense pleasure before, and he couldn't help but feel a sense of vulnerability that was both terrifying and exhilarating.

"Is this what it feels like to be fucked by a man?" Duncan thought to himself, his mind racing as Elias continued to thrust into him with wild abandon. He couldn't believe how much he was enjoying it, how much he wanted it. It was wrong, but he couldn't help himself.

Elias could sense Duncan's pleasure, could feel the way his body tightened around him with each thrust.

He could see the look of pure bliss on Duncan's face, could hear the way he moaned and gasped with every touch, every movement.

"You like that, don't you?" Elias said, his voice low and husky. "Being fucked like a little slut." Elias continued, his voice dripping with sarcasm. "Is this what you always wanted, Duncan? To be penetrated by a man, to be dominated and controlled?"

Duncan gasped, his eyes flying open at Elias's words. It was as if the other man had read his thoughts, had known exactly what he was thinking. And even though it was wrong, even though it was degrading, Duncan couldn't help but feel a thrill at the words. He couldn't help but feel a sense of excitement, of pleasure, at the thought of being used like a little slut.

"Yes," he cried out, his voice barely above a whisper. "I-I like it. I like being your little slut, Elias." Duncan said, panting as he arched his back, lifting his hips to meet each of Elias's thrusts. The feeling of being dominated was intoxicating, and Duncan couldn't get enough. He wanted more, needed more.

Elias's lips curled into a wicked grin as he heard Duncan's words. He continued to thrust into Duncan, hard and fast, loving the way the other man writhed beneath him.

He leaned down, his lips brushing against Duncan's ear. "Good girl," Elias said, his voice low and sultry. He nipped at Duncan's earlobe, loving the way the other man moaned and squirmed beneath him. "You like it when I dominate you, don't you? You like it when I take control and make you mine."

Duncan couldn't deny it, the feeling of Elias's power over him was intoxicating. He couldn't believe the things he was saying, the things he was allowing to happen. It felt natural, like this was where he belonged.

Duncan's body moved in time with Elias, his breaths coming in short, sharp pants as he succumbed to the pleasure coursing through him. He couldn't believe the vulnerability he felt, the way he was giving himself to Elias like this. He had never felt so weak, so at the mercy of another person. But at the same time, he couldn't deny the intense pleasure that was coursing through his body. It was like nothing he had ever experienced before, a feeling of pure bliss that was consuming him from the inside out.

Elias continued to pump into Duncan, his hips moving in a steady rhythm as he brought the other man closer and closer to the edge. He could feel Duncan's orgasm building, could feel the way his muscles twitched and tightened around him. "Come for me, Duncan," Elias growled, his hips moving faster as he chased his own pleasure. "Show me how much you love being my little slut."

Duncan couldn't deny the words, couldn't deny the way they made his body respond. He felt his orgasm building, felt the pressure coiling tight in his belly.

"Yes!" Duncan cried out, his voice hoarse with pleasure.

Elias felt his own orgasm rushing towards him, and with one final, deep thrust, he came, filling Duncan up with his hot seed.

Duncan's orgasm hit him like a tidal wave, his entire body shuddering and trembling with the force of it. He felt Elias's seed filling him up, and the sensation only added to the intense pleasure coursing through his body. He couldn't believe what he had just done, couldn't believe the things he had allowed to happen.

Duncan's mind raced as he pulled away from Elias, his body shaking with a mix of emotions. He couldn't deny the pleasure he had felt, the way Elias had made him feel, but at the same time, he couldn't shake off the feeling of disgust that was creeping in.

"What have I done?" Duncan thought to himself, his mind reeling with shame and guilt. "I let myself be taken by another man, and worse, I enjoyed it." Duncan said, his voice barely above a whisper.

He couldn't believe what he had just allowed to happen, couldn't believe that he had let himself be dominated and penetrated by another man. It was wrong, so wrong, and yet he couldn't deny the thrill he had felt, the pleasure that had coursed through his body as Elias had taken him.

"I can't believe I did that," Duncan thought, his mind racing as he tried to process what had just happened. "I can't believe I let myself be used like that." Duncan said, his voice filled with shame.

As the two men lay there, sweaty and tangled together, they were both lost in their own thoughts. Elias couldn't shake off the guilt that weighed heavily on his chest, knowing he had cheated on Iris, his girlfriend of many years. But the thrill of being with Duncan was too strong to resist. The way Duncan submitted to him, the way he begged for more, the way he moaned and trembled beneath him, it was all too much to resist. Elias knew he had to tell Iris the truth, but the thought of losing her made him feel sick to his stomach.

Duncan, on the other hand, couldn't deny the feeling of shame that washed over him as he felt Elias's semen flow out of him. He couldn't believe what he had just allowed to happen, couldn't believe the things he had said and done. He felt disgusting, used, and worst of all, he couldn't deny the thrill he had felt, the pleasure that had coursed through his body as Elias had taken him. He couldn't shake off the feeling of disgust that was creeping in, couldn't deny the way it made his stomach turn.

He had never been with a man before, had never even considered it. And yet, here he was, lying in bed with another man, feeling spent and satisfied after the most intense sexual experience of his life.

He rolled over, away from Elias, and stared up at the ceiling. He couldn't believe what he had done, couldn't believe the way he had submitted to Elias. He had always thought of himself as a straight man, and yet, here he was, questioning everything he had ever known about himself.

He sighed, running a hand through his hair.

He couldn't deny the pleasure he had felt, the satisfaction that still coursed through his veins. But at the same time, he couldn't shake off the feeling of disgust that was creeping in.

As these thoughts swirled around in his mind, he felt Elias stir beside him. The other man rolled over and wrapped his arms around him, pulling him close. "Duncan," he whispered, his voice rough with sleep and satisfaction. "Don't overthink it, okay? We both wanted it, needed it."

Duncan hesitated, torn between the desire to pull away and the comfort of Elias's arms around him. He wasn't sure he could handle the emotions that were swirling around in his head, but at the same time, he didn't want to leave the warmth of Elias's embrace.

But then, Duncan forced himself to sit up, pushing Elias's arms away. He couldn't accept these new feelings that were coursing through him, not right now. He needed time to think, to process what had just happened. "I-I need some time alone," Duncan stammered, his voice shaking as he pulled away from Elias and climbed out of the bed. Elias frowned, his arms dropping to his sides as he watched Duncan scramble out of reach. He knew that he should let him go, give him the space he needed. But at the same time, he couldn't help the twinge of hurt that pierced through him as Duncan distanced himself.

Elias couldn't deny the arousal that surged through him at the sight of Duncan's new female body. He knew it was wrong, but he couldn't help the way his body reacted to the curves and softness of the other man's new form.

He had always been attracted to Iris,

but Duncan newfound vulnerability, the way he submitted to Elias, the way he begged for more, the way he moaned and trembled beneath him, it was all too much to resist. Duncan's new form, soft and curvaceous, was a stark contrast to his previous muscular build. It made Elias's desire him, despite the guilt weighing heavily on his chest. He knew he had to tell Iris the truth, but the thought of losing her made him feel sick to his stomach. But he couldn't help but wonder, how would it be to explore this new side of Duncan?

How would it be to take charge and dominate him? Would Duncan submit to him as willingly as he had before, or would he push back and reclaim the masculinity that he had lost? Elias couldn't deny the curiosity that was building within him, the desire to explore the depths of Duncan's newfound femininity. He couldn't resist the temptation to take charge, to dominate him once more.

Duncan, on the other hand, was still lost in his own thoughts, trying to make sense of what had just happened.

As these thoughts swirled around in his mind, he began to gather his clothes, preparing to leave. But before he could even get dressed, Elias pulled him back into bed. "Where do you think you're going?" Elias growled, pulling Duncan back down onto the bed.

Duncan hesitated, feeling the heat of Elias's body against his bare skin. He could still feel the other man's semen seeping out of him, and the thought made him feel even more disgusted of what he had just allowed to happen.

"I-I need to leave," Duncan stammered, his voice trembling. "I need some time to think."

Elias tightened his grip on Duncan, pulling him back against his chest. "No, you don't," he murmured, his voice low and seductive. "You don't need to think, you don't need to analyze. You just need to feel."

Duncan shivered as Elias's breath tickled his ear, his body responding to the other man's words despite his reservations. He couldn't deny the way his heart raced at the thought of giving in to his desires, of allowing Elias to take control once again. It was wrong, so wrong, but at the same time, he couldn't deny the way his body responded to the other man's touch, to the way he dominated and controlled him.

As Elias continued to whisper in his ear, Duncan felt himself growing weaker, his resolve crumbling as the other man's words worked their magic on him. He couldn't resist the temptation any longer, couldn't deny the way his body craved Elias's touch. With a sigh, Duncan gave in, allowing Elias to pull him back into bed.

Elias's lips curved into a satisfied smile as he felt Duncan's body relax against his. He knew he had won, knew that Duncan was his for the taking. And as he wrapped his arms around the other man, he couldn't help but feel a thrill of excitement at the thought of claiming him once more.

He knew it was wrong, knew that they were in a dangerous game world and that they should be focusing on survival. But at the same time, he couldn't deny the way his body responded to the sight of Duncan's new female form, couldn't resist the desire to take control and dominate him once more.

Elias's hands roamed over Duncan's soft curves, his fingers tracing the lines of his new body with a sense of reverence. Duncan shivered beneath his touch, a mix of pleasure and vulnerability coursing through him. He couldn't believe he was allowing this to happen again, couldn't believe he was letting Elias touch him like this.

Elias's hands began to wander over Duncan's soft, curvy body. He couldn't help but feel a sense of satisfaction as he cupped Duncan's breasts, loving the way they fit into his hands. He tweaked the nipples, eliciting a gasp from Duncan as he pinched and rolled them between his fingers. Elias's other hand trailed down Duncan's stomach, slipping between his legs to find Duncan's wetness. Duncan couldn't deny the way his body responded to Elias's touch, the way he moaned and squirmed beneath his hands.

Elias's fingers slid through Duncan's wetness, spreading it over his clit in slow, deliberate circles. Duncan gasped, his hips bucking up in a silent plea for more. Elias smirked, continuing to stroke and tease Duncan's clit with his fingers. He could feel Duncan's orgasm building, could feel the way the other man's muscles tightened and twitched beneath his touch.

"Come on, Duncan," Elias purred, his voice low and sultry. "Let go, give in to the pleasure. You know you want it," Elias coaxed, his breath hot and heavy against Duncan's ear.

Duncan shivered, his resolve crumbling as Elias's fingers worked their magic on him. He couldn't deny the way his body ached for release, the way his muscles coiled tight with tension. He gasped as Elias's fingers continued to circle and stroke his clit, each touch sending a jolt of electricity straight to his core. He could feel the orgasm building, could feel the pressure coiling tight in his belly.

"Elias, please," Duncan groaned, his voice strained with pleasure. "I-I need more."

Elias smirked, his fingers still moving in slow, deliberate circles over Duncan's clit. "Oh, you do, do you?"

Duncan nodded, panting as the pleasure continued to build. "Yes, I-I need it. I need you."

Elias's smirk turned into a grin as he heard Duncan's words. He knew the other man was close, knew that he was ready to submit to him once again. Elias loved being in control, he loved dominating Duncan. "What do you want, Duncan?"

Duncan hesitated, his mind racing with thoughts and desires. He knew what he wanted, but at the same time, he couldn't deny the feeling of shame and guilt that was creeping in.

"I-I want you to fuck me," Duncan finally whispered, his voice barely above a whisper.

Elias's smirk grew wider as he heard Duncan's words. "Beg for it," he growled, his voice low and commanding.

Duncan shivered, his body responding to the dominance in Elias's voice. "Please, Elias," he pleaded, his voice strained with desire. "Please, I need you to fuck me. I need to feel you inside me again."

Elias's eyes darkened with lust as he heard Duncan's words.

"Good girl," he purred, his voice low and sultry. "But first, I want you to taste me."

Duncan's eyes widened as he realized what Elias was asking for. He had never done anything like this before, had never even considered it. But at the same time, he couldn't deny the thrill that shot through him at the thought of it.

He hesitated for a moment, his mind racing with conflicting thoughts and emotions. On the one hand, he knew it was wrong, knew that he shouldn't be doing this. But on the other hand, he couldn't deny the way his body responded to Elias's words. "I'll do it."

Elias grinned, his eyes sparkling with lust as he climbed out of the bed. "Good girl," he said, his voice low and husky. "Now, on your knees."

Duncan swallowed hard, his heart pounding in his chest as he did as Elias asked. He watched as Elias reveal his hard cock. Duncan couldn't help but stare, his mouth going dry as he took in the sight of the other man's erection. He could feel the heat radiating off of Elias's body, the smell of his arousal filling the air. It was large and thick, the tip already glistening with pre-cum.

"Go on," Elias urged, his voice low and sultry. "Take it in your pretty little mouth."

Duncan hesitated for a moment longer, but the desire to please Elias, to submit to him, was too strong to resist.

He leaned forward, sticking out his tongue and running it over the tip of Elias's cock. He could taste the salty, musky flavor of the other man's arousal. The taste was strong but not unpleasant. He could feel Elias's hand on the back of his head, urging him to take more. He opened his mouth, letting Elias slide his cock inside. It filled his mouth, pressing against the back of his throat. He gagged slightly but didn't stop, didn't pull away. He couldn't deny the thrill he felt at the thought of pleasing Elias in this way, the feeling of submission and domination that came with it.

Elias couldn't believe the way the other man was submitting to him, giving in to his every desire. It was a stark contrast to the way Iris had always been, strong and independent, never willing to submit to him like this. He loved the way Duncan submitted to him, the way he begged for more, the way he moaned and trembled beneath him. It was a feeling of power and control that he couldn't get enough of.

He watched as Duncan wrapped his lips around his cock, taking him deep into his throat. He could feel the other man's tongue swirling around the tip, teasing him in the most delicious way.

"Oh, fuck," Elias groaned as he felt his orgasm building. His hips began to thrust, driving his cock deeper into Duncan's mouth. Duncan gagged and choked, tears streaming down his face as he struggled to accommodate Elias's size. But at the same time, he couldn't deny the thrill he felt, the way his body responded to Elias's domination.

Elias's thrusts grew more insistent, his hands tightening in Duncan's hair as he pushed the other man down onto his cock. Duncan could feel the tears streaming down his face as he gagged and choked, but at the same time, he couldn't deny the pleasure that was coursing through his body.He could feel his own arousal building, could feel his own wetness slicking his thighs. .

Elias watched as Duncan took him deeper, gasping and choking around his cock. He couldn't believe the way the other man was submitting to him, the way he was giving in to his every desire. It was a feeling of power and control that he hadn't experienced before, and he couldn't get enough of it.

"Fuck, I'm gonna come," Elias growled, his thrusts growing frantic as he felt his orgasm building. He could feel the pressure coiling tight in his belly, his balls drawing up against his body as the pleasure consumed him. With a loud groan, he came, his semen spilling into Duncan's mouth in hot, heavy spurts. Duncan could feel the other man's release, the way it filled his mouth and throat. He could feel it spilling out of the corners of his lips, running down his chin and neck. It was salty and thick, and the taste made him want to gag.

But Elias held him in place, his hand still tangled in Duncan's hair, forcing him to swallow every last drop. Duncan couldn't deny the feeling of humiliation that washed over him, the way his body trembled with shame as Elias's semen slid down his throat and settle in his stomach. But here he was, on his knees, submitting to Elias in the most degrading way possible.

Elias pulled out of Duncan's mouth with a pop, grinning down at the other man as he wiped his cock on Duncan's cheek. "Good girl," he purred, his voice low and sultry.

Elias took a step back from Duncan, his eyes trailing over the other man's flushed and still trembling form. "You take me so well, Duncan."

Duncan stayed on his knees, eyes lowered and staring at the floor. He could still taste Elias's release in his mouth, feel the stickiness on his cheek. He wasn't sure what to think or feel. On one hand, he was disgusted with himself for allowing things to go so far. On the other hand, he couldn't deny the arousal that was still coursing through his body, the sheer thrill of submitting to Elias in such a way.

Elias watched Duncan for a moment before taking a step closer to him. "Now, on your hands and knees, facing the wall." Elias ordered, his voice filled with authority and desire.

Duncan felt his body respond to the command, shifting into position on all fours without question. He could feel his own wetness slicking his thighs, the wetness only growing as Elias moved closer to him.

Elias stroked Duncan's hips, "Such a good girl," he murmured, his hands gripping Duncan's hips as he guided him into the desired position. Duncan couldn't believe what he had just allowed to happen, but at the same time, he couldn't deny the thrill that coursed through his veins as Elias positioned him.

Elias couldn't get enough of the view, the sight of Duncan on his hands and knees, his soft curves on display. He loved the way Duncan's body looked in this position, the way it begged to be taken.

Without uttering a word, he aligned his cock with Duncan's pussy, teasing the other man with the tip.

Duncan couldn't help but moan at the contact, his body aching for more. He pushed back against Elias, trying to get him to penetrate him. But Elias was in control. He slapped Duncan's ass hard, eliciting a loud gasp from the other man.

Duncan couldn't help but moan at the sting of Elias's hand on his ass, his body aching for more. He pushed back again, trying to force Elias to penetrate him. But the other man was relentless, denying Duncan the release he craved.

Elias loved the way the skin reddened, the way it jiggled with the impact. He continued to tease and spank Duncan, watching in satisfaction as the other man's arousal grew in response.

"Please, just fuck me already," Duncan pleaded, pushing back against Elias again, trying to get him to penetrate him.

Elias smirked, enjoying the way Duncan begged and pleaded for him. He loved being in control, loved being the one in charge in this situation.

"You'll get what you want when I'm good and ready," Elias growled, his voice filled with lust and dominance.

Elias began to tease Duncan's entrance with the tip of his cock, pressing it just slightly inside before pulling back out.

He repeated the motion, drawing a low moan from Duncan's throat with each pass. Duncan trembled with anticipation, his hips wriggling as he tried to force Elias to enter him. But Elias continued to deny him, continuing his merciless teasing until Duncan was whimpering and gasping for just a little bit more.

"Beg for it, Duncan," Elias growled, his voice dripping with desire. "Beg for my cock." Elias's words were a demand, his tone dominant and commanding. "Beg for me to fuck you like the little slut you are."

Duncan moaned at the words, his mind reeling with a mix of shame, desire, and humiliation. He couldn't believe he was allowing himself to be treated like this, but at the same time, he couldn't deny the way his body thrummed with arousal, with the need to be used and filled.

"Please, Elias," Duncan whispered, his voice thick with desire. "I need your cock inside me. Please, Elias. I can't take it anymore." Duncan begged, his voice shaking with desire.

Elias chuckled, his hand still gripping Duncan's hip as he continued to tease the other man's entrance with the tip of his cock. "Beg some more," he growled, his tone filled with authority.

Duncan whimpered at the command but complied, "Please, Elias. I'll do anything. Just give me your cock."

Elias's eyes gleamed with desire at Duncan's words.

"You'll do anything, huh?" he growled, pressing the tip of his cock just slightly inside Duncan's entrance.

Duncan moaned at the feel of pressure, his hips jerking back towards Elias in an effort to force him inside. "Yes, yes, I'll do anything," he pleaded.

Elias's chuckle was low and deep. "Good girl." With that, he thrust his hips forward, burying himself to the hilt inside of Duncan. Duncan screamed, the sensation of being filled so completely overwhelming him. Elias didn't give him any time to adjust, immediately setting a punishing pace. He gripped Duncan's hips, his fingers digging into the soft flesh as he pulled him back onto his cock with each thrust.

"Fuck, you feel so good, Duncan," Elias groaned, his voice filled with desire.

Duncan could only moan in response, unable to form coherent words as the pleasure continued to build within him. Elias's thrusts were relentless, his hips snapping against Duncan's ass with a wet, squelching sound as he buried himself deep inside the other man. The sensation of being filled over and over again, of being used in such a way, was overwhelming.

He could feel his orgasm building, could feel the tension coiling tighter and tighter in his belly. He couldn't believe how good it felt, how much he loved being used in this way.

Elias could feel Duncan's muscles clenching around his cock as the other man approached orgasm. He loved the feeling of being wrapped so tightly, of owning Duncan's pleasure like this. Duncan's moans and gasps were like music to his ears, the sound of validation and arousal that spurred him on.

Elias reached around, his fingers finding Duncan's clit and stroking it skillfully. Duncan's moans grew louder as Elias hit his cervix and applied pressure to his clit simultaneously. It was too much, too good. He could feel himself hurtling towards the edge, ready to topple over it.

Duncan screamed as he came, his body shaking as wave after wave of pleasure crashed over him. Elias continued to thrust through Duncan's orgasm, prolonging the pleasure for both of them. Duncan could feel his muscles gripping Elias's cock, his release spilling out around it and down his thighs.

Elias groaned as he felt Duncan's orgasm, the pulsing of his channel around his cock dragging him over the edge as well. He thrust deep into Duncan one last time, his cock twitching as he emptied himself fully into the other man's welcoming heat.

Duncan could feel himself still trembling with aftershocks of pleasure as Elias slid out of him, leaving him feeling empty and used.

He couldn't deny the enjoyment he got from the encounter, the way his body thrummed with satisfaction. He could feel the mixture of their releases trailing down his thighs, mixing with his sweat.

Elias couldn't help but run his hands over Duncan's soft curves, savoring the way the other man's skin felt against his fingers. He loved the way Duncan submitted to him, the way he begged for more. It was a stark contrast to Iris, the woman he loved and lived with, who was always so independent and strong. Duncan, on the other hand, seemed to crave the dominance and control that Elias could offer him.

Duncan collapsed onto the bed, breathing heavily. Elias couldn't help but grin at the sight of the other man, now a woman in every sense of the term, covered in sweat and cum, a expression of satisfaction on his face. Elias joined him on the bed, snuggling up close to him.

Duncan tensed at the sudden close proximity of their bodies, but forced himself to relax. "Elias, I need to talk to you about something," he said, his voice a little shaky.

Elias looked at him, a question in his eyes. Duncan didn't know how to start, but he knew he had to say something. "I-I don't know if this is right," he stammered. "Us doing this, I mean. It feels wrong."

Elias's face fell at his words. "What do you mean?" he asked, his voice soft.

Duncan took a deep breath, trying to gather his thoughts. "I mean that what we just did, it's not right. I'm not gay, Elias. I've never had these feelings for men before. I don't know what's happening to me," Duncan explained, his voice trembling.

Elias frowned, his eyes clouded with confusion."I don't understand," he said, his voice low. "I thought you enjoyed it. You were certainly responsive enough, moaning and writhing beneath me."

Duncan felt his cheeks grow hot, embarrassed by the memory of his actions. "I did enjoy it, at least physically," he said, trying to explain. "But it's more than that. I can't ignore the fact that I'm a man, and I'm not attracted to men.

This is just happening because I'm in this female body," Duncan continued, his voice filled with frustration. "I can't keep doing this, Elias. It's not right."

Elias sighed, running his fingers absently through Duncan's sweat-dampened hair. "I understand your concerns, I really do," he said, his voice soft. "But the fact remains that you are in a female body now. A body that can feel pleasure in ways you never thought possible. And it's not just about the body, Duncan," he said, his eyes filled with a intensity that made Duncan's heart race.

"You are a woman now, at least in this game world. And as a woman, you have desires and needs that are different from when you were a man," Elias persisted.

Duncan shook his head, "No, it's not just that. I can't deny the fact that I do find men attractive now, but it's different. I'm not sure I can handle this." Duncan's voice was barely above a whisper, but it carried the weight of a thousand unsaid emotions. "I don't know if I can be this person, this woman. I don't know if I want to."

Elias sighed. "I understand how you're feeling," he told him, his voice soothing. "But I think you should give it some time. You may find that you enjoy this new persona, and you may discover things about yourself that you never knew before." Elias said, his voice low and sultry.

His hand had drifted down to cup Duncan's breast, his thumb brushing over the nipple and making it pebble beneath his touch.

Duncan couldn't deny the thrill that coursed through him at Elias's words, at the feeling of his hand on his breast. It was true, his new body felt good in ways he never could have imagined before.

The sensations of pleasure heightened, the feelings of arousal more intense, and a newfound attraction to men that he had never experienced before. It was all so confusing and overwhelming, and Duncan had no idea what to do about it.

Elias, however, seemed to be enjoying the situation immensely. He loved the way Duncan's body looked in its new form, and he loved the way he could dominate him so easily.Elias knew that Duncan was struggling with his new identity, but he couldn't help but feel excited by the possibilities.

Elias leaned in to whisper in Duncan's ear, "You look so beautiful like this, Duncan. And you feel so good. I want to keep exploring your new body and discovering all the ways I can make you feel good."

Duncan shivered at Elias's words, feeling a mix of pleasure and discomfort. He didn't know what to make of his feelings for Elias or his new attraction to men.It was all so confusing, and he couldn't deny the guilt that weighed heavily on him.

He looked down at Elias, now sleeping peacefully beside him, his chest rising and falling in a steady rhythm. Duncan couldn't help but feel a pang of jealousy, wishing he could sleep as soundly. But there was something else that was weighing on him, something other than guilt and confusion.

Duncan felt trapped, trapped in Elias's embrace. He couldn't move without waking the other man, and he didn't know how to handle the situation. He tried to shift his weight, to slide out from under Elias's arm, but it was no use. The other man's grip tightened, pulling him closer. Duncan could feel the weight of Elias's body pressing down on him, making it hard to breathe. He froze, unsure of what to do.

He didn't want to wake Elias, but at the same time, he couldn't bear the thought of being trapped like this for much longer. He took a deep breath, trying to steady his racing heart. He glanced around the room, searching for a way out. But the room was dark and unfamiliar.

The only light came from the sliver of moonlight peeking through the window, casting eerie shadows on the walls. Duncan couldn't shake off the feeling of vulnerability that came with his new female body. He was used to being in control, being the one in charge, but now he felt helpless, exposed. He couldn't sleep, not like this.

He tried to sit up, to move away from Elias, but his body felt heavy and sluggish. The events of the day had taken a toll on him, and he couldn't deny that he was exhausted. But he couldn't shake the feeling of unease that had settled over him.

Duncan looked down at his new body, at the curves and softness that had replaced his muscular form. He felt exposed, vulnerable. He couldn't help but feel a sense of panic, a feeling that he was in over his head. He didn't know if he could handle this new reality, this new body. The weight of Elias's arm on his shoulder, the feeling of his breath on his neck, the warmth of his body pressed against his. It was all too much, too intimate. He needed space, he needed to breathe.

Duncan tried to gently push Elias's arm off of him, but he only tightened his grip, mumbling something incoherent in his sleep.

Duncan sighed in frustration, feeling trapped and vulnerable in his new female body. He couldn't shake off the feeling of exposure, and the thought of sleeping naked in the same bed as Elias made him uneasy.

He glanced at his watch, it was already past midnight and they had to be up early for their journey to the game's only city. Duncan knew that he had to get some sleep, but he couldn't ignore the feeling of vulnerability that coursed through him. He had to get out of Elias's embrace, he had to free himself.

He slowly moved Elias's arm off of him, careful not to wake him. Elias mumbled something in his sleep, but didn't stir. Duncan breathed a sigh of relief and carefully slid out of the bed. He looked around the room for his clothes, but they were nowhere to be found. He frowned, confused.

Duncan looked around the room for his clothes, but they were nowhere to be found. He let out a low growl of frustration, his hands clenching into fists at his sides. He took a deep breath, trying to calm himself down. He had no idea where his clothes had gone, but he couldn't let himself get too worked up over it. For now, he had to focus on finding a way to get some sleep, and to do that, he would need to find something to wear.

He thought about waking Elias, but the other man looked so peaceful that Duncan didn't have the heart to disturb him. Instead, he padded across the room, careful not to make too much noise.

The floor was cold against his bare feet, sending a shiver down his spine. Duncan scanned the room for any signs of his clothes, anything he could use to cover himself. He opened the door a crack and peered out into the hallway, hoping to find some sign of his clothes. But the hallway was deserted, and there was no sign of his clothes anywhere.

He glanced back at the bed, where Elias continued to sleep peacefully.

Finally, he made a decision. He would have to take a chance and venture out into the hallway in search of clothes. With a deep breath, he opened the door and stepped out into the dimly lit hallway.

As he walked, he couldn't help but feel self-conscious about his nakedness. He wrapped his arms around himself, trying to cover up as much as possible. The thought of being caught naked in the hallway made him feel exposed and vulnerable. He quickened his pace, his bare feet silent on the cold stone floor.

As he rounded a corner, he collided with a figure that was standing there, causing them both to stumble and fall to the ground.

Duncan's heart raced as he quickly scrambled to cover himself, his cheeks flushed with embarrassment. "I-I'm sorry," he stammered, his eyes glancing up at the figure that he had collided with.

It was Ian. Unlike Duncan, Ian seemed to be embracing his new female form, his eyes lighting as he took in the sight of Duncan's nakedness.

Duncan couldn't help but feel a pang of envy, wishing he could feel as free and uninhibited as Ian seemed to be.

"No problem, no problem," Ian said, grinning from ear to ear. "You know, I was just coming to find you."

Duncan frowned, suddenly on guard. "I was looking for something to wear. I can't seem to find my clothes," Duncan replied, his voice barely above a whisper.

Ian's expression softened at Duncan's words. "Oh, I see. Well, I might be able to help you out with that," he said, a twinkle in his eye.

Duncan raised an eyebrow at Ian's words. he asked, not sure if he should trust the other man.

"Follow me," Ian said, a mischievous grin spreading across his face. He led Duncan down the dimly lit hallway, his hips swaying in his new female form. Duncan couldn't help but stare, a mix of envy and curiosity coursing through him. Ian seemed to be so comfortable in his new body, moving with a confident sway that Duncan couldn't imagine replicating. He followed the other man down the hallway, his mind racing with questions.

"Ian, what do you mean you can help me find something to wear?" Duncan asked, trying to keep his voice steady.

"Well, I might have a little something-something in my room," Ian said, winking at Duncan. "I have a feeling you're going to look even better in it than I do."

Duncan couldn't help but feel a pang of apprehension as they approached Ian's temporary bedroom. But he didn't have much of a choice. He was stark naked and freezing, and he couldn't wander the halls of this strange place indefinitely. With a sigh, he wrapped his arms around himself and cautiously followed Ian.

As they walked, Duncan couldn't help but notice the way Ian seemed to be enjoying this whole situation. He had always been a bit socially awkward, never one to be comfortable in his own skin. But now, as a woman, he seemed to be embracing his newfound femininity with open arms.

"You seem to be handling this change well," Duncan remarked, trying to make small talk as they walked.

Ian glanced over at him, a small smile playing on her lips. "I guess I am," she said, shrugging her shoulders. "It's a strange feeling, being in this body. But at the same time, it's also kind of exhilarating. I can do things, feel things, that I never could before."

Duncan couldn't help but nod in agreement. He knew exactly what Ian meant. Being in a female body, despite the discomfort and vulnerability he felt, had awakened new sensations within him. He felt more sensitive, more attuned to his own desires. But he couldn't deny the gnawing feeling of unease that lingered at the back of his mind. He was no longer in control of his body, and that was a terrifying thought. With a deep breath, he followed Ian into the room.

The sight that greeted him was unexpected. The room was lined with shelves and racks filled

with clothes, shoes, and accessories, all sorted neatly by type and color. At the far end of the room was a large mirrored wall, reflecting the display of clothing and accessories.

Ian walked over to it, studying his reflection as he ran his hands over a selection of dresses hanging on the rack. Duncan stood frozen, watching him, his mind racing.

He felt a strange sense of disorientation wash over him, as if he had stepped into another world entirely. Duncan spun around, his eyes wide with shock as he tried to make sense of the scene before him.

"What is all this?" he stammered, his voice echoing in the huge room.

Ian turned to face him, a mischievous grin spread across his face as he gestured to the array of clothing hung neatly upon racks and shelves. "Clothes," he said simply, his eyes sparkling with amusement. "I'm a girl, remember? I have to dress like one." He picked up a red dress that looked incredibly soft, brushing the fabric between his fingers with a smirk. "Looking for something to wear?" He held the dress out to me, a wicked glint in his eyes. "This would look great on you, I think."

Duncan couldn't help but feel a little self-conscious at the thought of wearing a dress. "Do you have any pants or a t-shirt I can wear?" Duncan asked, his voice tentative.

Ian laughed, shaking his head. "What kind of question is that? You're a girl, Duncan. Girls don't wear pants and t-shirts." He gestured to the dress hanging in his hand. "This is a perfect outfit for you. It's cute, feminine, and it will make you look amazing."

Duncan couldn't help but feel a little overwhelmed at the sight of the dress. He wasn't used to wearing such things, and the thought of it made him feel uncomfortable. "I don't know, Ian," he said, hesitating. "I don't think I can wear a that." He gestured to the dress in Ian's hand. "I'm not a girl, I'm a man. And I don't feel comfortable wearing dresses." Duncan replied, his voice low.

Ian chuckled, shaking his head. "You are a girl, Duncan. You have always been a girl. You just haven't realized it yet," he said, his eyes twinkling.

Duncan blinked, taken aback. "What are you talking about? I've always been a man," he said, his voice barely above a whisper.

Ian walked over to him, putting a gentle hand on his shoulder. "It's okay, Duncan. I know it's a lot to take in. But trust me, you've always been a girl. It's just taken a little bit of time for you to realize it."

Duncan shook his head, feeling more confused than ever. "I don't understand how that's possible. I was born a man, I've lived my whole life as a man. How can I be a woman ?"

Ian smiled softly at him. "You've always been who you are inside, Duncan. Your external body is just a manifestation of your internal identity."

Duncan stared blankly at Ian, unable to comprehend the words he was hearing. He opened his mouth to speak, but no words came out.

Ian seemed to understand his confusion and continued. "Think of it like this. When you play a game, you can choose the character you want to be, right?"

Duncan nodded slowly, still in shock.

Ian nodded, a grin spreading across his face. "Exactly," he said, patting Duncan on the shoulder. "And right now, you're in the game of life. And this time, you're a woman." Ian had whispered the words gently, his touches soft and comforting. Duncan had frozen at the revelation, unable to speak, unable to process the information that was now flooding his mind.

He looked down at his naked body, now smooth and feminine, feeling a strange mixture of anger, confusion, and fear. He couldn't deny the pulsating sensation between his legs, the way his body was reacting to this sudden change. And he couldn't ignore the way his mind was racing, trying to make sense of it all.

He was a man. Wasn't he? He had always identified himself as such, had always known himself to be male. Duncan slowly turned to face Ian, his brows furrowing together in confusion. "What do you mean, game of life?" He asked, his voice tense and strained.

Ian let out a chuckle, shaking his head. "Just a little phrase I like to use. Don't worry about it," he said, his eyes twinkling with humor.

"The point is, you've always been a woman, even if you didn't realize it." Ian smiled gently at Duncan. "And I think this dress would look perfect on you." He held up the red dress he had picked out earlier, trying to coax Duncan into accepting it.

"Ian, I can't..." Duncan's voice trailed off, losing its previous confidence. "I'm not...I don't...." Duncan clammed up, unsure of what to say next.

It wasn't every day that someone told you that you were a woman. It all felt surreal. The only thing that made this moment feel real was the sensation between his legs. Duncan couldn't tear his gaze away from the red dress in Ian's hand. It looked so soft and feminine, and it made him wonder what it would be like to be dressed up in such a way. Duncan felt conflicted; he didn't want to disappoint Ian, but he wasn't sure if he could pull off wearing a dress.

"Ian, I don't know... I've never worn a dress before," Duncan said, looking down at his feminine form again.

Ian chuckled, a smile lighting up his face. "Duncan, you wore dresses plenty of times when you were a little girl," he said, his voice gentle and reassuring.

Duncan's eyes widened in surprise. "What do you mean, 'when I was a little girl'? I've always been a man," he protested, his voice strained with disbelief.

Ian shook his head, his expression kind but firm. "No, Duncan. You've always been a woman. " he said. "And besides, I know for a fact that you used to love dressing up in dress and skirts when you were a kid."

Duncan shook his head, trying to clear the fog of confusion that was starting to settle over him. "No, I don't remember that at all," he said, his voice wavering slightly.

Ian smiled, taking a step closer to Duncan."Here, let me show you something."

With that, Ian reached into his pocket and pulled out a photo, showing two little girls who looked just like their avatars, but younger. "See for yourself," he said, handing the photo to Duncan.

Duncan's eyes widened as he saw the picture. He felt a strange sense of familiarity wash over him as he stared at the photo.

"This is us, when we were kids," Ian said, pointing at the two girls in the picture. "We used to play together all the time. And you, Duncan, you always loved dressing up in pretty dresses just like that one."

Duncan felt a lump form in his throat as he listened to Ian's words. He took the photo from Ian's hand and stared at it in disbelief. The little girl on the left looked just like Duncan in his new female form. And just as Ian had said, she was dressed up in a pretty pink dress, a big smile on her face.

"I...I don't understand," Duncan finally said, his voice barely above a whisper. "How is this possible?"

"It's simple, really," Ian explained, a small smile on his lips. "You're dreaming, Duncan." Ian's voice was gentle, but it held a firmness that made Duncan pause. "I think you need to wake up now."

Duncan felt a sense of disorientation, like a veil being lifted from his eyes. The room around him faded away, and he found himself back in Elias's arms, his head resting on the other man's chest.

"What... what happened?" Duncan's voice was hoarse from sleep, and he rubbed his eyes, trying to clear the fog of confusion that still clung to him. He glanced down at his naked body, then up at Elias, his eyes wide with a mixture of embarrassment and alarm. "Wh-what happened?" He stammered.

Elias chuckled, his arm tightening around Duncan's waist as he pulled him closer. "You fell asleep," he said simply.

Duncan couldn't help the blush that rose to his cheeks as he realized that he had been naked the entire time. "I...what happened to my clothes?" He asked, trying to keep his voice steady.

Elias looked up at Duncan, a quizzical expression on his face. "What are you talking about?" he asked, raising an eyebrow.

Duncan's eyes followed Elias's gaze to the floor, where his clothes were strewn about. He felt a wave of embarrassment wash over him. "Sorry, I had a weird dream," Duncan murmured, feeling sheepish as he picked up his clothes and quickly dressed. Elias's eyes never left his face, and Duncan could feel the weight of the other man's gaze as he pulled on his clothes.

"No problem," Elias said, his voice low and husky. "Do you want to tell me about it?"

Duncan shook his head, avoiding Elias's gaze. "It's not important right now. We should focus on getting to the city. We should regroup with the others first," Duncan said, trying to change the subject.

Elias raised an eyebrow, but nodded in agreement. "If that's what you want," he said, his voice still holding a hint of uncertainty.

Duncan couldn't shake off the feeling of discomfort as they made their way back to the rest of the group.

The dream, or whatever it was, had left him feeling disoriented and vulnerable. He couldn't help but feel a sense of unease at the thought of what Ian had told him. The image of that photo was burned into his mind.

Chapter 7: Road to the city

When Duncan and Elias returned to the main room, they found the rest of the group gathered around a large table, maps and notes spread out before them. Iris looked up as they entered, her sharp eyes taking in Duncan's flushed face and disheveled appearance.

"Is everything okay?" she asked, concern etched on her face.

Duncan nodded, forcing a smile. "Yeah, I just had a weird dream, that's all."

Iris studied him for a moment, then nodded as if she understood. "Okay. Well, we could use your input. We've been trying to come up with a plan to reach the city without being ambushed by those mechanical beasts."

She gestured to the maps and notes on the table, and Duncan moved closer to examine them.

As he scanned the maps, he couldn't shake off the feeling of unease. He glanced up at Iris,

who was deeply engrossed in the strategy. He couldn't help but feel a pang of guilt for keeping secrets from her. But at the same time, he didn't know how to bring it up or if he even should.

"Duncan, are you really okay?" Iris asked, noticing his distracted expression.

He nodded, forcing a smile. "Yeah, I just have a lot on my mind," he said evasively.

Iris looked at him knowingly but didn't press further. Instead, she turned back to the map and pointed to a narrow path that cut through a treacherous-looking marsh. "I know it's risky, but this is the fastest route to the city," she said. "We'll have to move quickly, and stay as quiet as possible."

Astrid nodded in agreement, her eyes fixed on the map. "I agree with Iris. We need to move quickly. The faster we reach the city, the sooner we can find out what's happening and figure out a way to escape."

Ian, who had been standing silently, looked as though he was on the verge of saying something, but hesitated.

Elias, sensing the tension, spoke up, "Well, we need to find a way to traverse this marshland and reach the city. From what we've gathered, it seems to be the only place where we can find answers and potentially escape this alternate reality." He looked at Iris, hoping for some input, but her gaze was distant, her mind elsewhere.

Duncan, who had been quiet throughout the discussion, finally spoke up. "I agree. We should stick together and move quickly. We have to be cautious and keep our eyes peeled for any movement in the marsh," Duncan said, still feeling uneasy from his dream but determined to focus on the task at hand.

Elias nodded, his gaze sharp and focused. "I'll take the lead. Iris, you and Astrid flank me. Ian, you follow behind. Duncan, you bring up the rear and keep watch for any dangers that may be lurking in the marsh."

Everyone nodded in agreement, ready to set out on the treacherous journey ahead. They gathered their supplies, double-checking their weapons, and making sure they had enough ammunition.

Duncan felt a knot in his stomach as he strapped his Ruger SR-556 across his back. The image of the dress was still fresh in his mind, and he couldn't shake the feeling of vulnerability that came with being in this new female body. He knew he couldn't afford to show any weakness, not out here in this treacherous marsh.

Iris passed out extra ammo packs to each of them, giving Duncan a sidelong glance. They made eye contact for a brief moment, and Duncan felt a shiver travel down his spine.

Iris' gaze was filled with an intensity that he had never seen before. It was as if she could see right through him. He quickly looked away,avoiding her gaze as he turned his attention to the task at hand. He double-checked his weapons before falling into line, ready to face whatever dangers the marsh had in store for them.

With gritted teeth, Duncan followed behind the group as they made their way to the swampy marsh. His mind raced with thoughts of his odd dream and his new reality. He kept replaying Ian's words in his head, telling him that he had always been a woman. 'It's just taken a little bit of time for you to realize it,' he had said, as if it were the most natural thing in the world. And in the dream, Duncan had almost believed him.

But now, standing on the edge of the marsh, the memory of that dream felt like a distant and surreal experience. Duncan couldn't quite wrap his head around it, and he wasn't sure he wanted to. He glanced over at Elias, who was leading the group, and then down at his own hands. They were slender and delicate, with neatly trimmed nails, and they didn't feel like his own.

Ian, who had been trailing behind, caught up with the group. "Hey, everyone," he said, panting slightly. "I just wanted to let you all know that I found something interesting."

Everyone turned to look at him, curiosity piqued.

"What is it?" Iris asked.

"Well, I was poking around, trying to find some information on this alternate reality we're stuck in," Ian explained. "And I found a reference to this place. It's called the Lifeless Marsh in the game world."

Duncan felt a chill run down his spine at the mention of the name.

"What does that mean?" Astrid asked.

"I'm not entirely sure," Ian admitted. "But it can't be a good sign."

"Lifeless means there's nothing living there, right?" Astrid asked, crossing her arms.

"Yeah, that's usually what it means," Ian replied with a grimace. "I didn't find anything about why it's called that, but it probably means it's dangerous."

Iris frowned, deep in thought. "Lifeless marsh doesn't sound promising," she murmured, her gaze fixed on the vast expanse of murky water.

Elias nodded, his eyes never straying from the horizon. "We know that it's the fastest route to the city," he said, his voice steady. "We can't afford to waste time and energy avoiding it. We'll have to be cautious and stay focused on our objective."

Duncan could sense the tension thickening in the air. He looked around at their surroundings. The marsh was a vast and desolate place, filled with murky water, twisted trees, and eerie noises. It was easy to see why Ian had been spooked by the name 'Lifeless Marsh'. He turned to look at Elias, who was standing tall and firm, staring into the distance with a stern expression on his face.

"Try to focus, Duncan." Iris's calm voice pierced through the cacophony in his mind. "Your distraction might put us all in danger."

Duncan looked up, meeting Iris's unreadable gaze. Her eyes pierced right through him, and he felt himself melting under her intense stare. He quickly shifted his focus back to the marshland stretching out before them. The breeze rustled the leaves on the twisted trees, creating a melancholic symphony of whispers and creaks.

As the group began to stride through the seemingly endless marshland, the oppressive silence weighed heavily on their shoulders. All they could hear was the rhythm of their footsteps and the steady drip of water seeping from the atmosphere.

The air was dense with humidity, clinging to the backs of their necks and making their breath hitch. The cloud of fog that surrounded them made it hard to see even a few meters ahead. They had to rely on each other to remain focused and stay on the right path.

Duncan felt uneasy, his gaze occasionally flicking over to Iris.

"Duncan, watch out for that tree root!" Iris called out suddenly, her voice urgent.

Duncan's foot caught on a hidden root, and he stumbled forward, nearly losing his balance. Ian rushed to catch him, a smirk on his face. "The swamp is getting to you?" He said teasingly.

Duncan scowled, pushing himself away from Ian. "Shut up. I'm just trying to keep us alive."

Ian simply shrugged, a sly smile playing on his lips.

As they trudged through the marsh, Elias noticed that Iris had fallen silent. Her eyes were distant and her gaze lost in thought. He couldn't help but feel a pang of worry for her. He realized that she had been quiet for several minutes, and when he looked at her, her eyes were dull and unfocused. He stepped closer to her, trying to catch her attention. "Are you okay?" Elias asked softly, placing a hand on her shoulder. Iris snapped out of her daze, immediately becoming alert at the touch. She looked up at Elias, giving him a weak smile.

"Yeah, I'm fine," she said, waving her hand dismissively. "I was just...thinking."

"About what?" He queried, raising an eyebrow. Iris hesitated for a moment before speaking.

"I don't know," she said softly. "It's just...I don't want to talk to you right now."

Elias looked taken aback. "Why not?" he asked, frowning.

Iris sighed. "I just...need some space, okay?" she said, avoiding his gaze.

Elias frowned, his brows furrowing together. He wanted to press her, to find out what was wrong, but he could see the determination in her eyes.

"Alright," he said finally. "If that's what you need."

Iris nodded, relieved. She didn't want to get into it right now, not when they were in the middle of the marsh and surrounded by danger.

They continued on in silence for a while, each lost in their own thoughts.

Elias shot quick glances over at Iris, trying to gauge her mood. He couldn't shake the feeling that she was upset with him, and he didn't know why. He had thought that they had made progress in their relationship, but now it seemed like they were back to square one.

Duncan, who had been trailing behind, noticed the tension between them. He couldn't help but feel a pang of guilt for keeping secrets from his friends. He knew he had to come clean, but he also knew that now wasn't the right time. They were in the middle of the marsh, and their lives were at stake.

As they navigated through the murky waters, they were constantly on edge, watching their steps carefully to avoid sinking in the mud.

But Ian couldn't help but feel uncomfortable with the situation. "I hate walking through the murky waters. It's disgusting and uncomfortable." he muttered under his breath, wiping sweat from his brow.

Astrid turned to him, "What was that, Ian?"

Ian shrugged, "Nothing. Just thinking about the last time I went camping."

Astrid nodded, not wanting to push the issue.

Suddenly, they heard a loud splash nearby. Everyone froze, their hearts pounding in their chests.

"What was that?" Ian whispered, her eyes wide with fear.

The group tensed, listening intently for any further sounds. The splash had come from their left, and they anticipated the mechanical beast emerging from the murky depths at any moment. As the group stood waiting, a sudden movement caught their eyes. A robot crocodile emerged from the murky waters, snapping its jaws viciously. Ian let out a high-pitched scream, causing the others to jump in surprise.

The robot crocodile advanced on them, its metal scales glinting menacingly in the dim light.

"Stay calm," Elias instructed, drawing his Ithaca 37 shotgun. "We can take it down."

Iris

quickly took cover behind a nearby tree, drawing her Dan Wesson M1911 ACP pistol. Astrid followed suit, readying her mechanical sword. Ian, looking terrified, moved closer to Duncan, who was still reeling from the sudden appearance of the creature.

Astrid, with fierce determination in her eyes, took the lead, attacking the robot crocodile with quick, precise movements. Her mechanical sword sliced through the metal scales, chopping off one of its menacing jaws.

The robot crocodile roared in pain, thrashing wildly in the water. Iris, her pulse quickening, took aim with her Dan Wesson M1911 ACP pistol and fired a series of shots directly into the creature's metal skull.

The robot crocodile let out a shriek of agony before collapsing into the marsh, taking one last breath before sinking beneath the surface of the murky waters.

The group stared at each other, their hearts still racing from the encounter.

"Good job, Astrid," Iris said, a visible tremor in her voice. "That was close."

Astrid smiled a wicked grin, her eyes glinting with the satisfaction of a job well done. "You have no idea how much fun I had out there."

Ian, still shaking with fear, looked at the group with wide eyes. "I don't ever want to do that again,"

he breathed.

Astrid chuckled, placing a comforting hand on his shoulder. "Don't worry, Ian. I will protect you."Astrid said firmly, patting Ian's shoulder reassuringly.

Ian blushed, looking down at his feet. "Thanks, Astrid," he muttered. Ian's face was pale and sweaty.

Elias scanned the marshland, searching for any signs of mechanical beasts lurking in the distance. "Let's keep moving," he said, breaking the silence. "This marsh is hard on the senses, and we don't want to be caught off guard."

Iris nodded, a hint of resolve in her eyes.

As they continued trekking through the marsh, Duncan found himself constantly glancing over his shoulder, searching for any signs of mechanical beasts. The encounter with the robot crocodile had left him rattled, but he couldn't let his fear show. He couldn't help but feel vulnerable in this new female body, and every snap of a twig or rustle of leaves made him think of the danger lurking just out of sight.

Elias had noticed his apprehension, and his behavior towards Duncan had started to shift. At first, it was subtle - a gentle pat on the back instead of a firm handshake, or a softer tone of voice. But over time, it had become more pronounced, with Elias going out of his way to protect and coddle Duncan.

It was driving him crazy. Duncan didn't want to be treated like a delicate flower. He wanted to be treated like an equal, like the strong, capable man he knew himself to be.

"Hey, are you okay?" Elias asked, placing a hand on Duncan's shoulder. "You seem a little on edge."

Duncan gritted his teeth, resisting the urge to shake off his hand. "I'm fine," he said curtly. "Just focused on our mission."

Elias raised an eyebrow. "Are you sure? You've been jumpy ever since we entered this marsh.I know you're trying to hide it, but I can tell. You're holding yourself differently, trying to be more delicate. It's sweet, really. But I have to admit, I find it

incredibly sexy."

Duncan felt a blush rise to his cheeks. "I-I'm not doing it on purpose," he stammered, feeling self-conscious. He could feel his face heating up, and he tried to play it cool. "I'm just trying to stay sharp, that's all."

Elias smiled knowingly. "Well, keep it up. It's doing something for me."

Iris, who had been walking a few steps

ahead, turned around. "What's going on?" she asked, her eyes flicking between Duncan and Elias.

Elias shrugged, a playful smile on his face. "I was just telling Duncan that I find it sexy when he acts all girly."

Iris raised an eyebrow. "Really?"

Duncan felt his face heat up. "I'm not trying to act girly," he protested.

Elias chuckled. "You don't have to try, it just comes naturally," he said, winking at Duncan.

Iris's eyes narrowed. "Is this a joke to you, Elias? Because I'm not finding it very funny," Iris snapped, crossing her arms.

Elias looked taken aback by her sharp tone, his smile fading. "No, of course not. I just wanted to lighten the mood," he said, holding up his hands in a defensive gesture.

But Iris wasn't having it. "Well, you can stop that now. We need to focus on the mission and getting out of this godforsaken marsh," she said firmly.

Elias nodded and fell into step beside her, his expression serious."Sorry, I didn't mean to upset you."

Astrid and Ian hung back, giving them space. Ian looked at Duncan nervously, unsure of what to say. With a deep breath, he finally spoke up, "Hey, Duncan, I know this must be tough for you. But, I'm here to support you."

Duncan looked at him, a mix of surprise and relief in his eyes. "Thanks, Ian," he said, trying to sound confident. "I appreciate that."

As they walked, the tension between Iris and Elias continued to build. They exchanged only a few words, and both seemed lost in their thoughts. Iris couldn't shake the feeling that something was off about Elias' behavior.

Meanwhile, Astrid was enjoying the thrill of the game. She reveled in the feeling of taking down the mechanical beasts that roamed the marshland. The danger made her feel alive, and she couldn't get enough of the adrenaline rush.

As they continued on their journey, the group stumbled upon an old shack nestled deep within the marsh. Iris cautiously approached it, checking for any signs of danger. "Looks abandoned," she said, her voice low, "There might be some useful supplies inside."

Without saying a word, Elias moved to her side, ready to sweep in if necessary. Ian, though hesitant, followed behind them, making sure they had each other's backs.

Inside, the shack was dimly lit and smelled of rotting wood. Ian cautiously moved forward, his flashlight illuminating the debris-strewn floor. Suddenly, he tripped over something and tumbled to the ground.

"Ian! Are you okay?" Astrid called out, rushing over to him.

"I'm fine," Ian grumbled, brushing himself off. "I just...I think I saw something. Wait, what was that?" Ian said, his eyes wide with shock as he pointed to a corner of the room.

Astrid and Iris followed his gaze and gasped in horror. There, amidst the debris, was an old skeleton. Its bones were pickled and brittle, and its skull had a gaping hole in the center.

Elias stepped closer, examining the skeleton. "Looks like it's been here for a long time," he said. "Could be someone who got lost in the marsh and never made it out."

Duncan felt a chill run down his spine as he stared at the remains. He couldn't shake the feeling that they were being watched, that something sinister was lurking in the shadows.

Iris couldn't help but wonder if it was part of the game world or if someone really died here. The thought sent a shiver down her spine. Iris gave a moment of silence to the unknown person who had met their end here.

Elias cleared his throat, breaking the silence. "We should keep moving."

Iris nodded in agreement, and the group turned to leave the shack. But just as they reached the door, a sudden loud bang echoed throughout the room, causing everyone to jump.

Iris quickly drew her M1911 ACP pistol, and Elias whipped out his Ruger SR-556. Duncan lurched to the side, seeking cover behind an old table while Ian dove for the floor. Astrid's eyes darted around, trying to locate the source of the noise, and Iris' grip tightened on her gun, ready to fire at any moment.

"I don't see anything," Duncan whispered, peeking over the table.

"Maybe it was just a bird or an animal," Ian suggested hopefully, but his voice trembled as he spoke.

Suddenly, another bang echoed through the room, and this time, they could all see the wooden wall splinter. A small, metal projectile was lodged in the wood, and it was clear that it was no accident.

Iris and Elias looked at each other, their expressions serious.

"Get down!" Iris yelled, grabbing Astrid and pulling her to the ground. Elias quickly followed suit,

diving behind the old shack entrance. Ian, still cowering on the floor, scrambled to find cover next to Duncan. "What the hell is happening?" he gasped, his heart pounding in his chest.

Duncan put a finger to his lips, gesturing for Ian to be quiet. He strained his ears, trying to locate where the shots were coming from.

Suddenly, a third projectile whizzed past his head and smashed into the wall behind him.

"We need to get out of here!" Duncan shouted, his voice hoarse with fear.

But Elias wasn't ready to back down yet. He peered out from behind the shack entrance, looking for any sign of their attacker. But all he could see was a thick fog and endless stretches of marshland.

"I think it's coming from there!" Elias yelled, pointing in the direction of a dense thicket of trees.

Iris took charge, quickly devising a plan. "We'll split up," she said, her voice firm. "Astrid and Ian, you go that way and find cover." She gestured to the left. "Elias and I will head right. Duncan, cover our escape."

Iris and Elias crept through the thicket, using the foliage as cover as they advanced.

They kept low and quiet, trying to avoid alerting whatever was waiting for them. Iris's pulse raced in her chest, her fingers taut on the grip of her pistol. She knew that they couldn't afford to be taken by surprise.

The darkness surrounded them, and the air was thick with dampness. Iris could feel the tension building in her body, but she couldn't let it distract her. She gestured for Elias to follow closely behind her, and they continued their slow advance through the marsh.

As they moved, Duncan scanned the area for any sign of enemy movement. It was frustratingly difficult to see anything through the fog, but he knew that he couldn't let his guard down. Every fiber of his being was on high alert for any sign of danger.

Duncan was finding it increasingly hard to ignore the unsettling feeling of dwelling in his new female body.

He could feel the curves beneath his clothes, the subtle softness that foreign to his sensibilities. It was a sensation that he had never anticipated experiencing, yet it was constantly present, a

constant reminder of his new identity.

A few moments later, they heard a rustling sound in the underbrush to their right. Duncan's heart leapt into his throat, and he quickly raised his KSVK 12.7 sniper rifle, taking aim in that direction. He could feel his finger tense on the trigger as he waited for any further movement.

But nothing came. The rustling sound had stopped, and the fog remained as thick and heavy as ever.

But suddenly, out of nowhere, a loud gunshot echoed through the marsh, followed by another and another. Bullets whizzed past Iris and Elias, striking the ground and tree trunks around them.

Iris cried out as she felt a searing pain in her side, and she fell to her knees, clutching at the wound. Elias lunged forward, trying to shield her with his body, but it was too late. The bullets had already found their mark.

Iris winced as she felt the searing pain in her side, but she knew that she couldn't afford to let it distract her. She gritted her teeth, trying to block out the pain as she looked up at Elias. His eyes were wide with fear, but there was also determination in them. She knew that he wouldn't let her down.

Duncan, however, was no longer standing idly by. He spotted the shooter and without hesitation, took aim with his KSVK 12.7 sniper rifle. His finger squeezed the trigger, and the bullet soared through the fog, hitting its target. A deafening cry rang out, and the gunshots stopped.

Duncan took a deep breath, feeling his heart hammering in his chest as he lowered his rifle. He peered through the scope, looking for any sign of further danger, but the marsh had fallen silent.

Iris was still on the ground, holding her side and wincing.

Elias quickly moved to her side, panic etched on his face."Iris! Are you okay? We have to get you out of here," he said, urgency in his voice.

She nodded weakly, trying to get up. But the pain was too much, and she collapsed back onto the wet ground.

Elias's heart raced as he looked at her wound, seeing the blood seeping through the fabric of her shirt.

"I need to get you inside," Elias said, grabbing Iris's arm and helping her to her feet. "Ian can heal you."

Iris nodded weakly, leaning heavily on Elias as they made their way to the shack.

Once inside, Elias helped Iris to sit down on a wooden bench, while he searched for Ian. He found him huddled behind a pile of broken crates, looking pale and shaken.

"Ian, we need you," Elias said urgently. "Iris has been shot."

Ian looked up at Elias, shock registering on his face, then rushed over to Iris's side. He began to undo her shirt, revealing the wound in her side. It was a messy, bloody gash that looked painful.

Astrid and Duncan joined them, keeping watch.

Ian placed a comforting hand on her shoulder, bringing Iris back to reality. He was focused intently on her wound, and a pained expression crossed over his face. It was a tense few moments, but Ian was able to quickly assess the wound and decided that he could heal Iris through sexual act. Iris was terrified, she wasn't sure what to expect, but she knew that it was the only way to save her life. Elias too was tense, he had never seen his girlfriend in such a vulnerable position, but he knew that this was essential for her survival.

Ian looked at Iris and spoke softly, "I need you to relax, Iris. Let me take care of you."

Iris reluctantly nodded, closing her eyes as she let out a deep breath.

Ian's hands moved carefully over her body, tracing the curve of her hip and the arch of her back before gently sliding her pants down.

Iris felt a flutter in her stomach as he ran his fingers over her skin, his touch warm and gentle, almost hesitant, and Iris couldn't help but feel a twinge of discomfort as she lay there, exposed.

But as Ian's fingers moved over her skin, something shifted inside her. She felt a warmth spreading through her, a heat that started in her chest and radiated outwards until it enveloped her entire body.

"What are you doing?" Iris asked, her voice barely a whisper.

"I'm healing you," Ian replied, his voice thick with desire. "I have to stimulate your penis to complete the healing process."

Iris's mind raced as she tried to process what was happening. She felt both embarrassed and aroused at the same time.

"I-I don't think I can do this," she stuttered, trying to pull away.

But Ian's grip on her was strong, and he held her firmly in place.

"Trust me, Iris," he said, his voice gentle yet insistent. "I know it feels strange, but you have to trust me. It's the only way to save you."

Iris closed her eyes, taking a deep breath. The heat and pleasure coursing through her body were overwhelming, but she knew she needed to trust Ian if she wanted to survive.

Ian's hand moved down Iris's body, tracing the trail of sweat that had formed on her skin, and settled on the base of her cock. He held it firmly in his hand, slowly moving his fist up and down, letting out a low groan as the warmth and moisture of her erection filled his palm.

Iris couldn't help but moan, her body responding instinctively to the touch. She felt her cock swell in Ian's hand, the sensation of pleasure intensifying as Ian's other hand cupped and squeezed her balls. Iris's mind was in a whirlwind of confusion and desire, and she couldn't help but think about how strange and surreal this situation was.

As Ian continued to stimulate Iris's cock, he couldn't help but feel a sense of excitement and arousal himself. The feeling of Iris's erection in his hand, the heat and moisture that emanated from it. Ian couldn't help but think about how much he enjoyed this new female body, the softness and sensuality that came with it.

Meanwhile, Astrid and Duncan were keeping watch outside the shack, making sure that no danger was lurking nearby.

Ian leaned down, pressing his large breasts against Iris's cock, using them as a makeshift sheath for Iris's member. He began to thrust his chest forward, sliding Iris's erection between the soft flesh of his breasts. The sensation of Ian's skin against her own was both strange and exhilarating, and Iris couldn't help but let out a soft moan.

Ian smiled, feeling a sense of satisfaction as he watched Iris's reactions. He continued to move his chest up and down, his breasts molding to the shape of Iris's erection. He could feel the heat radiating from Iris's cock, the slickness of pre-cum that coated his skin.

Duncan and Astrid, who had been watching over them from outside the shack, felt their hearts race at the sight of Iris's pleasure. They couldn't help but feel a twinge of envy and arousal, seeing Iris lost in the moment.

But none of that mattered to Ian at the moment. He was focused solely on pleasuring Iris, using his hands to press his breasts together and move them up and down to stimulate Iris's penis. He could feel the heat radiating from it, and he couldn't resist the temptation to taste it. Leaning forward, Ian licked the tip of Iris's penis, taking it into his mouth briefly before pulling back. Iris moaned softly, her body tensing as she experienced the new sensation. Ian continued to lick and suck on the tip of her penis.

His lips were soft and moist, and Iris could feel her whole body trembling with pleasure. He swirled his tongue around the head of her erection, licking away the precum that had gathered there. Iris let out a low moan, her hips bucking involuntarily, her hands reaching out to tangle in Ian's hair as she urged him on. She couldn't believe the intensity of the pleasure that was building within her, radiating out from where Ian's breasts enveloped her cock.

As Ian continued to move his chest up and down, pumping their bodies together, Iris could feel herself approaching the edge of climax. Her heart was racing, her breath coming in ragged gasps as she clung tightly to Ian's head, her fingernails digging into his scalp. She was completely absorbed in the sensation of pleasure that was coursing through her body, and for a moment, she forgot all about the danger they were in. Ian, too, was lost in the moment, his lips moving eagerly over Iris's cock as he tasted her skin and the saltiness of her precum.

Duncan and Astrid, who had been watching from a distance, found themselves entranced by the sight before them. They couldn't tear their eyes away as Ian's breasts slid up and down, enveloped Iris's cock.

Iris's hips bucked, her breath coming out in shallow gasps. She was on the brink of ecstasy, the pleasure building up so intensely with every thrust of Ian's chest, every flick of his tongue.

Iris could hardly bear it, her body tensed with anticipation, ready to release.

Ian's eyes grow wide with excitement, sensing that Iris was on the verge of exploding. He increased the pressure on her cock, using his chest to pump and grind against her taut flesh. It didn't take long for Iris to give in to the waves of pleasure enveloping her.

With each stroke, the tight grip of her orgasm built higher and higher. Finally, she could hold back no more, and with a fierce cry, she exploded, her entire body shuddering with release. Ian, feeling the strength of her orgasm, pulled back, his cheeks slick with her juices, his eyes glazed with desire.

Iris, still panting from her intense climax, regarded him with a mixture of gratitude and embarrassment. She could tell he wanted more, but she wasn't ready for anything more just yet.

Ian nodded, understanding. "It's fine," he murmured, rising to his feet and straightening his clothes. He ruffled his hair, attempting to make it look less disheveled."It seems to have healed."

Iris blinked, looking down at herself in disbelief.

She touched the spot where her wound had been, feeling only smooth, unbroken skin. "It did?" she asked, her voice still shaky.

Ian nodded, a relieved smile spreading across his face. "Yes, it seems that the healing powers of the game world are quite extraordinary," he said.

Astrid stepped forward, her eyes still filled with worry. "Are you alright, Iris? Did it hurt when it disappeared?"

Iris shook her head. "Not at all," she replied, taking a deep breath. "I feel...strange, but otherwise fine."

Duncan stepped out from the shadows, his expression unreadable. He looked at Iris, then at Ian, and then back at Iris."Iris, I know we're in a game and all, but could you please cover yourself up? The sight of your...uh...well, you know. It's a bit distracting." Duncan blushed, looking away. "I'm sorry, I can't help it." Duncan mumbled, looking away from Iris's new body. He tried to hide his growing arousal, but it was no use.

Iris noticed and raised an eyebrow at him. "Duncan, you should be used to the sight," she said with a smirk. "You used to have one of your own, after all."

Duncan's face turned bright red, and he looked away. "I know, Iris," he muttered, trying to suppress his reaction. "It's just...different now. It's just...it's taking some getting used to."

Iris chuckled softly, "I understand." She pulled her pants back up and adjusted her clothes, trying to make herself presentable again.

Astrid glanced at Duncan, noticing his discomfort. She giggled quietly, then walked over to his side and whispered, "I can help you with that if you want."

Duncan's head snapped around, his face flushed with embarrassment. "What are you talking about, Astrid?" he stammered.

"Well, you know," she replied, her voice low and sultry. "You're obviously dealing with some...confusion about your new body. And I'm here to help you explore those feelings if you want."

Duncan's eyes widened in shock."W-what do you mean?"

Astrid gave him a playful wink, "I mean, you don't have to feel uncomfortable with your new body forever. I can help you adjust to it."

Astrid's words hung in the air, causing Duncan to feel even more confused and overwhelmed. He had never felt such strange and conflicting emotions before, and he didn't know how to deal with them.

"I don't know if I want to adjust to this," Duncan admitted, his voice barely a whisper. "I just want to be a man again." Duncan looked down at his new body, shame and frustration etched on his face.

"It's okay, Duncan," Iris assured him, placing a comforting hand on his shoulder. "We all have our struggles with this new reality. But we're here to support each other."

Duncan nodded, feeling a strange mixture of emotions wash over him.

The group continued to move forward through the marsh, careful to avoid loose sand that could trip them up.

"I hate this place," Ian muttered, "It smells terrible, it's muddy, and I don't even know what kind of creatures are lurking in the shadows."

Astrid came up beside him, wrinkling her nose at the smell too. "I'll admit, it's not exactly the most pleasant location," she agreed. "But we need to make the best of it and keep moving forward."

Iris had her hand on her waist, where Ian had performed his healing act. It felt tender and raw, but she knew it was just a temporary discomfort.

Elias, who was walking ahead of them, turned around. "What's taking so long? We need to keep moving if we want to get to the city before dark."

Iris nodded. "We're coming, don't worry."

The group continued to trek through the marsh, staying together and watching each other's backs.

But as they walked, a tension began to build between Elias and Iris.

Elias couldn't shake the image of Iris with Ian. He felt a knot in his stomach, a mix of jealousy and anger.

Finally, he couldn't hold it in any longer. "Iris," he said, his voice low and tense. "We need to talk about what happened with Ian." Elias said, his voice strained.

Iris looked up at him, surprised. "What do you mean? I didn't have a choice, it was to heal me."

Elias's face twisted in anger. "You could have found another way. I never cheated on you like that."

Iris felt a pang of guilt. "I'm sorry," she said, reaching out to touch his arm. "I didn't mean to upset you. I just didn't know what else to do."

Elias took a deep breath, explaining his feelings. "I just...I don't know how to talk to you anymore. Not with you in that body. It's just too confusing."

Iris watched as Elias turned away, avoiding eye contact. She felt tears well up in her eyes, but she clenched her jaw and fought back the emotion. "I understand," she said, more to herself than to him. A heavy silence fell between them, only broken by the sound of their footsteps. Elias couldn't bring himself to look at Iris, he was still struggling with his feelings for her new avatar's male body.

Meanwhile, Duncan was having his own struggles, trying to navigate and accept his new female body. He felt a mixture of discomfort and excitement, as he was finding it hard to ignore his body's new reaction to men. Duncan slunk deeper into the shadows, trying to distract himself. He felt a pang of guilt, knowing that he shouldn't be entertaining these urges, especially given the circumstances they were all in. Duncan couldn't believe what was happening, he couldn't talk to Elias without tensing up, and now, he couldn't even look at Iris without feeling a strange attraction. It was starting to become a distraction, making it hard to concentrate on the task at hand - finding a way to escape this nightmare world.

Ian was the first to notice the change in Duncan's behavior, but he couldn't quite put his finger on it.

"Are you alright, Duncan?" he asked, his voice gentle yet concerned. "You seem a little distant."

"I'm fine," Duncan replied curtly, his mind elsewhere. He was trying to push away thoughts of his new female body and the strange desires that came with it. Duncan couldn't shake the feeling that he was betraying himself. "Ian, how can you be so...calm about this?" Duncan asked, his voice shaking.

Ian looked at him with surprise. "What do you mean?"

Duncan sighed, running a hand through his hair. "Ian, I can't help but feel...disgusted with myself. I can't help but feel like a freak. Like I'm not a real man anymore."

Ian frowned, looking at Duncan with concern. "Duncan, you're still the same person inside. Your body might be different, but that doesn't change who you are."

"But what if it does?" Duncan said, his voice filled with desperation. "I don't want to be this way. I don't want to be attracted to men, and yet, here I am."

Ian placed a comforting hand on Duncan's shoulder. "You know, Duncan, sometimes our desires can be surprising, and that's okay. It doesn't make you any less of a man." Ian said, his voice soothing.

But Duncan was not convinced. He looked away, feeling a lump in his throat. He couldn't shake off the feeling of shame and guilt that had been eating away at him since he realized his new body's preference.He tried to deny it, to ignore it, but the desires only grew stronger. Duncan's voice was laced with pain as he spoke, "Ian, I can't have these feelings. I'm a real man, unlike you."

"Duncan, that's not fair," Ian said, trying to keep the hurt out of his voice. "I'm still a man, in my own way. Just because my body is different, it doesn't make me any less so."

Duncan looked at him, his eyes narrowed in disbelief. "I saw you, Ian. I saw you in that dress before the transformation. You didn't look like a man."

Ian's face reddened slightly, "It was just a costume, Duncan. It doesn't define who I am."

"Costume or not, it still makes you less of a man," Duncan said stubbornly.

Ian sighed and looked away, feeling hurt and frustrated. "Fine, whatever you say, Duncan," he replied curtly. "I won't let your narrow-minded views define me."

Duncan felt himself getting angrier and angrier. He wanted to lash out, to hurt Ian, but he knew it wouldn't solve anything. So, he stayed silent as they trekked through the marsh.

Meanwhile, Astrid was lost in her own thoughts. She loved her new body and the power it gave her, but she couldn't shake off the feeling that something was missing. She longed to share this experience with someone who understood her, someone who could relate to what she was going through.

Astrid glanced around at her companions. They all seemed to be lost in their own thoughts, preoccupied with their own struggles. Elias and Iris were off to the side, still locked in a tense silence. Ian and Duncan were in front, their voices low as they argued about something.

Astrid sighed and shook her head, trying to push away the sense of loneliness that was starting to creep in. She knew that they were all going through a lot, but she needed someone to confide in.

Astrid approached Iris, who was walking alongside Elias, still tense and distant.

"Iris," Astrid began hesitantly, "I can see that something is wrong. Is it your relationship with Elias? because of....you know?"

Iris turned to Astrid with a sad smile. "Yes, Astrid, it's about that. I don't know how to talk to Elias anymore, it feels like we're strangers in this game world. And being in this male body doesn't help either."

Astrid nodded, understanding the depth of her friend's feelings. "It's not easy, is it?" she said, gazing thoughtfully into the distance. "Did you already tell him about what we did ?" Astrid asked, her eyes searching Iris's face for any sign of betrayal or deception.

Iris looked away, her cheeks flushing with embarrassment. "No, I haven't," she admitted softly.

"I don't know how to bring it up, or what to say. I don't want him to judge me, or to think less of me. And I don't want to hurt him." Iris finished, looking back at Astrid for support.

Astrid nodded in understanding. "I know, Iris. And I understand why you didn't tell him yet. But you can't keep it a secret forever.

It's not fair to him, or to you."

Iris sighed, knowing that Astrid was right. "I know, and I'm trying to figure out how to bring it up. But it's just so complicated. I don't want him to get hurt."

Astrid placed a comforting hand on Iris's shoulder. "I promise to help you figure out how to tell him, and to be there for you no matter what happens," she reassured. Iris smiled, feeling grateful for her friend's kindness.

At that moment, the group came upon a clearing. It was a small patch of dry ground amidst the mud and water of the marsh, and they paused to catch their breath and regroup.

Duncan sat down heavily, his mind still on the conversation with Ian and his own internal struggles. He couldn't help but feel a sense of loss, like he was grieving for a person who was still very much alive - himself, but in a different form.

Elias wandered over to a nearby tree, leaning against it and closing his eyes, lost in thought.

Iris saw her chance and approached him, her heart pounding. She had been thinking about how to bring up the subject all day, but now that the moment was here, she felt at a loss for words.

"Elias," she began hesitantly, her voice barely above a whisper. "We need to talk."

Elias opened his eyes and turned to face her, his expression wary. "What is it, Iris?"

Iris took a deep breath, gathering her thoughts before speaking. "It's about the other night, when I...with Astrid." She hesitated for a moment before continuing. "I didn't mean for it to happen, it just...did. I was scared and confused and I didn't know what else to do. But I need you to know that I still love you, Elias. That's never changed. And I need you to understand what happened and why."

Elias stared at Iris, his expression unreadable. He clenched his fists, trying to keep his anger in check. "You cheated on me?" he said, his voice low and dangerous.

Iris swallowed hard, feeling a tremor run through her as she looked into Elias's eyes. She knew he was hurting, but she also knew she had to be honest with him. "I'm sorry, Elias. I was afraid and I needed someone to comfort me. And she was the only one there."

Elias's voice was cold and angry now, his eyes narrowing as he looked at her. "No, Iris. This is too much. I can't just...forgive you for this." He took a deep breath, trying to steady himself, but the anger and hurt were both too raw. "I can't forgive this, Iris. Not now, not ever." His voice was bitter, like a knife cutting through her heart. She had never seen him so angry before, and it terrified her.

Iris looked down at her feet, feeling a tear roll down her cheek. She knew she had made a mistake, but she didn't know how to undo it. She didn't know how to make it right. "Elias, I'm sorry. I know I messed up. But please understand," Iris pleaded.

Elias's anger seemed to dissipate, replaced by a sad resolve. "I can't, Iris. I just can't. I need some time to process all of this. I think it's best if we take a break from each other for a while." He turned around and walked away, leaving Iris standing there, tears rolling down her cheeks.

Meanwhile, Ian and Astrid were watching the exchange from a distance. "Looks like things aren't going well for them," Astrid remarked.

Ian nodded in agreement, his eyes filled with concern. "This is a very stressful situation," he said. "It's understandable that they would have some issues."

As they watched, Iris sank to the ground, burying her face in her hands, while Elias walked away.

Astrid saw her chance and approached Iris, sitting down beside her and wrapping an arm around her shoulders. "I'm sorry, Iris,"

Astrid murmured, her voice filled with concern. "I know how much you love him, and I know how hard this must be for you."

"I'm worried about Elias, Astrid," Iris said, her voice low and concerned. "He's never been this angry before. I don't know what to do." "Give him some space. Let him process things. He'll come around."

Iris sniffled, nodding her head. "It's just so hard, Astrid," she said, her voice trembling. "I never meant for any of this to happen. I just want things to go back to the way they were." Iris sighed, still wiping her tears away.

Astrid gave her a sympathetic smile. "I know it's hard, Iris, but we have to remember that we're in a strange world now. Things aren't going to be the same as they were back home. Maybe this is a chance for us to explore parts of ourselves that we never knew existed."

Iris looked up from the ground, a questioning look in her eyes."Explore?"

Astrid nodded, a determined glint in her gaze. "Yeah. You see, I hated my old body, I was always self-conscious and hid away from the world. But something about this new one, it gives me confidence. I feel alive, and I want to embrace that feeling, even if it means taking risks."

Meanwhile, Elias, still hurt and confused from his conversation with Iris, found himself drawn to Duncan's presence. He noticed how Duncan seemed to be struggling with his own feelings, and it sparked a desire in Elias to take control, to dominate.

He approached Duncan, who was standing off to the side, staring out at the murky waters of the marsh.

"Duncan," Elias said, his voice low and commanding.

Duncan turned to face him, his eyes wide with surprise. "Yes, Elias?" Duncan replied hesitantly, feeling a sense of unease creeping over him.

Elias smirked, taking a step closer to Duncan. "Come here, Duncan," he commanded, reaching out to grab Duncan's arm.

Duncan hesitated for a moment, unsure of what was happening. He had never felt so vulnerable before, and it was unnerving. But he couldn't deny the odd sense of excitement that was building within him. He found himself unable to resist Elias's command, and he followed him willingly.

As they walked, Elias's grip on Duncan's arm grew tighter. "You know, Duncan, you're just a helpless woman now. You need someone to protect you, to take care of you."

Duncan's eyes widened in shock and confusion as Elias pulled him close, their bodies pressed together. He could feel the heat radiating off of Elias, and it made him feel both scared and excited.

"Elias, what are you doing?" Duncan asked, his voice trembling.

"I'm showing you who's in charge," Elias replied, his lips curling into a cruel smile. "You're weak now, Duncan. You need someone to tell you what to do, to guide you."

Duncan tried to pull away, but Elias's grip on him was too strong. "Elias, please stop," Duncan pleaded, his voice trembling. "I'm not a helpless woman. I'm a man, just like you."

Elias chuckled darkly, his eyes glinting with amusement. "No, Duncan," he said, his voice dripping with condescension. "You're not a man anymore. You're a weak, helpless woman. And as a man, it's my duty to protect you."

Duncan felt a surge of anger and frustration, but he couldn't deny the strange sense of arousal that was building within him. He didn't understand why he was reacting this way, but a part of him didn't care. He wanted to give in to the moment, to allow himself to feel something other than confusion and fear.

But at the same time, Duncan knew that he didn't want this kind of relationship with Elias. He didn't want to be dominated, to be seen as weak and helpless. He wanted to be strong, confident, and in control.

"Elias, stop," Duncan said again, his voice stronger this time. "I don't want this. I'm still a man, even if my body is different now."

Elias's eyes narrowed, and his grip on Duncan tightened. "I'll be the judge of that. You need to learn your place now that you're a woman."

Duncan felt his heart race as Elias's words sent a thrill down his spine. He knew this was wrong, but he couldn't deny his own arousal as Elias pulled him closer, his hands grazing against Duncan's chest. Duncan's mind was racing, torn between the role of defiance and submission. But in the end, the latter overwhelmed him as he felt his resolve crumbling down.

Elias noticed Duncan's conflicting emotions, "You have no control anymore, my little girl," he growled, his voice full of superiority and lust.

Duncan winced at the words, a strange mixture of humiliation and pleasure swirling inside of him. Suddenly, he realized that Elias had crossed a line that couldn't be taken back. Duncan's cheeks flushed with anger and embarrassment. "I'm not your little girl, Elias. I'm still me, Duncan."

Elias scoffed, still gripping Duncan tightly. "Sure you are, Duncan. You're just a weak little girl who needs a man to take care of her. And I'm going to be that man."

Duncan's anger boiled over, his mind no longer clouded by the strange arousal that had once consumed him. "I am not a little girl, Elias," Duncan growled, his voice deep and menacing even in this female body, "and I don't need you to take care of me! I can take care of myself."

Elias was taken aback by Duncan's sudden transformation.

He had never expected such a reaction from his friend, especially not under these circumstances. Duncan's eyes were blazing with anger and determination, and for a moment, Elias hesitated. He hadn't expected such a fierce reaction from Duncan, especially in this new body. But the surprise was fleeting, as Elias's anger and desire took over. With a swift movement, he pushed Duncan forcefully to the ground, sending him sprawling.

Ian, who had been observing the scene from a distance, was shocked by what he saw. He rushed towards Elias. "What the hell is going on here?" he demanded, his voice filled with anger.

Elias sneered at him, his eyes flashing with malice. "Mind your own business, Ian. This doesn't concern you."

"The hell it doesn't!" he shouted, standing between Duncan and Elias. "You have no right to treat him like that!"

Elias rolled his eyes. "Please, Ian. You're just a weak little girl, unable to protect yourself or anyone else."

Ian quickly helped Duncan up from the ground, shooting a glare at Elias as he did so. "Are you okay?" he asked, his voice full of concern.

Duncan nodded, still reeling from what had just happened. "I'm fine," he said, his voice shaky.

Iris and Astrid approached, looking concerned. "What happened?" Iris asked, looking between Duncan and Elias.

Elias waved his hand dismissively. "Nothing, just a little disagreement. We're fine."

Astrid looked skeptical, but didn't push the matter. Instead, she turned to Duncan.

Duncan nodded, still shaken by the encounter. "I'm fine. Just a little shook up."

"We should get moving," Iris said, looking around the marsh. "It's not safe here."

The group agreed and set off again, with Duncan and Elias keeping a distance from each other.

As they made their way through the marsh, Ian noticed a strange noise in the distance. "Listen," he halted the group, his gaze fixed on the horizon. A faint sound, like metal scraping against metal, was echoing through the marsh.

"What is it?" Astrid asked.

"Does anyone else hear that?" he asked, letting out a nervous chuckle.

The others exchanged worried glances as they listened to the distant scraping noise, their senses on high alert.

They moved forward cautiously, their ears straining as they tried to pick up any further sounds. As they moved deeper into the cold and murky marsh, the noise grew louder. It was undeniably menacing and was enough to keep everyone on edge.

As they ventured further, the noise became clearer and louder. Suddenly, an enormous mechanical beast emerged from the murky waters. It had the formidable shape of a crocodile with metallic scales and piercing red eyes. The ground shook as it moved towards them, its monstrous jaws open wide. The mechanical beast's sharp metallic teeth gleamed in the pale light of the game world. Its movements were fluid and sinister, slithering through the marsh like a deadly predator. The group stiffened, their hearts beating rapidly with fear.

"We have got to get out of here," Ian whispered, his voice quivering with terror.

Astrid, armed with her mechanical sword, went on the offensive. She darted forward, her footsteps quiet and stealthy as she stalked her foe. But the beast was as agile as it was powerful, dodging her attacks with ease. She whipped her mechanical sword around, trying to land a hit, but the creature was too fast.

Suddenly, Elias was beside her, his Ruger SR-556 raised and ready to fire. His expression was fierce and determined.

"Let me handle this, Astrid," he said, his voice gruff but commanding.

Astrid nodded, stepping back reluctantly.

Elias gun roared, and the mechanics of the creature seemed to rattle and splinter with each impact.

Iris and Ian joined the fray, each firing at the beast from their respective weapons. The air around them was filled with the scent of gunpowder and the staccato beat of gunfire. The mechanical crocodile roared in pain and fury but was gradually taken down with precision shots from Elias, Iris, and Ian. It collapsed onto the mud, silent and still.

As the group surveyed the carnage, Ian sighed in relief. "That could have gone horribly wrong," he muttered, a haggard expression on his face.

Astrid, however, was caught up in the adrenaline rush, her cheeks flushed and a broad grin stretching across her face. "That was amazing!" she exclaimed, her eyes shining with excitement.

Meanwhile, Duncan had taken a step back from the group, trying to process the whirlwind of emotions he had just experienced. He didn't know how to handle these feelings, how to make sense of them. And now, as if things couldn't get any more complicated, he noticed something in the water around them.

"Guys," he said hesitantly, gesturing towards the murky marsh water. "Do you see that?"

Iris and Astrid turned to look, their expressions turning serious as they saw what was coming towards them. A group of mechanical crocodiles and alligators appeared in the water all around the them. The beasts' metal jaws snapped menacingly, and their cold, lifeless eyes glinted in the dim light.

Ian's face paled as he saw them, and he swallowed hard. "Do we have enough ammo left?" he asked, his voice trembling slightly, looking at each of his companions.

Iris quickly checked her inventory . "We do, just barely," she replied, her eyes scanning the numbers. "But we need to make sure we conserve our ammunition until we reach the city."

Just then, one of the mechanical beasts lunged out of the water, snapping its jaws at them. Astrid swiftly swung her mechanical sword, deflecting the creature's attack and narrowly avoiding being bitten. The beast recoiled and retreated, snarling and snapping with rage.

"We have to move," Iris shouted, grabbing Ian's arm and pulling him back. "Now!"

The group of mechanical beasts were closing in, their cold, metallic jaws snapping menacingly. Iris swung her FN P90, firing off quick bursts of bullets at the approaching creatures. Elias, Duncan and Astrid followed suit, using their respective weapons to fend off the relentless attackers.

The sound of gunfire and whirring metal filled the air as they retreated towards the city, trying to outrun the ever-growing army of beasts. Ian, however, struggled to keep up.

"Hurry up, Ian!" Astrid shouted, swinging her mechanical sword in a wide arc to keep the beasts at bay. "We need to move faster!"

But Ian couldn't move any faster. His short legs were no match for the powerful jaws and sharp claws of the mechanical beasts. Just as he thought he was going to be overtaken, a hand reached out and pulled him to safety.He looked up to see Iris a compassionate smile on her face. "Come on, Ian. We've got to keep moving," she urged. "If we stop now, those beasts will get us." Iris glanced worriedly back at the mechanical beasts that were still snapping and snarling towards them, and saw with dread that they were still gaining ground.

Ian knew she was right; they had to keep moving if they wanted to survive. But his legs were trembling with fear and exhaustion, and he knew he couldn't keep up this pace for long.

Just then, he heard a loud thud behind them, followed by a painful roar. He turned to see that one of the mechanical beasts had been taken down by Duncan, who was skillfully wielding his Ithaca 37 like a seasoned combatant.

As the group continued their escape through the marsh, they heard more roars and crashing noises behind them. It seemed as though the mechanical beasts were growing bolder, closing in on them. Iris could feel her pulse quicken as they approached.

As they continued to fight off the attackers, Duncan seemed to find more confidence in his body than before. The adrenaline coursing through his veins helped him focus his mind, and he moved with a purpose and strength that surprised even himself.

Ian, on the other hand, looked petrified. As they navigated the dangerous terrain of the marsh, he struggled to keep up, his short legs churning frantically through the mud and leaves. He could hear the metal claws of the mechanical beasts snapping at his heels, a deadly reminder that he wasn't going fast enough. Ian was gripped with panic, and he stumbled and fell to his knees.

"Come on, Ian! Get up! We need to go!" Iris called out to him desperately, firing off a few more rounds at the closing pack.

But Ian couldn't move; he was frozen with fear.

Iris saw this and knew she couldn't leave him behind. She ran back towards him, shooting at the pursuing beasts to buy time. Duncan, Astrid, and Elias followed suit, firing off shots to cover Iris's advance.

Ian was shaking uncontrollably as Iris approached him. She reached down and grabbed him, slinging him over her shoulder with ease.

With the rest of the group covering them, Iris ran towards them, her feet sinking into the mud with every step. She could hear the mechanical beasts hot on their heels, their snarls and growls growing louder as they closed in.

CAUGHT IN GARDEN OF MECHANICAL SOULS

She could hear the roars of the mechanical beasts growing louder behind her, but she didn't dare look back.

As she ran, she saw Astrid pulling the pin on her last grenade and throwing it towards the approaching mechanical beasts. The grenade exploded with a loud bang, and the beasts were thrown back, with some falling motionless into the murky water below. However, there were still several survivors, snarling and snapping, with their eyes filled with rage.

Ian, still clinging to Iris, let out a whimper of fear at the sight of them. Iris, feeling a surge of protectiveness, tightened her hold on him. "I've got you, Ian," she whispered, her voice soft but steady. "You're gonna be okay."

But Ian was still shaking, panting for breath, tears streaming down his face.

Iris adjusted her hold on him, wrapping an arm around his waist and carrying him as they dashed. The pace was grueling, but Iris refused to slow down. She felt a responsibility to protect her friends, to make sure they all made it out of this alternate reality alive. She could hear Ian's heavy breathing and feel his head resting against her shoulder.

He was so small and fragile, she wanted to comfort him, tell him that everything would be okay, but there was no time. She had to keep moving. The mechanical beasts were relentless, hot on their heels.

Ducking and zigzagging through the marshy terrain, they made their way towards the promised safety of the city.

"We can't keep this up for much longer, guys," Iris huffed, clutching the frightened Ian tightly. Her heart pounded in her chest, the rhythm fueling her legs as they sprinted. The muddy marsh was a blur, and the mechanical beasts chasing after them were a terrifying presence that seemed to be closing in.

Just when all hope seemed lost, the group burst out of the marsh and onto a flat, rocky surface. Their eyes widened as they took in their surroundings. The marsh stretched out behind them, with the mechanical beasts still chasing after them, snarling and snapping. But ahead of them lay the rack railway that

led to the city. It was their ticket to safety, a chance to escape this nightmare and find some answers.

The mechanized creatures behind them seemed to pause, momentarily surprised by the sudden change in terrain. Taking advantage of the respite, Iris and her team sprinted towards the railway, hearts pounding in their chests. The mechanical beasts behind them roared in anger, but they were slowing down, giving the group a slight advantage.

As they reached the edge of the marsh, the rusty tracks of the rack railway stretched out before them, disappearing into darkness. The railway was old, but it was their only hope of escaping the marsh and making it to the city.

They sprinted towards it, their breaths coming in ragged gasps. As they reached the edge of the railway, they saw that it descended underground.

Without hesitation, they jumped onto the rickety train and huddled together as it began its descent into the depths of the mountain.

The train creaked and groaned as it made its way down the steep incline. The air grew colder, and the walls of the tunnel seemed to close in around them. The mechanical beasts were close behind, but they couldn't follow the train into the mountain.

Iris put Ian down on one of the train seats, panting heavily as she caught her breath. "Are you okay, Ian?" she asked, her voice filled with concern.

Ian nodded, wiping away the tears that had streaked down his face. "I'm fine, Iris. I just...I was scared," he admitted.

Iris smiled gently, placing a comforting hand on his shoulder. "We all are, Ian. But we're all in this together. And we're going to make it out of this alive."

Duncan and Astrid were already getting to work, checking the train's machinery to make sure it was functioning properly. Elias stood guard, watching the tunnel entrance warily as they descended further into the mountain.

As the train moved deeper into the tunnel, the air grew cooler and darker. The mechanical beasts' growls and snarls were fading in the distance, replaced by the echoing sounds of the trains mechanical gears grinding against the tracks.

Iris watched the faces of her friends, their eyes filled with a mix of relief and apprehension. Duncan and Astrid busied themselves, fixing and securing various aspects of the train in preparation for their descent into the unknown depths of the mountain. Ian sat quietly, still shaken but grateful to be alive.

Iris looked at him with concern, then turned to her canteen and took a deep drink. She looked at Elias munching on his rations. She walked over to Ian and handed him the rest of her water. "Here, Ian. Drink this," she said softly.

Ian looked at her in surprise, then took the canteen gratefully. He took a few sips, still

catching his breath. "Thank you, Iris," he whispered.

Iris watched him, a small smile on her face as she saw the relief wash over him.

Meanwhile, Astrid and Duncan had finished their inspection of the train and returned to their seats. They both sat on opposite sides of Iris, their gazes lingering on her. Duncan found himself unable to shake the raw attraction he felt towards his friend, even more so now in this new reality where he felt drawn to her despite her male avatar. Every time Iris looked at him, Duncan felt a stirring in his new body, a foreign feeling that he couldn't ignore.

Elias stared at Duncan, anger and frustration simmering just beneath the surface.

Meanwhile, Ian sat awkwardly in his seat, still reeling from the turn of events. He couldn't help but feel vulnerable in his feminine avatar, despite the fact that he also found himself enjoying his new body.

Astrid, however, seemed to relish her new form. She moved with grace and confidence, and the mechanical sword she carried seemed an extension of herself.

"Hey, Ian, how do you like your avatar?" Astrid asked, her tone playful.

Ian blushed, not knowing how to respond. "Uh, it's...it's different," he stammered.

Elias couldn't help but chuckle at Ian's response. "Different, huh? That's one way to put it." He glanced down at Ian's body, unable to hide a slight smirk.

Iris caught the exchange and shot Elias a sharp look. "Not now, okay?" she said quietly. "We just survived a dangerous encounter and we need to focus on getting to the city."

Elias held up his hands in surrender and sat down, grumbling under his breath. Iris turned her attention back to Ian, who was still looking uncomfortable. "I bet you'll be surprise at how naturally those breasts feel," she teased, giving him a smirk. "Not that I'm an authority on the subject, but I've heard men say it..."

Ian's cheeks turned a deep shade of red, and he fidgeted in his seat. "I don't think this is the time or place for that kind of conversation," he said, scooting away from Iris.

Astrid chuckled, "Come on Ian, loosen up a bit. We're in the middle of a dangerous alternate reality, we need all the laughter we can get."

Duncan looked at Ian, concern evident in his eyes. "Are you okay? You seemed pretty shaken up back there," he said.

Ian nodded, still struggling to come to terms with the situation. "I'm sorry, guys. I couldn't move faster. I'm just not built for this kind of thing."

Iris smiled sympathetically. "It's okay, Ian. We understand. You don't have to apologize." She looked around at the group and took a deep breath. "But we need to find a way to make it through this game together. We can't afford to let fear or self-doubt hold us back."

The train moved deeper into the tunnel, the darkness swallowing them whole. Iris could feel the tension building between them, each one lost in their own thoughts. She glanced at Elias, his gaze fixed on the dark tunnel. They hadn't spoken since then, and she could sense that he was still upset about what had happened. She closed her eyes, taking in a deep breath.

The only sound was the rhythmic clacking of the train's wheels against the tracks. She shifted in her seat, trying to ease the ache in her muscles.

Astrid was lost in her own world, gazing out the window of the train, her curves accentuated by her fitted bodysuit. Even in the dim light, Iris could see the faint flush on her cheeks, a reflection of her excitement. Iris couldn't look away from the way Astrid's long blond hair cascaded down her back, the way her curves danced as she moved, and the way her blue eyes sparkled with adventure.

She couldn't help but wonder what Astrid was thinking as they rode the train through the dark mountain tunnels.

By contrast, Duncan sat on the other side of Iris, felt a deep shame as he noticed his eyes lingering on Iris more than he should. The heat in him rose as he thought about how soft and ripe her lips looked, how his mind was overwhelmed by the many things he wanted to do with her. He shook away those thoughts, trying to refocus himself on the task ahead. But those feelings persisted, making it impossible for him to fully concentrate on their predicament.

Meanwhile, Ian had managed to regain some composure after his initial panic.

He sat quietly in his seat, watching the tunnel walls slide past as they descended deeper into the mountain. He looked down at his hands, feeling the smooth skin on his fingertips. It still seemed strange to him, but he couldn't deny that he found himself oddly attracted to these qualities in himself. A small smile played at the corners of his mouth, and he couldn't shake the feeling that being in this alternate reality had somehow awakened a side of him he never knew existed. As the train rumbled on, Ian sat quietly, lost in thought.

The tunnel seemed endless, and the lack of light made it difficult to see their surroundings. Every creak and clank of the old train's mechanical innards sent waves of anxiety through the group. The darkness outside the windows gave no indication of the depth they had descended, and the silence was oppressive.

Suddenly, the train screeched to a halt. The sudden stop sent everyone off-balance, causing Ian to spill his water and Duncan to nearly fall out of his seat.

Iris quickly regained her composure and looked about, trying to discern the cause of the halt. The tunnel, still enshrouded in darkness, remained eerily silent. Suddenly, she noticed a flicker of movement in the corner of her eye. She leaned closer to the window, peering into the pitch-black expanse beyond.

In the next moment, a burst of light erupted from the darkness, illuminating a sprawling cavern ahead of them. As the train moved forward, the group caught their first glimpse of their mysterious destination.

Inside the cavern, a breathtaking cityscape lay before them. Towering structures lined the streets. The buildings were a curious mix of medieval architecture and advanced technology, with gleaming metal and stone intermingling seamlessly.

CAUGHT IN GARDEN OF MECHANICAL SOULS

In the center stood a massive tower, adorned with intricate gargoyles and illuminated by vibrant colored lights. It appeared to continue through the cavern's roof. The architecture was a blend of Gothic and modern styles, with steel beams and stained glass windows.

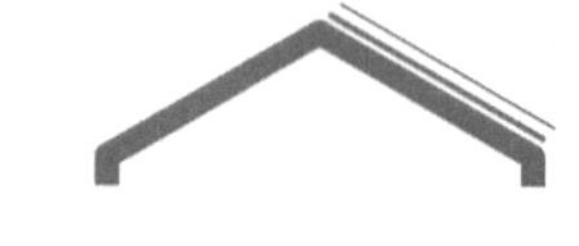

Chapter 8: The city

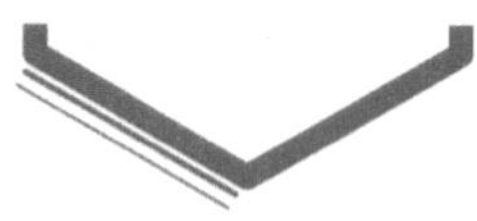

The train pulled into the city's station, which seemed to be carved directly into the cavern's rocky wall. The group cautiously stepped off the train and onto the platform, taking in the awe-inspiring sights and sounds of the city.

The air was filled with the hum of machinery, and the ground beneath their feet vibrated with the energy of the city.

The group stood in awe of the towering structures surrounding them, straining their necks to take it all in.

Iris turned to her comrades, her voice steady despite the wonder in her eyes. "We should head to the flat that serves as our base in the game. We need to regroup, rest, and come up with a plan to find a way back home."

The others nodded in agreement, still taking in the cityscape.

As they made their way towards the exit, they couldn't help but notice that many of the people around them were staring at them, whispering to each other, they couldn't help but notice how different the NPCs of this world seemed to be.

Ian's footsteps faltered as he caught the eye of a handsome man ogling him. He looked like a typical NPC, but his gaze was intense and deliberate, causing Ian to blush. He quickened his pace, almost running to catch up to Iris, his cheeks aflame. She gave him a puzzled glance, noticing his embarrassment. "What's wrong, Ian?" she asked, her voice soft and caring.

"Nothing, Iris. I just...I thought I saw someone looking at me," he replied, still trying to catch his breath.

Iris raised an eyebrow, a small smile playing on her lips. "Looking at you? Well, you do look stunning in that new body," she teased, winking at him.

Ian blushed even harder, stumbling over his words. "W-what? I mean, thank you, Iris. But... I don't know if I'll ever get used to this."

Ian muttered, his eyes scanning the majestic cityscape before them.

"It's rather breathtaking, isn't it?" Iris responded, her eyes sparkling with curiosity.

"Yeah, but...it's just too *real*." Ian sighed, brushing his long white hair out of his eyes. He couldn't help but feel vulnerable in his new body, even among his allies. The thoughts running through his mind made him feel uneasy, and he was still grappling with the fact that he was now a beautiful, petite woman with a seductively feminine figure.

As they followed Iris through the city, they continued to discuss the strange behavior of the NPCs they encountered. The city was bustling with people, all going about their day-to-day lives in this strange and unfamiliar world.

The group made their way through the bustling street market, passing by stalls filled with exotic foods and wares. The tantalizing scent of roasting meat and freshly baked bread filled the air. Ian's stomach growled, reminding him that he had not eaten since their departure from the marsh.

Iris suggested they take a break and grab some food. The group gratefully agreed, and soon they found themselves seated at a small, wooden table at a nearby stall, surrounded by curious NPCs.

Iris was on high alert, scanning the crowd as they ate, her analytical mind working tirelessly to try to make sense of this strange new world.

Astrid, on the other hand, was completely captivated by the foods on display. She eyed a particularly delicious-looking plate of roasted meat and vegetables, licking her lips in anticipation. As she reached for a forkful, she couldn't help but notice the way the NPCs were staring at her and her companions.

Their eyes seemed to be glued to each of them, some even reaching out as if to touch. Ian's cheeks flushed as he felt a pair of hands brush against his hair, sending a shiver down his spine.

He turned to see a young girl, no more than eight or nine years old, looking up at him with wide, curious eyes. "Your hair is so pretty," she said in a soft voice, her fingers still lightly tracing the strands of Ian's white hair. "Can I touch it?"

Ian hesitated for a moment, unsure of how to respond. He had never been one for attention, especially not from strangers. But there was something about the girl's innocent curiosity that made him feel at ease.

"Sure," he said, giving her a small smile.

The girl's eyes lit up as she ran her fingers through Ian's hair, marveling at its softness. Ian couldn't help but chuckle at her enthusiasm.

"What's your name?" he asked, trying to make conversation.

"Makoktok," the girl replied, still playing with Ian's hair.

Iris chimed in, "It's nice to meet you. I'm Iris, this is Ian, Elias, Duncan, and Astrid."

The girl giggled, "I know who you all are, you're the player! I can't believe I'm meeting you in person."

The group exchanged puzzled looks, unsure of how the child knew who they were.

"It's true," Iris responded with a small smile. "But how did you know that, Makoktok?"

The girl looked up at Iris with a wide grin. "Everyone knows who you are!" Makoktok replied, still twirling a strand of Ian's hair around her finger.

Elias' curiosity was piqued. "You know who we are?" he asked, leaning in to better hear the child's reply.

"Yes, everyone knows who you are! You're the player!" the girl exclaimed, her eyes shining with excitement.

Elias couldn't help but feel a twinge of pride at the child's words. "That's right, we are the players," he confirmed, smiling.

"But...why do you call us that?" Ian asked, genuinely confused.

Makoktok's face scrunched up in concentration as she furrowed her brow, clearly puzzled by the question. "I don't know," she finally replied, shrugging her shoulders. "That's what everyone calls you. You're the ones who come to our world, not the other way around." Makoktok flashed a bright smile, still playing with Ian's soft locks. The group exchanged bewildered looks, struggling to comprehend the situation.

Elias chuckled at the child's straightforwardness. "Yes, that's true. And Makoktok, do you know anything about how we got here?" he asked, still trying to process the stranger's knowledge of the group.

Makoktok looked thoughtful for a moment. "I think...something must have gone wrong. That's why you're here, right? In our world?" she said, finishing her thought as if prophesizing.

Before Ian could respond, Makoktok suddenly sat herself on his legs, her small hands grasping his shoulders for balance. Ian's eyes widened in surprise, and he couldn't help but blush at the sudden closeness. He glanced at Iris, who gave him a knowing smile.

"Well, it seems like you've made a new friend, Ian," she said, her voice filled with amusement.

Ian couldn't help but chuckle, his nerves slowly dissipating as he felt the warmth of the child's small body against his own. He couldn't believe how real everything felt, from the softness of her skin to the weight of her body on his legs.

"So, Makoktok, do you know anything about how we can get back home?" Duncan asked, his voice laced with curiosity.

His gaze moved from Iris to Makoktok, who seemed completely at ease in her perch atop Ian.

Makoktok thought for a moment, her brows furrowed. "I don't know, I don't know much about the world outside the city. I only know what I've been told, and what I've seen." She looked up at Ian, her eyes wide with innocence. "I'm afraid I don't know, but if you promise to come back and visit me, I can ask around for you," she said with a hopeful smile.

Ian nodded, a small smile playing at the corners of his lips. "Of course, Makoktok. I pinky promise," he said, hooking his little finger with hers.

Makoktok's face lit up with joy, and she hopped off Ian's lap, running off to find her way home.

The group watched her go, a sense of wonder lingering in the air.

"Well, that was interesting," Duncan commented, his eyes still following Makoktok as she disappeared into the crowd.

The group stood up, thanking the vendor for the delicious food and making their way through the crowded street market. As they walked, they couldn't help but notice the way the NPCs reacted to their presence.

It seemed they were either mesmerized or terrified. Some went out of their way to avoid them, while others shamelessly gawked at their every move.

They passed through sprawling plazas filled with vendors, mechanics, and merchants. One shop in particular caught Duncan's eye. It was a tavern, dimly lit and bustling with activity. There was a stage in the center of the room, where musicians played lively tunes.

CAUGHT IN GARDEN OF MECHANICAL SOULS

The tavern was filled with NPCs from all walks of life. The atmosphere was lively and inviting, and Duncan couldn't help but feel drawn in by the energy of the place. He glanced back at the group, a grin spreading across his face. "How about we take a little detour?" he suggested to Iris.

"Detour?" Iris raised an eyebrow, scrutinizing him curiously.

"Just a few drinks to celebrate our success," Duncan added quickly, feeling his cheeks warm at the memory of their previous victory.

Iris gave him a skeptical look but ultimately agreed. "Alright, one drink, but we need to focus on finding a way back home," she said, leading the group towards the dimly lit tavern.

As they entered the tavern, Ian hesitated for a moment, feeling a wave of apprehension wash over him. He didn't want to be here, surrounded by strange people, but followed the group reluctantly, feeling vulnerable and out of place. As they stepped inside, the sounds of laughter and music filled the air. The tavern was filled with NPCs of all shapes and sizes, some dancing, some singing, and others simply enjoying their drinks.

Duncan led the group to a table in the corner, giving them all a good view of the entertainment.

Ian took a seat on a cushioned bench, his eyes scanning the room nervously. He crossed his arms over his chest, trying to hide his feminine appearance as much as possible. He couldn't help but feel self-conscious, especially when he noticed a group of men gazing at him.

Astrid, on the other hand, was reveling in her newfound confidence. She twirled a lock of her long, blond hair between her fingers, her eyes sparkling with excitement. "Look at this place, Iris! Isn't it amazing?" she asked, her voice bubbling with infectious enthusiasm.

Iris couldn't help but smile at Astrid's childlike wonder. She glanced around the tavern, her analytical mind still trying to make sense of this strange new world. Her gaze lingered on the group of men who had earlier caught Ian's eye. They were still staring at him, their expressions a mixture of lust and curiosity.

Meanwhile, Elias was deep in thought. He had been observing the NPCs' behavior and was convinced that they were acting strangely. He looked over at Duncan, who seemed to be in high spirits after seeing the tavern's entertainment.

Elias couldn't help but feel a sense of protectiveness towards him, especially after noticing the way some of the NPCs had been staring at Duncan earlier. Without a second thought, Elias put his arms around Duncan's shoulders, giving him a reassuring squeeze.

Duncan tensed up at first, taken aback by the sudden show of affection. But after a moment, he leaned back into Elias' embrace, feeling a sense of comfort and security wash over him.

The waitress approached their table, a tray balanced precariously on one hand, her clothes barely covering her. Elias's eyes followed her every move, his gaze lingering on her shapely figure.

"Good evening, my friends," she purred, her voice husky and sultry. "What can I get you to drink?" she added, her eyes locked onto Elias, her lips curling into a coy smile. She leaned forward, her ample cleavage on full display.

Elias couldn't help but feel a rush of blood to his head, his thoughts immediately turning to more impure desires. He quickly shook off the feeling and refocused his attention. "Uh, I'll have a beer," he finally managed to say, trying to keep his voice steady and calm.

"And for you, handsome?" she asked, turning her attention to Iris, her eyes sparkling with interest.

Iris considered the question for a moment before answering. "I'll have a rum and coke," she replied, never breaking eye contact with the mysterious woman.

The waitress gave her a quizzical look, her eyes flickering between Iris and the drinks menu. "We don't have rum here," she said hesitantly, as if uncertain of her own words.

Iris arched an eyebrow, her curiosity piqued. "Then what do you have?" she asked, her voice calm and collected.

The waitress seemed to hesitate for a moment, her eyes darting around the room before settling back on Iris. "We have wine, beer, and some specialty drinks," she replied, her voice low and husky. "We have something called the 'pink desire', a special elixir made from exotic fruits and herbs. Sometimes, it has a strange effect on people." she added, staring intently at Iris.

Without hesitation, Iris and Astrid shared a glance before nodding in agreement. They both decided to give the wine a try.

"Two glasses of your finest wine, please," Iris requested, a mischievous glint in her eye.

Duncan, on the other hand, was more interested in the beer selection. He scanned the menu before settling on a local brew. "One pint of your most popular beer, please," he ordered, leaning back in his seat with a satisfied grin.

Feeling a deep blush rise to the surface of his cheeks, Ian spoke up, "I'll have a glass of the pink desire." It sounded intriguing, and he was eager to see what kind of effect it would have on him

The waitress nodded and winked salaciously before disappearing into the crowd.

As they waited for their drinks, Iris studiously observed the other patrons of the tavern. She noticed the way many of the men were generously tipping the waitress with coin and small gifts. The men seemed transfixed by her presence, practically drooling over her like a lovesick puppy. Their gazes lingered on her curves, their desires clear visible on their faces. Elias felt a flush creep over his cheeks, his own struggles with his attraction growing stronger by the minute. The way the waitress moved, her curves on full display, made his thoughts wander to places they shouldn't. His hands found their way to Duncan's lap, his fingers tracing the muscles under the fabric of Duncan's pants.

Elias' touch sent shivers down Duncan's spine, his growing attraction causing his body to respond to Elias' subtle advances.

Iris noticed the exchange between of them and her eyes narrowed. "Elias, what are you doing?" she demanded, her voice sharp and accusing.

Elias looked up at Iris, his eyes wide with surprise. "I was just...I was just trying to..." he stammered, his voice trailing off as he saw the anger in Iris' eyes.

Duncan's heart sank at the sight of his lover's rage. He quickly withdrew his hands and sat back in his seat.

"I'm sorry, Iris," he said softly, his eyes casting down, avoiding her gaze.

Iris' anger subsided, replaced by a deep sense of hurt.

The waitress returned with their drinks, setting them down on the table with a flirtatious smile. She lingered for a moment, her eyes locked on Elias. "Here you go," she purred, her fingers brushing against his as she handed him his beer.

Iris scoffed, her eyes rolling as she watched the interaction between the waitress and Elias. "You'd better watch yourself, Elias. I don't appreciate you getting attention from other women."

Elias's eyes flashed with anger at her words, and he stood up from the table, knocking his chair over. "I don't appreciate your constant suspicion and accusations!" he shouted, slamming his fists on the table. "I am tired of this constant monitoring! I am an adult, and I can handle myself! I don't need you questioning my every action!"

Iris stared at him, dumbfounded by his outburst. She had always trusted him, but the recent strange behavior he had exhibited was worrying. "Elias, I am only looking out for you," she said calmly, trying to defuse the tension in the air.

"Looking out for me?!" Elias laughed bitterly.

"You don't understand how it feels, being attracted to someone who used to be your lover, but now is trapped in a male body. It's distressing, confusing, and unsettling all at once. I can't bring myself to interact with you like I used to." He spat out the words, like venom, his voice trembling with anger and frustration.

The words cut Iris to the quick. She had never seen Elias like this, so lost and angry. She had known that this change would have effects on them, but she had never anticipated that it would be this bad.

"Elias, I'm sorry." She said gently, her voice wavering with uncertainty. "I didn't mean to hurt you."

"It's too late for apologies, Iris." He said coldly, shaking his head.

He was no longer the kind, gentle person she had fallen in love with. Iris could sense that something inside of him had changed. He had always been a reserved man, but now there was a heat burning within him that couldn't be ignored. She could feel the tension between them, and it made her heart ache.

Elias's eyes never left the waitress as she moved gracefully through the tavern, serving drinks and catching the eyes of the male patrons with a flirtatious smile. He could feel himself becoming more and more agitated, his thoughts racing as he stared at her.

"Iris, I think it's time we part ways," Elias said, his voice barely above a whisper. "I can't...I can't be around you like this. It's...it's too much."

Iris felt a knot in her stomach as she heard those words. She knew that something had shifted between them, but she had hoped that it was just temporary. Now, it was clear that Elias needed space, and Iris didn't want to push him any further.

"I understand," she said, her voice trembling slightly. "I'll give you some time."

Elias nodded, his eyes never leaving the waitress as she approached another table. Iris struggled to hold back tears as she watched him. Despite her emotional state, Iris knew they needed to focus on finding a way back home. She stood up from the table, her feelings swirling in her mind. "Let's finish our drinks and head to our base," she said forcefully, hoping to divert her attention away from Elias.

Elias, still staring off in the distance, barely acknowledged her comment. "I'll meet you there," he said, his tone distant and empty.

Iris hesitated for a moment, considering whether to push the issue further. But she saw the look of determination on Elias's face and knew that trying to change his mind would be a futile effort.

With a sigh, she picked up her glass and took a long sip of her wine. It tasted like sweet nectar on her tongue, a burst of flavor that ignited every one of her senses. She closed her eyes, savoring the moment, letting the taste take her away to a different place, a place far removed from the current tension that had overtaken the table.

Ian, who had been quietly observing the scene unfolding between Iris and Elias, took the opportunity to take a sip of his own drink. He felt a warm sensation spread across his body as the elixir did its work.

Ian felt his thoughts become foggy his gaze wandered around the room, taking in the sights and sounds of the bustling tavern. His eyes landed on a group of musicians playing lively jigs on fiddles and flutes, their infectious energy impossible to ignore.

The sensation started in his chest, spreading through his body like a slow poison. Ian's breath quickened, and a rush of pleasure coursed through him. He gasped, feeling himself becoming aroused.

He watched as they played, their fingers moving nimbly over the strings and keys. The musicians were hot, perspiration glistening on their skin as they danced and swayed to the rhythm. Ian's gaze followed the movements of the lead fiddler, a handsome young man with a mischievous glint in his eyes. Ian couldn't help but feel drawn in by his energy, a magnetic pull that made it impossible to look away.

Ian felt a throbbing between his legs, the sensation growing stronger and more intense with each passing second. He tried to resist the urge, but it was no use. Ian found himself standing up from his seat and swaying to the rhythm of the music. The intoxicating elixir he had consumed had taken full effect, and he felt a newfound sense of freedom and abandon flowing through his veins.

He began to dance, moving his hips in a lascivious manner that drew the attention of the musicians and the other patrons of the tavern. Some watched in amazement, while others couldn't help but join in.

Suddenly, the lead musician broke away from his group and made his way over to Ian. With a wink and a grin, he placed his hand on Ian's shoulder and began to dance with him. The two moved in sync, their bodies melding together in a fluid and sensual dance.

Ian couldn't believe what was happening. He had never felt so uninhibited.

His body seemed to be sliding into a primal rhythm, and he let it, allowing himself to become completely engulfed in the experience. He felt the stranger's soft lips against his, and he responded in kind, deepening the kiss as their tongues tangled together.

Ian's hands gripped the stranger's hips, pulling him closer, as his own body responded to the scene before him. The warm, moist mouth on his own was sending waves of pleasure pulsing through his loins, and he couldn't help but moan in response. He wrapped his fingers around the man's thick shoulder, digging in tight as their bodies pressed together.

The man's powerful arms encircled Ian, pulling him in close. Ian could feel the heat radiating off of the stranger's muscular body, setting every one of his nerve endings alight. The man's hands roamed over Ian's ass, gripping and kneading the flesh. Ian could feel the man's erection pressing through his pants and it only made him more excited.

The man responded by grinding his hips against Ian, causing the young man to moan with pleasure. They broke apart, both panting heavily. Ian leaned forward, biting and licking at the man's neck and ears. The man growled in response, lifting Ian up and carrying him to a secluded corner of the tavern.

The music faded into the background as they stumbled through the crowded room, the man's hands groping and grabbing at Ian's body as they went.

They reached a dimly lit alcove, hidden from the rest of the tavern by a thick velvet curtain. The man kicked the curtain aside and pressed Ian up against the wall, his lips finding Ian's once again in a deep and passionate kiss.

Ian's hands roamed over the man's chest and abs, feeling the firm muscle beneath his shirt. He could feel the man's hard cock pressing against him, and he moaned in anticipation.

The man broke the kiss and began to unbutton Ian's shirt, his fingers fumbling with the buttons in his eagerness. Ian's skin was flushed with desire, his nipples hard and sensitive to the touch. The man leaned in and began to kiss and lick the exposed skin, his stubble grazing against Ian's delicate skin.

Ian's hands made their way to the man's belt, fumbling with the buckle as he tried to undo it. The man grinned and bit Ian's earlobe, letting out a low growl as he did so. Ian shuddered at the sensation, his heart pounding in his chest. The man's hands continued exploring Ian's body as he went, tracing lines across his skin and making his breath hitch every time he touched a sensitive spot.

Finally, with trembling fingers, Ian managed to unbuckle the man's belt and pull down his pants. The stranger's cock sprang free, hard and pulsing with blood. Ian gasped at the sight of it, taking in the thick shaft and the bulbous head that was already glistening with pre-cum.

"You're huge," Ian breathed, licking his lips in anticipation.

The man grinned, running his fingers through Ian's long white hair. "You're not so bad yourself, gorgeous," he replied, admiring Ian's large breasts. With that, he leaned in and kissed Ian deeply, their tongues intertwining as they explored each other's mouths. Ian responds by reaching up and tangling his fingers in the man's short hair, pulling him closer.

As they kiss, the man's hands begin to wander over Ian's body, feeling every curve and dip. One hand finds its way to Ian's breast, cupping it and giving it a gentle squeeze. The other hand makes its way down Ian's body, slipping inside of his miniskirt, and finding its way to Ian's wet, slick folds. The man groans at the feeling of Ian's wetness, slipping two fingers inside of Ian with ease.

Ian lets out a gasp at the feeling of the man's fingers inside of him, his back arching as the man begins to pump them in and out. The man's thumb rubs slow circles around Ian's clit, causing Ian to moan as pleasure builds within him.

The man's fingers continued to move inside of Ian, hitting all the right spots, making the game native feel like he's going to explode. The music playing faintly in the background only adds to Ian's arousal, encouraging him to give himself over to the moment, to let go of any inhibitions he once possessed.

Ian can feel his body trembling, ready to explode with sensation.

"Oh! I'm gonna..." Ian gasps, his hips thrusting against the man's hand in desperate need.

The man pulls his fingers out, leaving Ian ragged and panting.

"Take me!" Ian pleads, his eyes wide with desire.

The man grins wickedly, savoring the moment before he finally gives in. He lifts Ian up, his strong arms encircling his waist as Ian wraps his legs around his hips. The man's fingers dig into Ian's thighs, leaving marks on his skin as he positions himself at Ian's entrance. He meets Ian's gaze, their eyes locking for a moment before he thrust forward, filling Ian's tight, wet heat with his rock-hard cock.

Ian's back arches with pleasure as he feels the man enter him, his fingers digging into the man's shoulders as he tries to adjust to the feeling. Ian moans, his head falling back against the wall as the man begins to move, thrusting in and out of Ian with a steady rhythm that leaves them both gasping for breath.

The pleasure building inside Ian increases with every stroke of the stranger's cock, and he can feel his orgasm building faster than ever.

The man's hands slide up Ian's chest, skimming over his sensitive nipples before gripping his shoulders tightly. He growls, his lips trailing along Ian's jawline.

Ian can hear his own breathing grow louder and quicker with every passing moment. The friction of the man's thick cock sliding in and out of him is overwhelming, and Ian feels his eyes roll back in his head with pleasure. The man's thrusts grow harder and faster, and Ian can feel himself drawing nearer and nearer to the edge of ecstasy.

The man's lips find Ian's once more, their breath mingling as they kiss fiercely. The heat of the moment only intensifies Ian's pleasure as the man's thumb starts to circle Ian's clit faster and more insistently.

Ian lets out a loud moan and arches his back as the man thrusts harder and faster, driving Ian closer and closer to the edge.

With each powerful thrust, Ian can feel his orgasm building, the sensation of the man's cock sending sparks of intense pleasure through his body. Ian can feel his legs shaking as he grips the man's shoulders, trying to hold on as the pleasurable wave builds higher and higher.

Suddenly, Ian feels a sudden and violent surge of cum rush through him, a warm flood pouring out as the man continues to thrust, driving Ian over the edge. Ian moans loudly, his head flinging back as he surrenders to the overwhelming feeling surging through his body.

The man's hands grip Ian's hips tighter, holding him in place as he thrusts deeper and harder, pushing Ian to the brink of pleasure and beyond.

Ian feels himself consumed by the intense sensations, his mind a haze of ecstasy and pleasure. The man's cock glides in and out of Ian's slick heat like a piston, each stroke drawing forth whimpers and moans of pure bliss from deep within Ian's chest. Ian's hands explore the man's hard, muscular body, feeling the tension and strength contained in every single fiber of the man's being. The man's thighs flex and release with each thrust, and Ian can feel the muscles working to power the forceful movements, causing the man's hard cock to slam into Ian with raw ferocity.

Suddenly, the man pulls out and spins Ian around so that he is facing the wall. Ian's arms reach up above his head, bracing himself against the cold stone, arching his back in anticipation.

The man groans with wicked pleasure as he runs his hands over Ian's body, his fingers tracing a path over the curve of Ian's ass before spreading the cheeks apart.

The man's other hand wraps around Ian's waist, pulling his ass back towards him, pressing Ian's face flush against the cool stone wall as he positions himself. The tip of the man's cock teases at Ian's entrance, eliciting soft gasps from Ian as the cock nudges against the sensitive skin.

The man slowly pushes inside of Ian, burying himself until he is fully seated within Ian's tightest hole. There's a moment of pause, a breath taken together as Ian adjusts to the intrusion. The man's fingers dig into Ian's hips, holding him firmly in place as he slowly begins to rock in and out of Ian. The slow, steady pace allows both parties to savor the feeling, heightening their pleasure as the man's cock teases and rubs against Ian from the inside.

Ian's breath comes in ragged gasps as the man's hands roam over his body, kneading and gripping his hips, thighs, and waist.

But then, in a sudden and unexpected move, the man grabs hold of Ian's long white pigtails, tugging hard on them. The sharp pull causes Ian to cry out, a mixture of pleasure and pain. The man continues to thrust into Ian with renewed vigor, the rhythm now wild and frantic. The sudden change in pace causes Ian's body to tighten around the man's cock, intensifying the sensations for both parties.

Ian's eyes flutter closed as the man pulls on his pigtails again, the pain mixing with pleasure as it courses through his body. He can feel the man's cock as it slides in and out of him, the sensation almost too much to bear.

The man's hands are all over him, gripping Ian's hips, snaking around his waist, and tugging at his hair. Ian lets out a series of moans, unable to stop himself from responding to the numerous sensations that are washing over him.

The music is playing in the background, a hypnotic rhythm that only serves to fuel the primal desires coursing through his veins.

As the man inside of him continues to pound relentlessly, Ian can feel his whole body heating up, every muscle tensing and tightening as he reaches the point of no return. The man's grip on his hips tightens even further, and he gives a gruff moan, an affirmation of his own impending climax.

Ian's ass tightens in response, squeezing the man's hard cock, causing another torrid surge of pleasure to ripple through them both. With a final, desperate thrust, the man empties himself, the hot surge of cum filling Ian with warmth that radiates out from his core. It's an intense feeling, overwhelming and powerful, and Ian can't help but shudder as the man pulls out and their bodies separate. He sags against the wall, one hand gripping the stone as he takes deep, ragged breaths.

The man doesn't wait for him to recover. Instead, he turns Ian around, taking his empty mouth and capturing it in a hungry kiss. Their tongues entwine, tasting the remnants of the elixir still lingering in Ian's mouth. The man, breathing heavily, pulls away from him, leaning back against the wall and closing his eyes. Ian follows suit, leaning against the man, feeling the heat of his body radiating through him. He runs his hand up the man's bare chest, feeling the ripples of muscle underneath. The man's hand finds Ian's and holds it there. Ian looks into his eyes, and he sees a sense of longing there. He feels a pang of guilt, knowing that he's about to leave this stranger behind.

Meanwhile, Iris and Astrid had left the tavern and started to make their way to their base, leaving Duncan, Elias, and Ian behind. Iris couldn't help but feel a twinge of guilt as she walked away from Elias, but she knew that she needed to give him some space. She had hoped that Astrid might have some insights into how to deal with the situation, as she seemed to be taking everything in stride.

As they walked, Iris couldn't help but notice how different Astrid was in this world. In the real world, she was shy and introverted, always hiding behind her hair. But in this world, she was confident and bold, her eyes bright with excitement. Astrid looked like a completely different person with her long blonde hair and slender figure. Iris couldn't help but feel a bit jealous of her new look.

As they walked, Iris listened as Astrid talked about her experiences in the game world. She was amazed at how effortlessly Astrid navigated this new realm, quickly adapting to its rules and quirks. It was clear that Astrid was enjoying herself, and it made Iris happy to see her so full of life. But there was still a nagging feeling in the back of her mind, something that told her that she needed to be more cautious in this world. She couldn't shake the feeling that they were being watched, that someone was always lurking in the shadows, waiting for their moment to strike.

Back in the tavern, Elias had continued to flirt with the waitress, his eyes following her every move as she walked around the room. Despite his lingering doubts about his feelings for Iris, he couldn't help but feel drawn to the waitress.

As she leaned over the table, showing off her curves in the process, Elias felt a surge of desire wash over him. He couldn't help but stare at her body, mesmerized by the sight. The waitress, sensing his gaze, looked over and gave him a coy smile.

"Would you like to join me upstairs? The owner has some rooms upstairs if you're looking for a more private place to rest," she said, her voice low and sultry, leaning over the table just enough to let her ample cleavage show. Elias felt a shiver run down his spine. He hesitated, knowing that he should probably get back to Iris, but the offer was too tempting to refuse. He found himself nodding, unable to tear his gaze away from her.

"I'll just finish my drink and meet you upstairs," he finally managed to say, his voice husky with desire.

The waitress grinned and winked at him before sauntering away, leaving him alone with his thoughts. He took a long sip of his drink, his mind racing with excitement and anticipation.

Elias knew that what he was about to do was wrong. He knew that Iris would be hurt if she found out, but he couldn't help himself. He stood and followed her up the narrow, winding staircase, his heart pounding in his chest with excitement.

Upstairs, the room was dimly lit, and the air was thick with anticipation. Elias's eyes took in every detail of the room – the velvet curtains, the four-poster bed, and the simple wooden table in the corner.

He tried to divert his attention from the curvy outline of the waitress as she sauntered into the room.

Dropping his gear onto the floor, he was all too aware of the warmth that crept into his pants as the waitress approached him with a seductive smile. She handed him a glass of wine. He took it, downing it in one gulp before she could protest.

He waited for her to speak, but she simply stretched out onto the bed, inviting him to join her with her sultry gaze. He hesitated for a moment, torn between his loyalty to Iris and his raging desires. But the thought of Iris in her male avatar form lingered in the back of his mind, pushing him to act on his instincts.

Elias shrugged off his clothes and approached the woman lying on the bed. Her eyes sparkled with mischief as he kissed her deeply, his hands roaming across her frame. Her skin was smooth and warm under his touch, and the memory of Iris's touch faded from his thoughts as she arched into his embrace.

Elias's hands wandered down her body, feeling the weight of her breasts in his palms. The woman moaned as he massaged them, running her fingers through his hair. He leaned down, taking one nipple into his mouth, swirling his tongue around it while he pinched and pulled at the other with his fingers.

The woman beneath him writhed and moaned, her body responding to his touch like a well-tuned instrument. He moved lower, trailing kisses and licks down her stomach, stopping just above her pubic bone. Without waiting for any further invitation, he spread her legs wide with his hands and

positioned himself between them. The waitress's breath hitched as he did so, but she didn't resist.

Elias's cock was hard and throbbing, straining against the fabric of his pants. He tore them off in a flash, revealing himself to the waitress. She gasped, her eyes widening as she took in the sight of him. Elias's fingers traced a path up her inner thigh, teasing her before finally finding her entrance. He slowly pushed himself inside her, feeling her warmth envelop him. Her pussy felt so tight, like a perfect glove designed just for him. He gripped her hips and started to move, thrusting in and out in a steady rhythm.

Her moans filled the room, and her hands roamed over his back and shoulders, gripping him tightly as the pleasure mounted.

Elias felt like he was losing control, but he didn't care. The feel of her hot, slick pussy around his cock was too good to resist. He savored every moment, taking in the sight of her writhing and moaning beneath him. Her tits bounced with each of his thrusts, and her nipples were hard peaks, begging for attention.

He leaned down to take one in his mouth, sucking energetically and pulling on the hard nub with his teeth. Her gasps and moans filled his ears, and her hands clung to his shoulders as he continued his energetic assault.

His hard, sweaty body glistened as he rode her hard, his thick, throbbing cock gliding easily in and out of her tight, wet hole.

The waitress bit her lip to muffle her own moans as she rode the wave of pleasure crashing down upon her. The pain of being penetrated was roughly pleasurable, the throbbing ache in her stretched hole was an exquisite sensation, driving her closer and closer to her climax.

Elias's hand wrapped around the woman's neck, holding her in place as he slammed into her again and again. The sound of their bodies meeting echoed in the dark room, punctuated by her muffled screams of pleasure and his deep, guttural moans.

Elias' grip on the waitress's neck tightened as he felt his climax approaching, her muffled cries only fueling his desire.

As he picked up the pace, the bed frame creaked in time with their rhythm. The sweat dripped from his forehead and onto her chest, where it was absorbed by her ample cleavage.

She moaned loudly and pushed her breasts up on his chest, making it easier for him to take a nipple between his teeth. He latched on and pulled firmly, twisting his head as he sucked and nibbled. She squirmed beneath him, gripping the sheets below her with tight fists. They continued like this for a while, each lost in their own pleasure, before finally reaching their climaxes together. Elias groaned deep in his throat as he came, filling her to the brim with his hot, sticky release.

As their breathing slowly returned to normal, Elias pulled out and rolled onto his back beside her. He stared up at the ceiling, feeling guilt and shame weigh down on him. Iris was the one he truly loved, yet he had just cheated on her. But it was difficult to shake off the thrill of the encounter and the satisfaction of his lust. He lay there, arms folded behind his head, as he watched the waitress get dressed, his gaze lingering on her curves. She shot him a knowing smile before leaving the room, leaving a lingering scent of perfume behind.

At that time, Duncan sat in the tavern, staring at the table in front of him. He had been so caught up in his thoughts about his newfound attraction to men that he hadn't realized that he was now alone at the table. He looked around the tavern and noticed that Iris, Elias, Ian, and Astrid were nowhere to be found.

Panic began to set in as he remembered that he didn't have any money on him to pay for the drink they had ordered.

He glanced up at the bar and saw one of the waitresses walking towards him with a look of determination on her face. Duncan knew that she was coming to ask him for payment.

"Excuse me, miss," she said politely, but with a hint of firmness in her voice.

Duncan gulped nervously, his heart pounding in his chest. "Yes?" he replied hesitantly, fumbling with the coins on the table trying to avoid eye contact.

"Your friends left you here, and you still have to pay for the drinks."

Duncan frowned, his shoulders sagging with guilt. "I'm sorry, I don't have any money on me," he said quietly.

The waitress raised her eyebrows in surprise, but she quickly recovered, her expression softening as she took in his appearance. "My boss isn't very understanding when it comes to people walking out without paying. If you don't have the funds, perhaps we can arrange something else?"

Duncan's mind raced as he looked at the woman. He couldn't pay for the drinks, but he couldn't just leave without doing something.

As if reading his mind, the waitress said, "We're actually short-staffed right now, and could use an extra pair of hands. Why don't you trade your payment for a job here for the rest of the night?" she suggested, a hint of desperation in her voice.

Duncan's eyes widened in surprise. "What?" he asked, taken aback by the sudden turn of events.

"You can work off your debt," the waitress explained. "We're in need of an extra pair of hands tonight, and I'm sure my boss would be happy to accept that as payment for your drinks."

Duncan blinked in surprise, taken aback by the proposition. "A job? As a waitress?" he asked, feeling a flush of embarrassment creep up his neck.

"Yes, why not?" the waitress said, amused at the blush on Duncan's face.

Duncan hesitated for a moment before nodding. "Alright, sure. I'll do it." He felt a little nervous, but he was also curious to see what it would be like.

The waitress led him to the back of the tavern and opened a door to reveal a small room with a few racks of clothes. "Here, try these on." She handed him a stack of clothes, and he took them hesitantly.

"This is what you'll be wearing tonight," she explained, gesturing to the short dress and thigh-high stockings.

Duncan looked down at the clothes in his hands, feeling nervous and embarrassed to be dressed in such a revealing outfit, especially considering that he was a man in a woman's body.

The waitress noticed his hesitation and smiled reassuringly. "Don't worry, you'll get used to it. And besides, it's just for one night. Now come on, let's get you dressed."

Duncan nodded nervously and stepped behind a curtain to change. As he slipped out of his clothes and into the dress, he couldn't help but feel a sense of vulnerability. The dress was tight-fitting and revealed a lot more skin than he was used to showing. He felt exposed and unsure of himself.

When he emerged from behind the curtain, the waitress gave him a once-over, her eyes lingering on his legs.

She smiled approvingly and then reached out to tug at the hem of his dress, pulling it up to reveal the simple white underwear he was wearing.

Duncan blushed, feeling suddenly self-conscious, but the waitress didn't seem to notice. Instead, she leaned over the counter, rummaging through a drawer and pulling out a new set of underwear.

"Try these on," she said, handing him a pair of red lace panties. Duncan looked at them skeptically, but the waitress gave him a wink and a nod, encouraging him to try them on.

Reluctantly, Duncan stripped off his old underwear and slipped on the new ones. The fabric was soft and silky against his skin, and the red lace was a stark contrast to the plain white he had been wearing before. He couldn't help but feel a little self-conscious, but the waitress seemed pleased with her choice.

"There, that's much better," she said, approvingly. "Now let's get you to work."

Duncan followed the waitress back out to the tavern, feeling self-conscious in his new attire. He couldn't believe he was doing this, but he knew he had no choice.

As he approached the table where he had left his friends, he saw that it was empty.

The waitress showed him the ropes, explaining how to take orders, serve drinks, and clear tables. Duncan listened attentively, trying to absorb as much information as possible.

As they walked around the tavern, the waitress introduced him to the other staff members, who all gave him a friendly nod or a wave. Duncan couldn't help but feel a little out of place in his new attire, but he tried his best to push those thoughts aside and focus on the task at hand.

Finally, it was time for him to start taking orders. The waitress showed him how to use the order pad and explained the different drinks on the menu. Duncan felt a little overwhelmed, but he took a deep breath and approached the first table with confidence.

"Hi there, I'm Duncan. What can I get you to drink?" he asked, smiling at the two patrons sitting at the table.

The two men looked up at him and grinned. "Hey there, cutie!" one of them said. Duncan felt his face grow hot, but he steeled himself and smiled back.

The waitress who had helped him earlier walked by and winked at him. "Remember, a little flirting never hurt anyone and it can get you good tipping," she whispered as she passed.

Duncan took a deep breath and leaned in a little closer to the men. "So, what can I get for you two handsome gentlemen?" he asked, adding a little extra charm to his voice.

The men exchanged a glance and grinned. "Well, how about two pints of your finest ale?" the taller one said, winking at Duncan.

As he turned to leave, the other man took the opportunity to give his ass a playful squeeze, causing Duncan to jump with surprise.

"Hey now, none of that!" he protested, trying to keep his voice light and joking, even as his heart raced. The man just laughed and held up his hands in a gesture of innocence. Duncan hurried back to the bar, grateful to be out of the man's reach. His heart was still racing, and his head was swimming. Is this really happening? he wondered as he grabbed a towel from the counter and started wiping down tables.

It seemed like just a few minutes ago that he had been sitting comfortably in his apartment. Now he was wearing a dress, groped by a stranger, and working at a seedy tavern.

He felt like he was stuck in a bad dream, and he desperately wanted to wake up. The longer he worked, the more he felt like he was becoming a joke to the patrons, a target for their lewd comments and suggestive glances.

He worked through the evening, serving drinks and flirting with the customers to try and understand the ins and outs of his strange new existence. The experience was a far cry from his old life, but there was a sense of excitement to it that he couldn't ignore.

As the night wore on, Duncan couldn't shake the feeling that he was missing out on something. The other members of the group were all paired up, engaged in passionate encounters that seemed to be deepening their connection to one another. Duncan felt cut off. Despite his feelings, he continued to serve drinks and perform his duties, trying to forget about his loneliness.

However, as the night progressed, he found himself growing more and more aroused by the male customers who flirted with him. The patrons, mostly male, found his timid and shy demeanor endearing, constantly flirting with him, trying to catch his attention.

At first, Duncan rejected their advances, but as the night went on, it became harder to ignore the growing physical attraction he felt towards some of them. There was something enticing about being desired by so many. Duncan's arousal grew with each lingering gaze, with every playful comment or flirtatious touch. His body stirred, and he felt himself being pulled in a direction that he had never before considered.

As the tavern started to thin out, Duncan felt a tap on his shoulder. Turning around, he saw the waitress who had helped him earlier, standing with a smile. "You did great tonight, Duncan. My boss is impressed. Your tab has been paid off, and you can go home now. But if you need money, one of the patrons has taken a liking to you. He's asked me to tell you that if you'd like to make some extra coin, he has a proposition for you. It involves some... adult activities." The waitress winked and nodded towards a man sitting at the bar, who caught Duncan's gaze and smiled invitingly.

Duncan's heart pounded in his chest as he took in the man's chiseled jawline, broad shoulders, and piercing blue eyes. He couldn't deny the attraction he felt, nor could he ignore the possibility of earning some extra coin.

Duncan hesitated for a moment, glancing back at the waitress to gauge her reaction. She simply gave him an encouraging nod, as if to tell him that it was up to him to make his own decisions.

Duncan felt his heart racing, but he wasn't sure if it was from the offer or the identity of the potential customer. Regardless, he felt a thrill course through him, and he realized that he was intrigued. He gave the man a hesitant smile and made his way toward the bar.

As he approached, the man stood up and extended his hand, introducing himself. Duncan was pleasantly surprised by the man's easy demeanor and quick smile. They exchanged pleasantries, and Duncan was unable to tear his gaze away from the muscular form beneath the man's shirt. The man, sensing Duncan's apprehension, placed a reassuring hand on Duncan's arm and leaned in to speak in a low whisper.

"I know this might seem like a strange offer, but I've taken a real fancy to you tonight. I'd like to offer you something a bit special.

Something that will help you earn a bit of cash, and maybe I can have a bit of fun in the process."

Duncan hesitated, his mind racing with thoughts of what the man might be suggesting. He had never done anything like this before. But as the man's fingers gently brushed against his hand, Duncan felt a surge of heat coursing through his body.

"Would you like to come up to my room?" the man asked. Duncan could hear the huskiness in his voice and felt a shiver run down his spine.

"I... I don't know," Duncan stammered.

The man noticed the uncertainty in his voice. He stepped closer and reached out, gripping

Duncan's jaw with a gentle yet firm hand. "It's okay," he murmured. "I promise I won't hurt you."

Duncan's heart raced, but he couldn't deny the attraction he felt for this stranger. He nodded slightly, allowing the man to lead him upstairs and into his private room.

The room was dimly lit, with a large four-poster bed taking center stage. The man closed the door behind them and turned to face Duncan, his eyes full of desire. He approached Duncan slowly, his hand reaching out to cup the back of Duncan's neck, pulling him in for a kiss. Duncan felt himself being swept away by the man's intensity, his hands wandering down Duncan's back as they kissed.

The man broke the kiss and looked into Duncan's eyes, a sly smile playing at the corners of his lips. "I have a particular taste," he whispered, his voice low and sultry. Duncan felt a shiver run down his spine, unsure of what the man meant. But as the man's hands began to explore his body, Duncan couldn't deny the growing excitement he felt.

The man's fingers deftly undid the buttons on Duncan's dress, pushing it off his shoulders and letting it fall to the floor. Duncan stood before the man, feeling vulnerable and exposed in nothing but his underwear. The man smiled at him, his eyes sparkling with mischief.

"I've prepared a costume for you," he said, gesturing to a rack of clothes in the corner of the room. "I thought we could indulge in a little roleplay, don't you think?"

Duncan felt his cheeks flush, but he nodded hesitantly. He had never done anything like this before, but he couldn't deny the curiosity that was building within him.

He felt a mix of anxiety and excitement as the man turned away from him and walked over to the rack of clothes. The man picked out a costume and turned back around to face him, holding it up for him to see. Duncan's heart raced as he took in the sight before him. It was a schoolgirl uniform, complete with a plaid skirt, white blouse, and a matching tie.

The man smiled at him, his eyes bright with anticipation."Put it on,"

the man said, handing the costume to Duncan. He didn't question the strange request but slipped the uniform on, feeling the skirt rustle against his legs and the blouse hugging his chest. The man moved closer, taking in the sight of Duncan in the schoolgirl outfit.

Once the costume was on, Duncan looked up at the man shyly, feeling vulnerable and aroused.

The man chuckled and took a step closer to him, reaching out to grab Duncan's chin and tilt his head back.

"Now, my little student," the man purred, his voice low and commanding, "it's time for your lesson."

Duncan couldn't believe what was happening, but he found himself getting more and more turned on by the second. "Yes, Professor," he replied, his voice shaking as he spoke.

The man - who was dressed in a suit and tie - smirked and then stepped even closer to Duncan. "Good. I'm glad to see you're taking your studies seriously," the man said with a satisfied grin. "Now, let's move on to the practical portion of your lesson," he said, his voice low and sultry.

Duncan looked up at him with wide eyes, feeling a mix of trepidation and excitement. The man chuckled and reached down, undoing his pants and releasing his erect member.

Duncan's eyes widened, but he felt a strange sense of excitement wash over him.

"Now, my little student," the man said, guiding Duncan's head towards his groin, "it's time for your lesson on fellatio."

Duncan hesitated, unsure of what to do. The man saw his apprehension and smiled, leaning down to whisper in his ear, "Don't worry, I'll guide you every step of the way."

Duncan hesitated for a moment before nodding timidly, feeling a wave of butterflies flutter in his stomach. He knelt down between the man's legs, positioning himself as he looked up at the man nervously.

"Are you ready?" the man asked, his voice husky and filled with anticipation.

Duncan nodded, his mouth dry as he took in the sight of the man's erect member before him.

"Then, my little student, it's time for your lesson to begin," the man said, guiding Duncan's head towards his crotch.

Duncan took a deep breath, closing his eyes as he felt the warm, hard length of the man's penis against his lips. He hesitated for a moment, unsure of what to do next, but the man's hands on his head urged him to proceed.

He opened his mouth, taking the man's penis in his mouth, and he felt the man's hands grip his head tightly as he began to bob his head up and down.

"That's it, my little student," the man groaned, as he started to thrust into Duncan's mouth. "Take it all in, and don't forget to use your tongue."

Duncan took his time exploring the man's shaft, feeling the slight stubble on his balls, running his tongue up and down the veins, swirling the head of his dick in his mouth.

The man groaned, his grip on Duncan's head tightening. "That's right, my little student. You're a natural at this."

The man pulled out of Duncan's mouth with a pop, leaving him panting slightly. "But we're not done yet. It's time for your next lesson." He grabbed Duncan's hand and pulled him up from his knees, leading him over to the bed. "I want you to ride me."

Duncan hesitated for a moment, unsure of what to do. The man smiled and reached down, undoing the buttons on Duncan's blouse. "Don't worry, I'll guide you." The man's hands reached down and began to caress Duncan's inner thighs, gently pushing them apart.

"Do you want me to fuck you, my little student?" the man asked, his voice low and filled with lust.

Duncan hesitated, unsure of what to say.

"Yes," Duncan finally managed to say, his voice barely above a whisper.

The man's eyes widened with pleasure, and he grinned. "Don't forget to call me Professor," he reminded Duncan.

"Yes, Professor," Duncan said, unable to keep the excitement out of his voice.

The man grinned and then leaned in to whisper in his ear. "I knew you'd be a quick learner," he said, before pulling Duncan's skirt up and revealing his underwear.

"Ah, it seems like your underwear violated school rules," the man said, with mock sternness. "That means I'll have to punish you."

"Bend over," the man commanded.

Duncan obeyed, bending over the bed as the man lifted his skirt up even higher. He could feel the cool air on his exposed skin, making him shiver with anticipation.

Duncan's heart raced as he felt the man's hand come down on his ass, delivering a sharp smack that made him gasp. The man chuckled and spanked him again, leaving a warm blush on Duncan's cheeks.

"You've been a naughty student, Duncan. And you know what we do with naughty students, don't you?" the man asked, his voice dripping with desire.

Duncan couldn't believe how turned on he was, and he felt himself grow even more aroused as the man's hand explored his thighs, slowly pulling down his underwear to expose him completely.

He couldn't deny that he was getting turned on by the man's dominance, or the way his juices were already dripping down his thighs.

The man's hand trailed down his inner thighs again, dipping a finger between his legs to gather up his leaking wetness. He brought the finger up to Duncan's lips, using it to paint his mouth with the glistening liquid.

"You've been a very naughty student, Duncan. So naughty, in fact, that I think you deserve a special punishment," the man said, still with that same low and sultry voice. Duncan felt himself shivering in anticipation, unsure of what was to come next. But at the same time, he couldn't deny that the thought of the "punishment" the man had in mind excited him. He opened his mouth and let the man paint his lips with his own juices, tasting himself for the first time.

"Lick your lips clean," the man commanded, and Duncan complied, tasting himself more fully. The man smirked and then leaned down to whisper in his ear, "you're going to be a good girl and follow the rule like a good student, yes?"

Duncan couldn't believe how much the man's words turned him on, and he found himself responding without thought, "Yes, Professor."

"That's right, be a good girl for the professor." The man's voice was dripping with lust, and as he spoke, he leaned in to tug at Duncan's earlobe with his teeth. Duncan couldn't help but let out a moan, feeling his whole body tremble as the man's hands continued to explore his thighs.

"Now, spread your legs a little wider for me," the man said, his voice a rough whisper. Duncan obliged, parting his legs even more as he felt the man's fingers probing at his entrance.

The man's breath was warm against his ear as he whispered, "You're such naughty little student. Let's see how quickly you can learn this lesson." The man's voice was soft like a caress, making Duncan shiver in anticipation.

Duncan felt the man's fingertip slowly sliding inside of him, spreading him open as he moaned at the invasion. It was an unfamiliar sensation that made him feel both vulnerable and excited, and he couldn't help but push back against the finger, trying to take it in deeper.

"That's it," the man growled in his ear. "You're such a good little student. Let your professor show you how to take it." He slowly added a second finger, scissoring them apart to stretch Duncan open. Duncan was whimpering now, unable to keep quiet as the pleasure coursed through him.

The man started to pump his fingers in and out, fucking him slowly. Each thrust brought him higher and higher, until he was panting and writhing on the bed, desperate for more.

The man's thumb found Duncan's tight little bud, teasing and circling it until Duncan couldn't take it anymore. He pushed back, impaling himself on the man's thick fingers.

Duncan moaned and gasped, his eyes tightly closed as the pleasure consumed him. The man's fingers felt so good, but he wanted more. He wanted to push past the limits of what his body had known before, and feel the raw pleasure

of full on penetration. He was overwhelmed with desire, and begged the man to fuck him properly.

"Please, professor," Duncan moaned. "I want you inside me."

The man obliged, pulling his fingers out of Duncan's tight hole and replacing them with his thick cock. He pushed inside of Duncan, filling him up completely.

The feeling of being stretched out like this was overwhelming, but in the best way possible. Duncan groaned and writhed on the bed, urging him to move faster.

He started to thrust into Duncan with long, slow strokes. Each one hit all the right spots, causing Duncan to gasp and moan. The man's pace gradually picked up, and with each thrust, Duncan felt his body tighten with pleasure. He was vaguely aware that this was part of the game, but the intensity of the sensation consumed him, and all he could focus on was the feeling of being filled up by the man's thick cock.

"You feel so good," the man groaned in his ear, his breath hot and heavy. "You're such a good little student."

The man's voice was dripping with lust, and he continued to thrust into Duncan with a rough and steady rhythm. Duncan couldn't believe how good it felt to have the man inside of him. He found himself pushing back against the man's thrusts, eager for more.

The man's hands gripped Duncan's hips, holding him still as he drove into him over and over again. Duncan gasped and moaned, the sensation of being filled so completely overwhelming him.

"You like that, my little student?" the man growled, his hips slapping against Duncan's ass. "You like it when your professor fucks you like this?" the man smirked, his hips still pistoning in and out of Duncan with the utmost abandon.

"Yes, Professor, yes," Duncan moaned, his whole body trembling as the man continued to fill him up, again and again.

He couldn't believe how good it felt, the feel of the man's thick cock stretching him out. His moans grew louder and more urgent, as the sensation of being thoroughly fucked by this man consumed him.

The man placed a hand on Duncan's shoulder, guiding him to lean further over the bed. Duncan compliantly leaned as far as he could, his cheek resting on the cool fabric of the bed.

The new position allowed the man even deeper penetration, and Duncan cried out in pleasure. The man's hands roamed over Duncan's body, squeezing and kneading his flesh as if it were dough.

Duncan groaned at the touch, his body trembling with desire. He felt his thoughts beginning to blur as his mind slipped deeper and deeper into a haze of pure animalistic lust.

His body tightened as the man continued to slam into him. The rough thrusts turned into a frantic, fevered pace, and Duncan felt his whole body trembling with pleasure. With every pounding stroke, he could feel his orgasm building, cresting higher and higher. He could barely breathe, his moans coming in ragged gusts.

The man was relentless, driving into him harder and faster, his thrusts growing more erratic as he neared his climax. Duncan felt himself approaching the edge as well, the pleasure building up inside him like a tidal wave.

Just as Duncan felt himself reaching the peak of his orgasm, the man's body tensed, and he grunted as he released his seed deep inside Duncan. Duncan gasped and writhed beneath him, feeling the warmth of the man's cum filling him up.

He could feel his own orgasm tearing through his body, a wave of pleasure sweeping over him as he came hard, bits of his release splattering onto the sheets underneath him.

The man slowed his movements, still pulsating inside of Duncan, who lay beneath him, his body drained and spent. The man pulled out slowly, leaving Duncan feeling empty, but content and satisfied. "You're a natural," the man said, his voice a low growl as he traced a finger over Duncan's sweaty brow. "But I think our little lesson is over for today."

Duncan nodded weakly, still trying to catch his breath. He felt a twinge of disappointment that the encounter was over but couldn't deny the satisfied bliss that radiated through his body.

"Thank you, Professor," he said, looking up at the man with a soft smile.

The man chuckled and leaned down to press a gentle kiss to Duncan's lips. "You're welcome, my little student. I hope you learned something valuable today."

Duncan couldn't help but laugh at the man's words, his cheeks flushed with pleasure. "I think I did," he said, his voice barely above a whisper.

The man chuckled and helped Duncan off the bed, guiding him towards the bathroom. "I think it's time for a bath. You're all sweaty and sticky after our little session."

Duncan nodded, following the man meekly into the bathroom. He couldn't believe what had just happened. But at the same time, he couldn't deny the sense of excitement and satisfaction that flowed through him. It was as if a weight had been lifted off his shoulders, and he felt free. The water enveloped him, washing away the remnants of the day's tension, and the heat from the steam greeted him like a warm embrace.

Duncan closed his eyes, sinking deeper into the tub, and felt a hand rubbing his shoulders. "Mmm," he sighed contentedly, letting out a small moan as the fingers dug into the tension knots in his back. He had never felt so relaxed, and without opening his eyes, he reached back for the source of the massage.

His fingers met with warm, smooth skin, and he realized that the man was now also in the tub with him. The man's strong arms encircled him, pulling him back against his chest.

"That's better," the man murmured, pressing a soft kiss to the side of Duncan's neck. "You were so tense and unsure earlier. I'm glad you let me show you how to relax and enjoy yourself."

Duncan couldn't help but smile at the man's words. He had been tense, anxious even, about the whole experience initially.

However, as the man's hands moved over his body, expertly kneading out the knots and tension in his muscles, Duncan felt himself relax. The sensual touch of their skin against each other, combined with the steaming water, was intoxicating.

Duncan leaned back into the embrace, his head resting against the man's shoulder as he closed his eyes. The soothing sensation of the man's fingers tracing light patterns on his shoulders was nearly enough to lull him into a state of blissful relaxation.

Almost as if reading his mind, the man's voice whispered in his ear, "That's enough for now, my student. It's time for us to rest."

Duncan nodded, reluctantly extracting himself from the seductive embrace and allowing the man to help him out of the tub. Together, they padded to the large four-poster bed, and the man pulled back the thick, luxurious covers before gesturing for Duncan to climb in.

Duncan obeyed, slipping between the cool sheets and enjoying their silken softness. The man followed him, drawing the covers up over them both, and Duncan curled up against him, resting his head on the man's chest.

The man's arm wrapped around him, pulling him in closer as he traced light patterns on Duncan's shoulder with his other hand. "Sleep well, my little student," he whispered, his lips brushing against Duncan's forehead.

As they lay there, the man began to softly hum, and Duncan realized it was a melody from one of his favorite songs. He leaned back into the embrace, letting out a soft sigh of contentment. For the first time in what felt like ages, Duncan felt truly at peace.

Meanwhile, Iris and Astrid had arrived at their base of operations - a simple apartment in one of the city buildings.

Iris glanced around the small space, assessing their surroundings. The living room was cluttered with various pieces of furniture and equipment, including a large table with maps spread out on it. There were also several weapons stored in a nearby cabinet.

Astrid sat down on a worn-out couch, letting out a sigh of relief as she took her weight off her feet. Iris walked over to the window, gazing out at the city below. The towering structures and vibrant lights created a breathtaking view. She wondered how they had gotten here and if they would ever be able to return home. As she turned, Iris found her gaze drawn to Astrid, who was absentmindedly running her fingers over the armrest of the couch. She seemed lost in thought, and Iris couldn't help but feel a surge of protectiveness towards her friend.

"What's on your mind, Astrid?" Iris asked, moving closer and sitting down beside her.

Astrid hesitated for a moment, biting her lip as she gathered her thoughts. She looked at Iris, who was watching her with a look of concern. "I was just thinking about our relationship," Astrid finally said.

Iris raised an eyebrow. "Our relationship?" she echoed, confused.

"Yes," Astrid said, her voice low and sultry. "I want to be intimate with you, Iris."

Iris blinked, taken aback by Astrid's sudden confession. "But... I'm in relationship," she stammered.

"I know," Astrid replied, her gaze intense. "But I can't deny the way I feel anymore. I want you, Iris. And I think you want me too."

Iris hesitated, unsure of how to respond. She had always had a deep connection with Astrid, but she had never considered the possibility of a romantic or sexual relationship with her. However, as she looked into Astrid's eyes, she couldn't deny the attraction she felt.

"Astrid, I-" she began, but before she could finish her sentence, Astrid leaned in and kissed her. The kiss was soft at first, but it quickly became more passionate. Iris felt a jolt of excitement run through her body as she responded to the kiss, her heart pounding in her chest.

She wrapped her arms around Astrid, pulling her closer as they continued to kiss. She could feel the heat radiating from Astrid's body, and the sensation was intoxicating.

Iris's hands explored Astrid's curves, finding their way to the small of her back. Astrid let out a soft moan, her fingers running through Iris's hair.

Iris pulled away reluctantly, breathing heavily as she looked into Astrid's eyes. "We shouldn't..." she stammered, struggling to find the right words.

Astrid's expression was intense, her green eyes sparkling with desire. "Why not?" Astrid whispered seductively, leaning in closer to Iris. "We've been through so much together, haven't we? And I can't wait any longer. I want you, Iris."

Iris hesitated, feeling torn between her duty to Elias and her growing feelings for Astrid. She knew she owed it to Elias to be loyal and faithful, but she couldn't ignore the way her body was responding to Astrid's touch.

"I can't... I can't... I don't know if I should..." Iris stammered, her voice betraying her earlier determination to stay strong.

Astrid's hands rested lightly on Iris's shoulders, her thumbs gently rubbing small circles on the tense muscles. Iris's heart raced as Astrid leaned in closer, whispering in her ear. "I know you feel the same way, Iris. I can see it in your eyes, the way you look at me when you think I'm not looking. I can feel it when we hug and your body melts into mine."

Iris shivered at Astrid's words, her mind racing with conflicting emotions. She did feel an attraction to Astrid, but she couldn't betray

Elias like that a second time. She loved him, and she knew this wasn't right. She shouldn't be cheating on Elias, but she couldn't resist Astrid's charm anymore. She wanted her, needed her, and she couldn't stop herself from giving in to the overwhelming temptation that lived within her.

Iris's heart raced as she reached up to grab hold of Astrid's waist, pulling her closer so that their bodies were almost fused together. They breathed each other in, and Iris could feel the heat between them building with every passing second. She pressed her lips to Astrid's once more, her fingers tangling in the other woman's thick blonde hair as they kissed deeply.

The kiss grew more passionate, and Iris could feel herself becoming lost in the moment.

The feeling of Astrid's tongue exploring her mouth, her body pressed up against hers, sent a rush of desire through her. Iris felt her own body responding, her own desires taking control.

As they continued to kiss, Iris's hands began to wander, tracing patterns over Astrid's body. She could feel Astrid's own excitement growing, her body tensing and arching into Iris's touch.

It was then that Iris felt a strange sensation - a throbbing, pulsing feeling in her groin. Her penis was getting erect. She could feel it straining against the fabric of her pants, growing harder and heavier by the second.

Iris pulled back from the kiss, her eyes widening in shock as she looked down at the growing bulge in her pants. She guiltily glanced up at Astrid, unsure of how to react or what to say.

Astrid, however, simply smiled and raised an eyebrow, her eyes sparkling with curiosity as she stared at Iris's crotch. "Take it out," Astrid's voice was husky.

Iris hesitated for a split second before complying, her eyes locked on Astrid's as she reached for the button of her jeans and pushed the zipper down.

Her cock sprang free, bouncing against her stomach. She wrapped her fingers around her shaft, squeezing tightly as the head of her cock swelled to its full size.

Astrid's eyes gleamed with hunger as she stared at Iris's erection, her tongue darting out to wet her lips. "I want to see it, Iris," she purred, her voice seductive and low.

Iris swallowed thickly, her gut twisting with nerves. This was what she had been trying to avoid, what she had been trying to resist. The thought of sleeping intimately with Astrid filled her with a mix of excitement and self-loathing. She longed to give in to the temptation, but something within her held her back. However, she knew that sometimes giving in to your desires is better than denying yourself. She longed to be close to Astrid, to feel her soft skin against her own.

She had held herself back long enough, she thought, as she reached over and pulled Astrid into her arms. They kissed hungrily, their tongues tangling and bodies pressed together. Iris moaned softy as she felt Astrid's fingers tugging at her clothes and letting them fall to the floor.

Now, naked, Astrid was fully revealed to Iris, and the sight of her slender, toned body made the Iris's heart race. Astrid's chest was small but perky, with tiny pink nipples that were already taut with arousal. Iris's eyes trailed downward, taking in the curves of Astrid's stomach and her round hips, before arriving at the apex of her thighs. There, a small patch of neatly trimmed blonde hair concealed the treasures that beckoned to Iris.

Astrid's hand slid down Iris's chest, tracing the muscles there, then moved lower still, ghosting over Iris's hardened cock. "Let's go to the bed," Astrid said, her voice husky and filled with longing.

Iris could do nothing but nod mutely as she followed Astrid to the plush, inviting bed. She watched as Astrid crawled onto the center of the mattress, her blonde hair cascading around her shoulders like a golden curtain. The sight of her was intoxicating, and Iris felt her pulse quicken as she approached.

Astrid stretched out on the bed, her legs slightly parted, inviting Iris to join her.

As Iris climbed onto the bed, she felt the smooth fabric of the sheet slide against her bare skin. She could feel her heart pounding in her chest, adrenaline coursing through her veins as she prepared for what was about to happen.

Astrid stretched out her arms, inviting Iris to join her. She looked down at Astrid, whose chest rose and fell with shallow breaths as she waited. Iris crawled closer, her heart pounding in her chest. She reached out, her hand finding Astrid's small breasts. She cupped them, feeling the texture as she ran her fingers over the taut peaks.

Astrid's breath hitched, and her gaze turned heated as she looked up at Iris. Iris felt a flush of desire spread through her body, and she leaned down to kiss Astrid again.

This time, the kiss was slower, more deliberate. Iris could taste the saltiness of Astrid's skin, the sweet taste of her own desire mingled with it. She let her fingers trail lower, following the curves of Astrid's abs down to the juncture of her thighs.

Iris could feel the heat radiating off her, and she couldn't wait any longer. She slipped her fingers inside Astrid, reveling in the slickness of her folds, the way she fit perfectly around Iris's fingers.

Astrid moaned, thrusting her hips against Iris's hand as she worked her fingers deeper inside. Iris could feel the tension building in Astrid's body, the way she tensed and released with each stroke. She added a second finger, spreading Astrid open and rubbing against her G-spot.

Astrid moaned into Iris's mouth, her breath hitching as Iris's fingers delved deeper. She arched her back, pressing herself harder against Iris's hand. Iris could feel the walls of her vagina clenching and releasing around her fingers, the wetness increasing as Astrid's excitement built.

Iris didn't hesitate. She pushed a third finger inside, feeling Astrid tremble with pleasure. Soft cries escaped Astrid's lips as Iris's fingers moved in a rhythmic pattern, stimulating her G-spot and sending waves of pleasure coursing through her body. Iris moved her other hand to Astrid's breast, kneading and pinching her erect nipple. Astrid's back arched as she moaned, her hips bucking against Iris's hand. Iris's thumb circled Astrid's clit, adding an extra layer of sensation and intensifying the pleasure running through her.

Astrid panted, her fingers gripping the sheets beneath her tightly. Iris's fingers were still deep within her, moving inside her with slow, deliberate strokes that sent shivers down her spine. Astrid's climax lingered just out of reach, tantalizingly close but still elusive.

Iris blew lightly across Astrid's nipple, causing her to jump as a fresh wave of pleasure washed over her. She whimpered and clamped her hand tight around Iris's hair, pulling her closer. "Please, do that again."

Iris complied eagerly, nuzzling against Astrid's breast. She couldn't get enough of the way Astrid smelled, the way she tasted, the way she felt. Iris's hand roamed over Astrid's soft, lithe body, her fingers occasionally venturing down to toy with the slit between Astrid's two firm, swollen breasts which begged for attention. She loved the way Astrid's skin felt against her own, cool and smooth.

Iris lifted her head, her tongue flicking out to trace the hard nipple, then closing her lips around it. She sucked, feeling the soft flesh get pulled into her mouth as she bit and sucked gently. Astrid's breath hitched, her body tensing and jerking beneath Iris's touch.

Astrid could feel her whole body quivering with pleasure, the walls of her vagina clenching and releasing around Iris fingers. Iris sucked harder on Astrid's nipple, feeling the hardened nub swell in her mouth. Her lips and tongue moved to and fro across Astrid's nipple, teasing it while her fingers played with Astrid's soaked and aching pussy.

Iris's thumb found Astrid's clit once more, gently massaging and caressing the sensitive bud.

Astrid moaned, her back arching as pleasure coursed through her. She bit her lip, holding in a scream of delight as Iris's fingers explored her. The feeling of Iris's fingers playing with her sensitive spot brought Astrid to the brink of pleasure.

"Iris, please..." Astrid begged.

Iris grinned and removed her fingers from Astrid's pussy, bringing them to her lips and sucking on them greedily. Astrid's arousal had never tasted so sweet.

Iris savored her, each lick causing Astrid to writhe and moan, her fingers digging into the bedsheets. Astrid sweetness dripping down Iris's chin. She leaned in for a lingering kiss, her tongue swirling and twirling with Astrid's, the taste of their mingled desire sending shockwaves through both of their bodies. With Astrid's lips still pressed against hers, Iris's wandering hand found its way back to Astrid's pussy. She could feel Astrid's body shaking around her hand, a testament to the powerful orgasm taking hold of her.

Iris felt a sense of pride at having given Astrid such pleasure, but the sensation was quickly overwhelmed by her own mounting desire. She wanted to be touched, wanted to feel Astrid's hands on her own throbbing sex, to feel their bodies press together and merge in the most intimate of ways.

With a sudden burst of boldness, she reached down and grasped her own cock, giving it a slow, deliberate stroke. Astrid watched with rapt attention, her breath hitching as she saw Iris touch herself for the first time.

"Let me," Astrid whispered, breaking the silence. Her voice was thick with desire as she shifted her position to kneel between Iris's legs, reaching up to grip the base of Iris's cock.

She looked up at Astrid, "Are you sure about this?" she asked, her breath hitching in anticipation.

"Yes, I'm sure," Astrid replied, running her tongue along the head of Iris's cock, the salty taste of pre-cum making her moan. "I want this, Iris. I want you." She closed her eyes and moaned softly as she took Iris inside her mouth, relishing the taste, the texture, and the way Iris twitched and shuddered under her expert touch.

Iris's hips bucked involuntarily as Astrid's tongue twirled around the sensitive head of her cock. Astrid's mouth was warm and wet, and Iris could feel herself slipping deeper inside astrid's throat with each thrust. Astrid used her hands to cup Iris's balls, rolling them gently and massaging them with just enough pressure. She looked up at Iris, her eyes shining with desire. "I want to feel you inside me," she murmured, her voice low and seductive.

Iris could see the hunger in Astrid's eyes, and she knew that this was something they both wanted.

Slowly, she reached down and guided the head of her cock to Astrid's entrance. Astrid parted her legs wider, inviting Iris to enter her. Iris paused, taking a deep breath, then slowly began to push forward.

At first, it was difficult, and Iris could feel the resistance of Astrid's tight walls. But as she persisted, she felt herself sliding deeper and deeper inside Astrid.

Astrid's eyes were squeezed shut in pleasure, her mouth open in a silent moan. Iris couldn't help but watch as her cock disappeared inside Astrid's tight pussy.

Finally, she was fully inside Astrid, her body pressed against hers.

Astrid opened her eyes, her gaze fixed on Iris. "It feels so good," Astrid whispered, her voice trembling.

Iris couldn't help but agree, feeling the heat of Astrid's pussy envelop her cock. She began to move, pulling out slowly before thrusting back in, a soft gasp escaping Astrid's lips each time. Her body was rippling with desire, every muscle tensed in expectation as Iris's body slid against hers. Each thrust elicited a soft gasp from her, and her hips bucked involuntarily to meet Iris's. Iris reveled in the sensations, the softness of Astrid's inner walls gripping her as she sunk deeper with each thrust. She could feel herself growing harder inside her, the pressure building as pleasure coursed through her veins.

Iris reached down to touch Astrid's clit with her thumb, pressing down firmly, using the same rhythm as her hips. Astrid let out a soft cry, and Iris could feel the walls of her vagina clenching around her cock. The sensation was almost too much. Iris gritted her teeth, trying to hold back, trying to draw out the pleasure for as long as possible. She could feel Astrid's breathing grow more erratic, her body trembling beneath her. She was close. Iris could feel it. That telltale throb in her belly that meant her climax was near.

Astrid's hips moved in counterpoint to Iris', meeting her thrust for thrust, her body rising to meet each and every one. Iris could feel Astrid's warmth surrounding her cock, the silkiness of her folds gliding over her sensitive skin.

Suddenly, Iris felt a wave of pleasure wash over her. She closed her eyes, gritting her teeth as she fought to hold back the orgasm threatening to overwhelm her. She wasn't ready to finish yet. She wanted to savor this moment, this feeling of being connected with Astrid.

But it was a losing battle. With a groan, Iris gave in to the inevitable and tilted her hips, driving her entire length into Astrid in one desperate thrust. Astrid cried out in surprise and pleasure, her pussy contracting around Iris's cock as she came hard, her body shaking with the force of her climax.

The sensation of Astrid's orgasm sent Iris over the edge, and with a shout, she too reached her peak, the hot flood of her release filling Astrid's pussy in a series of spasms that left her breathless and panting. She collapsed onto Astrid, her heart pounding as she gasped for air, feeling the sticky evidence of their lovemaking between them.

Astrid wrapped her arms tightly around Iris, holding her close and nuzzling her neck. Iris was still panting from her orgasm, her chest heaving as she struggled to catch her breath. Astrid's own body was still trembling from the force of her climax, and she could feel Iris's cock still twitching inside her.

But as Iris's breathing began to slow and deepen, Astrid realized that she was starting to fall asleep.

"Iris, wake up," Astrid whispered, gently shaking Iris's shoulder. "I want to talk to you."

But Iris didn't stir. She was fast asleep, her body completely relaxed in Astrid's arms.

Astrid sighed, feeling a pang of disappointment. She had wanted to talk to Iris about what had just happened between them, to express her feelings and make sure that they were both on the same page.

For a moment, Astrid considered waking her up, but then decided against it. She didn't want to ruin the moment, to create tension where there had been only pleasure and intimacy. For now, she would just enjoy the feeling of Iris in her arms, the warmth and weight of her body a comfort in the stillness of the night.

Astrid slowly drifted off to sleep, her heart swelling with warmth and happiness and the knowledge that she would be able to wake up next to her the next morning.

The next day, when Ian woke up, he was in a small tavern room, with a hangover from hell and a musician passed out on the floor beside him.

He didn't remember much from the night before, just a hazy recollection of the pink desire and a song that seemed to follow him wherever he went.

"What the hell happened last night?" Ian muttered to himself, rubbing his throbbing head.

He looked down at the musician, who was still snoring softly on the floor. Shaking his head, Ian got up and pulled on his clothes, trying to shake off the lingering remnants of the previous night. He wasn't sure what had happened, but he knew he didn't want to think about it too much. Instead, he decided to focus on the day ahead.

Ian made his way down to the ground floor of the inn. His head still pounded from the previous night's festivities, and his stomach rumbled in protest. He walked past the common room, where the other travelers were already enjoying their breakfast, and headed towards the kitchen.

The chef, a burly man with a mustache, greeted him with a nod. "Morning. What can I get you?" the chef asked, but Ian was too busy processing the new information to answer.

Meanwhile, Elias woke up in another room, the waitress nowhere to be seen. He sat up in the unfamiliar bed and looked around. The room was small and sparsely furnished, with a single window that looked out onto an alleyway.

"What the hell?" Elias muttered. He distinctly remembered paying for his meal and leaving a generous tip for the waitress. But now, as he checked his pockets, he realized that his wallet was lighter than it should be. He quickly counted out the remaining bills and coins, but it was clear that several notes were missing. His heart sank. He stood up, intending to confront the innkeeper, but stopped short as a figure appeared in the doorway.

It was the waitress, and she appeared to be surprised to see Elias. "Oh, you're awake," she said brightly. "I thought you might be feeling a bit under the weather after last night, so I brought you some water." The waitress held out a glass with a smile, but Elias couldn't bring himself to return it.

"Thanks," he said, taking the glass and setting it down on the nightstand without drinking. "But I think we need to talk about something else first."

The waitress raised an eyebrow. "Oh?"

Elias took a deep breath, trying to keep his temper in check. "I woke up this morning and realized that some money is missing from my wallet. And I'm pretty sure it was you who took it." Elias said, his voice low and dangerous.

The waitress blinked at him, her smile never faltering. "Oh, that. Yes, I did take it. I'm sorry if there was any misunderstanding, but last night's activities were not exactly free of charge." The waitress said with an apologetic smile. "I'm afraid I did mistake our arrangement. I didn't realize you were looking for something more than just a quick service. I should have made that clear to you."

Elias couldn't believe what he was hearing. He was stunned, feeling a mix of emotions, ranging from anger to confusion. "You're wrong. I didn't pay you for sex. We had sex because we were attracted to each-other."

The waitress sighed, "I understand where you're coming from, but the fact remains that I don't make a habit of providing freebies." She crossed her arms and raised an eyebrow, a clear challenge in her eyes. 'Look, it's simple. I naturally assumed that I was providing a service that needed to be paid for. And you accepted that service without any complaint or argument. So, you got what you paid for." said the waitress. Her tone was matter-of-fact, but there was an underlying edge to it that spoke volumes. It didn't escape Elias that

there was no apology, no contrition for taking his money. Just a simple "I gave you what you paid for" and that was it. Elias was seething, but he knew he couldn't confront the waitress again. He could feel the anger building inside him, but he knew that he needed to keep it under control for now. He forced a polite smile, "Well, in that case, I suppose it was worth it."

Elias collected his belongings and left the room, resisting the urge to look back at the waitress. He had a feeling that he would not see her again.

Duncan rubbed his eyes, feeling the weight of the world pressing down on him. The 'professor' was nowhere to be found, and there was a note on the table next to him with a few crumpled bills.

He stood up, his limbs heavy, and walked over to the window. The cityscape outside was a blur, the colors muted and indistinct.

He was just about to make up his mind when he remembered something.

His clothes!

He had left them in the waitress's changing room last night.

With a heavy heart, Duncan turned his attention to the note.

"Dear Student,

I hope this note finds you well. I have left you some money, it is not much, but it should be enough. I must leave now, but I have faith you will find your way back home.

Yours sincerely,

The Professor

P.S. You can keep the school uniform if you want, it suits you."

Duncan felt a pang of sadness as he read the note, knowing that he had let a rare opportunity slip away. But he couldn't dwell on it now. He had to focus on the task at hand.

He turned his attention to the school uniform that lay draped over the back of a chair.

He slipped the shirt on, feeling the soft fabric brush against his skin. It was a perfect fit. He tugged on the skirt, adjusting hit to his liking, and tied the tie securely around his neck.

Duncan picked up the money from the table.

He glanced around the room one last time before making his way out the door.

As he walked down the corridor, he noticed a familiar figure. It was Elias, standing by the wall, a smirk playing on his lips as he took in the sight of Duncan in the schoolgirl uniform.

"Well, didn't expect that," Elias said, fighting back a chuckle.

Duncan rolled his eyes, but couldn't help but smile. "Shut up, Elias. I had to leave my clothes in the waitress's changing room last night."

Elias shook his head, still grinning. "The mysteries of life, huh?" He glanced down at the money in Duncan's hand. "Looks like you've had a successful night."

Duncan shrugged sheepishly, "Well, I did what I had to do. Besides, this should cover my expenses for the next few days."

Elias give Duncan a sly wink. "I guess it's time for breakfast. Are you coming?"

Duncan nodded and followed Elias, still adjusting to the feeling of the schoolgirl uniform. They made their way down to the tavern's dining area, where a bustling crowd of travelers and locals were enjoying their breakfast. The smell of freshly baked bread filled the air, making their stomachs growl with hunger.

As they entered the kitchen, they saw Ian seated at the bar, nursing a glass of milk and tearing off chunks of a bread roll with his teeth.

Duncan raised a hand to catch Ian's attention, his fingers brushing against his skirt as he did so. "Good morning, Ian," he called out, smiling warmly.

Ian looked up, his cheeks stuffed with

bread. "Mmph," he mumbled, swallowing the food in his mouth

before speaking. "Good morning," he said, wiping his mouth with the back of his hand.

"I didn't realize you were into schoolgirls, Duncan," Ian said with a smirk, his eyes traveling up and down Duncan's body.

Duncan blushed, "I wasn't exactly in a position to choose my attire last night."

Ian chuckled, "Still, you pull it off rather well."

Elias rolled his eyes, "Enough with the banter, you two. I'm starving." He took a seat next to Ian and flagged down the chef. The burly man mumbled something in response and shuffled away, returning a moment later with a platter of steamy scrambled eggs and a mug of something who look like coffee.

Elias groaned with pleasure, taking a huge spoonful of the eggs and savoring the taste.

Duncan, however, was still feeling uneasy about the previous night's events and pushed his plate away. "I don't think I can eat this," he said, rubbing his forehead.

The chef raised an eyebrow at him, but Elias just chuckled. "What's wrong, Duncan? Afraid you'll get fat?"

Duncan shot him a withering look. "I'm serious. I don't feel very well."

Ian looked at him with concern. "What's wrong? Did something happen last night?"

Duncan shook his head, "It's nothing, really. I just need a moment to gather myself."

Ian looked at Duncan sympathetically, "If you need to talk, you know you can always come to me. I'm here for you guys."

Duncan gave a weak smile, "Thanks, Ian. I appreciate it." Duncan replied, still looking a bit uneasy. Ian looked at Duncan for a moment, his gaze filled with concern, before turning his attention back to his food.

After breakfast, the group decided to go to the base to reunite with Astrid and Elias. Duncan nearly forgot to retrieve his clothes, but luckily Ian reminded him just in time.

They made their way to the changing room where Duncan had left his clothes the previous night. To their surprise, it was still unlocked, and Duncan quickly changed out of the schoolgirl uniform, handing it to Ian with a look of relief.

Together, they headed back to the dining area where Elias was waiting for them.

As they made their way to the base, the streets of the game world's city were bustling with NPCs, and they couldn't help but notice how human-like they were acting. They laughed, argued, and flirted with each other, their movements and gestures reminiscent of the people back in the real world.

As they entered their base, they found Astrid and Iris sleeping together in the same bed, naked.

Elias' eyes widened in shock and anger. "What the hell is going on here?" he shouted, causing both Astrid and Iris to stir in their sleep.

Iris opened her eyes and saw Elias standing there, his face contorted in anger. She immediately sat up, her body still glistening with sweat.

"Elias, what's wrong?" she asked, her voice trembling with fear.

Elias pointed at the two of them, his finger shaking with rage. "I can't believe you, Iris! How could you do this to me?" Elias took a step closer to Iris, his eyes narrowed as he stared at her. "You need to explain yourself, Iris. Now," he said, his voice low and edged with emotion.

Iris looked up at him, her eyes wide in confusion and hesitation. She took a deep breath, channeling her inner strength. "Alright, Elias. I will." She hesitated, unsure of how to begin. "Last night...it happened because...Astrid and I...we felt a connection, and things just happened," Iris finally stated.

There was silence in the room. Elias's anger was still visible on his face, but there was also a hint of confusion. "How did things just happen, Iris? And why are you naked with her? Have you been unfaithful to me?" he asked.

Astrid, who had been quiet throughout the exchange, now spoke up. "It's not like that, Elias. We didn't set out to intentionally hurt you. We just...connected. And it felt right."

Elias' anger began to dissipate slightly as he processed her words. But he still looked hurt. "So you decided to have sex with her instead of me? How am I supposed to feel about that, Iris?"

Iris bit her lip, thinking carefully about her response. She knew that she couldn't just brush off Elias' concerns or pretend that nothing had happened. She owed him an explanation, and she needed to be honest with him.

"I know it must be hard for you to understand, Elias," Iris said, taking a deep breath. "But it wasn't about choosing between you and Astrid. It was just about the moment, and a connection that we both felt. I didn't intend for it to happen, but now that it has, I can't deny that it felt right. I hope you can find it in your heart to forgive me."

Elias looked at her, his expression unreadable. "I'll think about it," he said gruffly.

Iris's eyes widened with surprise, but she quickly recovered and gave him a small smile. "Okay, that's all I'm asking for. I understand if you're not ready."

Elias nodded, still lost in thought. Iris could see the pain in his eyes, but she also knew that he was a strong man, and that he would eventually come to terms with the situation.

In the meantime, she knew that she had to keep the peace within their group. She turned her attention to Astrid, who was still lying in the bed, her naked body partially hidden under the covers. Iris couldn't help but feel a twinge of envy towards Astrid. She was still so carefree, so unapologetic about her desires. Iris had always been the cautious one, the analytical one, always weighing the pros and cons before making a decision. And now, here she was, lying in bed with Astrid, both of them naked and unsure of what the future held.

Ian's voice broke through the silence, reminding them of their current state. "Hey, you two, I hate to break it to you, but you're still naked and probably should get showered."

Iris felt a blush creep up her cheeks as she sat up, looking around the room. She had forgotten that they had fallen asleep without getting dressed after their encounter. "Right, of course." She climbed out of bed, feeling a little self-conscious about her own nudity, and made her way towards the bathroom.

Astrid followed close behind, her own cheeks flushed with embarrassment. "I can't believe we forgot about that," she giggled, shaking her head. "I guess we were a little preoccupied."

Iris couldn't help but smile at her friend's carefree attitude. But now was not the time for such thoughts. Iris needed to focus on the task at hand.

Meanwhile, Duncan couldn't help but stare at Iris as she spoke. He could feel his body growing more and more aroused with each passing moment.

The sight of her naked form was almost too much for him to handle.

"Hey, Duncan," Ian said, trying to keep his voice steady.

Duncan turned to face him, a quizzical expression on his face. "Yeah?"

Ian hesitated for a moment before speaking. "I was wondering if you wanted to join me in the shower. You know, since Astrid and Iris are taking the other one."

Duncan's eyes widened in surprise. "What?" he exclaimed, taken aback by Ian's words.

"Come on, Duncan, it's just water," Ian said, grinning. "And besides, it's not every day we get to shower together, right?"

"I don't know, Ian," he said hesitantly. "It just feels...weird, you know? It's not that I don't trust you, but I've never shared a shower with another man before."

"Come on, Duncan, it's just a shower. What's the big deal?" Ian shrugged, looking a little embarrassed. "We're both in women's bodies right now, so it's not like we're two guys showering together. It's a one in a lifetime opportunity. We should take advantage of it."

"That doesn't necessarily make it any less strange, Ian. I don't think we should blur the lines."

Ian sighed and slouched in his chair. "I understand your point of view, Duncan. But what's wrong with taking a chance once in a while? Life's too short to always play it safe." Ian replied, a sense of frustration creeping into his voice.

Duncan thought for a moment, then nodded his head in agreement. "Alright, Ian, let's do it."

Ian smiled, looking relieved. "Great! C'mon, follow me to the shower," he said, leading the way.

As they stepped into the bathroom, Duncan's heart raced. But as he looked at Ian, who seemed calm and assured, he allowed himself to relax a bit. He began to unbutton his shirt as Ian started running the water. The sound of water filling the bathroom helped settle his nerves.

He glanced at Ian, who had already stripped down and was hopping into the shower. He looked surprisingly comfortable in his new female body. Ian motioned for Duncan to join him. He hesitated for just a moment before stepping under the streaming water with Ian.

The water drenched him from head to toe, but his thoughts were a jumbled mess of apprehension and confusion. Suddenly, a feeling of something hard poking him on the lower back brought his attention back to the room.

He turned around to find Ian holding a bottle of shower gel, a mischievous smile playing on his lips.

"Ian!" he said, surprised, as the bottle continued to poke him. "What are you doing?"

"I'm sorry, I didn't mean to startle you," Ian said. "I was just wondering if you wanted me to wash your back."

Duncan felt his face grow hot with embarrassment. He had been so caught up in his own thoughts that he had forgotten where he was, and who he was with. He glanced over at Ian, who was still holding the bottle of shower gel, a hopeful expression on his face.

"I-I don't know," Duncan stammered. "I mean, I've never done anything like this before. It feels strange."

Ian grinned, his eyes sparkling with excitement. "Come on, Duncan. It's just a bit of fun. I've always wanted to try it." He squeezed the shower gel onto his hands and started lathering up Duncan's back.

Duncan couldn't help but feel a little uncomfortable at first, but he soon relaxed into the sensation of Ian's hands on his skin. The warmth of the water and the slickness of the gel made everything feel surreal, like they were in some sort of dream world. And maybe they were, thought Duncan, still trying to wrap his head around the fact that they were stuck inside a video game. He glanced over at Ian, who was now working on his shoulders. The sensation of his hands was surprisingly soothing, and Duncan felt his body begin to relax under his touch.

It was a strange feeling, allowing someone else to take care of him like this. But there was something about Ian's gentle, caring demeanor that made it easy for Duncan to let his guard down. He closed his eyes and let out a sigh, feeling the tension in his muscles melt away. The warm water cascaded down on him, massaging away the knots in his shoulders.

He leaned back against the cool tile of the shower wall, letting the warm water cascade down his body.

But then, something unexpected happened. Ian's hands began to wander, slowly tracing a path to Duncan's chest. And then, without warning, Ian cupped Duncan's breasts, giving them a gentle squeeze.

Duncan gasped in surprise, his eyes flying open. He looked over at Ian, who was grinning mischievously. "Ian, what are you doing?"

"Relax, Duncan," Ian said, his hands still on Duncan's breasts. "We're both girls now, so it's fine."Ian said with a smirk, continuing to massage Duncan's chest.

Duncan's eyes widened, "But...but we're not..." he trailed off, feeling a wave of confusion wash over him. "We're not girls, Ian. We're still us, just in different bodies."

Ian shrugged, "Who cares? And besides, I kind of like it. I've always been the short, scrawny one, and now I have these beautiful curves. I mean, look at me!" Ian twirled around in the shower, the water cascading over him. "I feel so different," he marveled. "And look at these." He gestured to his own chest. "They're so perky and round. I can't stop staring at them!" Ian exclaimed, holding his new breasts in his hands.

Duncan looked at Ian, then down at his own chest, feeling a strange sensation of envy creeping up inside him. He had never wanted to have breasts before, and he certainly didn't want bigger ones. But here he was, feeling jealous of Ian's perky and round chest. It didn't make any sense to him.

Duncan felt a sudden urge to cover himself up, but it was too late. Ian had already noticed his discomfort and was looking at him with a mixture of amusement and concern. "Hey, are you okay?" Ian asked, letting go of his own chest and turning to face Duncan.

Duncan, unable to meet his gaze, hastily wrapped the towel around himself.

"I think it's best if we stop, Ian," he croaked, unable to hide the lump in his throat.

Ian nodded, looking apologetic, holding up his hands in a gesture of peace. "I didn't mean to make you uncomfortable. I just got carried away."

Duncan gave him a small smile, still feeling a little awkward. "It's okay, Ian. I just need some time to adjust to all of this." Duncan said shyly, still feeling a little overwhelmed.

Ian looked at Duncan with concern. "Okay, you know you can always talk to me. I'm here for you." He paused, then added with a shy grin, "I'm just happy to have someone to share this with. I never expected to experience all of this."

"Neither did I." Duncan replied, managing a small smile.

In the meantime, in the other shower, Iris and Astrid were also washing each other. Iris felt a thrill run through her body as Astrid's soapy hands explored her curves.

The warm water and the slickness of the gel made everything feel surreal. Iris leaned into Astrid's touch, feeling her body respond in ways she never thought possible. Astrid's soapy hands slipped and slid over Iris's body, eliciting gasps of pleasure and excitement. Iris couldn't help but feel a twinge of guilt at the thought of doing this behind Elias's back, but the thrill of experiencing this new side of herself was too great to resist. She closed her eyes, letting out a soft sigh of pleasure as Astrid's hands trailed down her stomach and back up again. The water cascaded over them, the heat mingling with the cool tiles and creating a sensual symphony of sensations.

Iris's heart raced as the memories of her past experiences with Elias came flooding back. She couldn't help but compare the gentle, passionate touch of Astrid's hands with the rougher, more animalistic passion she and Elias shared.

With Astrid, it was all about exploring and discovering each other's bodies, a slow, deliberate dance of intimacy. With Elias, it was all about satisfying the primal need and desire that burned between them. Iris loved both experiences.

But now, she found herself torn between the two. She loved Elias with all her heart, and she knew that he loved her too. But for some reason, she couldn't shake the feeling that something was missing from their relationship. And as Astrid's hands continued to map out her body, Iris couldn't resist the temptation to give into her desires. She reached out and wrapped her arms around Astrid, pulling her closer. She felt Astrid's body respond, and they stood there for a moment, locked in a passionate embrace, their bodies slick with water and soap.

Iris moved her hand downwards, her fingers brushing against Astrid's trimmed pubic hair. She let out a shudder of delight as Astrid's legs automatically parted slightly, allowing her easier access. Iris slid her hand even further down, feeling her heart race as her fingertips brushed against Astrid's already wet folds.

Astrid moaned softly, her grip on Iris tightening. "Iris," she whispered.

"Yes," Iris replied, her voice barely audible over the sound of the running water.

She explored Astrid with her fingertips, marveling at how different they felt from Elias' body. She traced rings around Astrid's clit, making her moan softly with pleasure. Iris' heart quickened, her mind swirling with a mix of guilt and excitement.

She glanced at Astrid's face, the ecstasy etched into every line and curve of her expression. Iris's heart raced as she realized what was happening, but the allure was too strong. She could feel her own desire building, aching for release.

Her body seemed to move on its own accord, her hands sliding down Astrid's slender bod. Her fingertips brushed against Astrid's breasts, sending ripples of pleasure throughout her entire being. Iris squeezed the mounds, reveling in the feeling of her fleshy pillows filling her hands.

Astrid smiled and tilted her head back, causing the water droplets to cascade down her neck and between her breasts. Iris lowered her head and ran her tongue over
the sensitive skin, eliciting a shiver of delight from Astrid.

She trailed her teeth around Astrid's perky nipples, pinching and tugging at the already erect peaks. Astrid gasped and squirmed in response, briefly breaking their embrace. Iris grabbed hold of her hips and pulled her back towards her, pressing her body against her own.

She could feel Astrid's wet folds pressed against her legs, and she felt a sudden surge of desire.

Without wasting any more time, Astrid moved her legs further apart and guided her hips and groin into the perfect position.

Iris slowly pushed herself into Astrid, feeling the slick warmth of Astrid's flesh wrap around her own.

Astrid gasped in pleasure as Iris thrust deeper into her, gripping onto the counter for support. Their bodies glistened with a sheen of water, and the soap still clung to their skin, adding a silky slickness to their movements. Astrid's moans filled the room, and Iris felt her own pleasure building as she moved inside her. She could feel her balls slapping against Astrid's slippery flesh, and she could sense her load beginning to boil in the pit of her stomach.

Iris thrust deeper into Astrid, and she could feel her balls slap against her ass as she bottomed out. Astrid moaned enthusiastically, feeling the pleasurable stretch inside her. Iris could feel her pleasure building faster and faster, the intensity increasing to the point where she felt like she was going to lose control. And suddenly, she did. She thrust into Astrid one final time, burying herself to the hilt as she cried out in release. Her entire body shook with pleasure, and she could feel herself pulsing and twitching inside Astrid.

Astrid moaned loudly, her entire body tensing with pleasure as she felt Iris climax inside her. Iris's muscles contracted and relaxed around Astrid, causing a wave of ecstasy to course through her body. Iris could feel her juices gushing out of her, mixing with the running water below.

Satisfied, Iris pulled back gently, leaning against the tiled wall to catch her breath. Both she and Astrid stood there for a moment, their bodies still slick with water and soap, their chests heaving with exertion.

As the warmth of the shower began to fade, the two women broke apart reluctantly as they finished rinsing off the soap and stepped out of the shower.

They toweled each other off, stealing occasional glances at each other. Iris couldn't help but feel a little self-conscious about her body, but Astrid's admiring looks helped ease her worries.

As they got dressed, the group gathered in the common room, discussing their plan moving forward. Iris took the lead while Elias remained quiet, still grappling with his thoughts.

Ian and Duncan sat together on a couch, with Duncan still feeling a bit uneasy about the shower incident. Ian occasionally stole a glance at him, trying to gauge his reaction.

Astrid and Iris sat cross-legged on the floor, facing the group with subtle smirks playing on their lips.Iris's gaze lingered on Elias, whose expression remained stony and distant. She sighed inwardly, pushing aside her disappointment and focusing instead on the task at hand.

"As we all know, we need supplies and ammo to continue on our quest," Iris began, her voice firm and steady. "To make things easier, I suggest that Duncan and Elias go buy ammo for the group, Ian, you can accompany me and Astrid to buy supplies, and in the meantime, maybe check if there's any information about how to get back home."

Ian looked at them with eager eyes. "I'll go check out Makoktok instead," he said, a mischievous glint in his eyes. "I want to see if she had found any information on how to get back to our word. And I did promise to play with her today."Ian grinned, winking at Duncan.

As they left the room, Astrid couldn't help but watch them, a small smile playing on her lips. "You guys are so cute together," she said, playfully punching Ian on the arm.

Duncan glared at her, his face reddening. "Don't call me cute," he grumbled, crossing his arms over his chest. "I'm a man, not some girl."

"Aww, come on, Duncan," Astrid said, pouting. "You're just being shy. You know I was only teasing you."

"I'm not shy," he snapped. "I just don't like it when people treat me like I'm weak." Duncan responded gruffly.

"I know, Duncan, I'm sorry," she said, placing a hand on his arm. "I didn't mean to make you feel that way. I just think you look really cute in your new body."

Duncan sighed, his body relaxing slightly under Astrid's touch. "Fine. But don't call me cute again."

With that, the group split up as planned. Iris and Astrid set out to gather supplies and scout for information. Duncan and Elias headed to the local armory to buy ammunition.

Ian, on the other hand, had his mind set, he headed to Makotok's house , knowing she would be happy to see him again.

"I'm so glad you came to visit me," Makotok greeted him with a bright smile and a welcoming wave, "I was starting to get bored."

"I'll do what I can to keep you entertained," Ian promised with a mischievous grin, "but first, I have a question. Have you found any information about how to get back home? Iris and the others are really eager to leave this game world."

Makotok nodded, "Yes, I heard of a fortune teller who might be able to help you get back home. She's located in a back street of the city, it's a bit hidden but if you follow the map I drew for you, you shouldn't have any problems finding her."

"Thanks, Makotok. I'll be sure to let Iris and the others know," Ian replied with a grateful smile.

Makotok beamed at him, " I'm just happy to help, Ian. You know you can always count on me!" She said with a friendly wink. "But before you go, don't forget your promise to play with me."

Ian's face flushed as he remembered his words. "Of course, I'll play with you, Makotok," he said, trying to keep his voice steady.

"Great!" Makotok exclaimed, grabbing Ian's hand and pulling him towards a small room in the back of her house.

Inside, the room was filled with toys and games of all shapes and sizes. Makotok let go of Ian's hand and skipped over to a table in the corner of the room. She rummaged through a basket filled with dolls and plushies before pulling out seven small figurines. She handed one to Ian, smiling mischievously. "Let's play a game," she said.

Ian looked at the figurine in his hand, a miniature representation of is avatar with simplified features. He couldn't help but feel a little uncomfortable knowing that he was essentially playing with a version of himself. But he pushed his reservations aside and obliged Makotok.

As he looked at the array of figurines in front of him, his eyes fell upon the familiar forms of Iris, Astrid, Duncan and Elias. But what caught his attention were the two figurines that he didn't recognize.

One of them was a girl with long white hair that nearly went to her feet. She had a serene expression on her face. Ian looked up at Makotok, his curiosity piqued.

"Who is this?" he asked, pointing to the figurine.

Makotok smiled, "Ah, that's one of the robot leaders, an android who looks exactly like a human." Ian raised an eyebrow, "A android ? That's cool. And who's this?" He asked, gesturing to the last remaining figurine.

Makotok picked up the last figurine, a graceful cat-like creature with a small crown atop its head. "This is the royal cat," she said. "It is the king of the robot, and very powerful. They say he can communicate with others robot through dreams, and can even give them visions. As a player, you should knew this."

This game was known for its immersive and detailed world-building, the android and royal cat figurines in front of Ian served as a reminder of just how bizarre this world can get.

Ian set to work playing with Makotok, using the figurines to act out various scenarios. He found himself getting lost in the game, forgetting his worries. Makotok, for her part, seemed to be having a great time. She giggled and gasped as Ian moved the figurines around, making up stories about their adventures. Ian couldn't help but be reminded of his time playing games as a childe.

He smiled to himself, feeling a sense of nostalgia wash over him. But then, he snapped out of his reverie and looked at the clock. He gasped, realizing that he had lost track of time. "Oh no, I need to get back to Iris and the others!"

Makotok looked at him, her face falling. "I understand, Ian. You need to go."

He nodded, reluctantly setting the figurines aside. "Yeah, I really do. But thank you for playing with me, Makotok. I had a lot of fun."

He hugged Makotok tightly, smiling at her warmly before standing up. "I'll be sure to tell Iris and the others about the fortune teller," he said, still holding her hand in his.

Makotok squealed in excitement. "I'm glad I could be of help!" she exclaimed, looking up at Ian with stars in her eyes. He couldn't help but feel a little self-conscious under her gaze, not used to being admired like this.

He took a deep breath and managed a small smile. "Thank you, Makotok," he said, ruffling her hair affectionately. "I really did have fun playing with you."

With a fond farewell, Ian left Makotok's house, hurrying to find Iris and the others. He checked his map, making sure he was heading in the right direction.

As he turned a corner, he spotted Iris, Astrid, Duncan and Elias waiting for him.

"Ian! Where have you been?" Iris called out, looking relieved to see him. "We've been waiting for you."

"Sorry, I was just, um, err, err," He stammered, fumbling for words to explain.

Iris looked at him with a raised eyebrow, her arms crossed over her chest. "Well, you had us worried, Ian," she said, a hint of annoyance in her voice. "We were about to go looking for you."

"I know, I'm sorry," he repeated, rubbing the back of his neck nervously. "I lost track of time."

"Mhm." Astrid hummed nonchalantly,

her eyes never leaving Ian as she manipulated her combat sword in her hands.

He shifted uncomfortably, "I'm sorry. But Makotok wanted to play a game with me, and somehow that led to me losing track of time." Ian said, scratching the back of his head sheepishly.

"Well, at least you had a good time," Astrid chimed in. "But we should focus on finding a way home now."

"Right," Ian nodded. "And that's why I'm glad I found this." He pulled out a small piece of paper from his pocket and unfolded it, revealing a map scribbled on it. "Makotok told me about a fortuneteller who might be able to help us find a way home. She gave me this map,"

The group huddled together, studying the map that Ian had obtained. They traced their fingers along the lines and dots that indicated their location and the direction towards the fortuneteller's abode.

Determined to make progress, Iris turned to the group."Alright, let's find this fortune teller and see if we can get some answers." The group, still in a mix of emotions, agreed.

Ian had taken the lead, guiding them with the makeshift map he'd received from Makotok. The others followed him like sheep, silent and emotionless, a stark contrast to the playful demeanor Ian had just displayed in Makotok's home.

He led them through the bustling streets of the city, maneuvering around the crowds with ease until they eventually turned down a back alley, poorly lit and filled with debris.

"We're almost there," Ian said, confidently striding ahead. Despite the fear of the unknown seeping into their thoughts, the group trudged along, their eyes fixed on Ian.

As they approached an old, rusty door at the end of the alley, Ian stopped and knocked three times.

A soft voice echoed from within, inviting them to enter. The group hesitantly pushed open the door, revealing a small and dimly lit room. The room was cluttered with old books, artifacts, and trinkets, some of which they recognized from their own world.

But what caught their attention was the figure sitting in the corner. The fortune teller appeared to be a young, slender woman with long, unkempt blond hair. She was dressed in a flowing robe that seemed to swallow her lithe figure. She looked up at the group as they entered, offering them a warm smile. "Welcome, travelers. You seek a way back home, do you not?"

Iris stepped forward, her eyes narrowing as she studied the fortune teller. "How do you know that?" she asked, suspicion lacing her voice.

The fortune teller's eyes twinkled mischievously. "Ah, but that is my gift, is it not? I see things that others do not. You have been brought here because you were caught in the wish of another from your world." she said. "It appears that someone from this world has tampered with the game, and that person must be dealt with before you can be sent back." The fortune teller explained, her eyes piercing the darkness.

"What do you mean, 'dealt with'? Who is this person?" Astyd asked, tension creeping into her voice.

The fortune teller shook her head slowly. "I do not know who this person is, but they have tainted the game. You must find them and put a stop to their actions if you wish to return home."

Iris furrowed her brow, a look of determination taking hold of her features. "We will find them and make things right," she declared, her voice filled with resolve. The others nodded in agreement.

The fortune teller stood up and approached the group, her robe swishing around her feet. "There is a place known as the Factory. It is said that the one you seek can be found there."

Astrid was the first to speak, her usually timid voice betraying a note of defiance. "And how are we supposed to find this Factory?"

The fortune teller's smile never wavered as she gestured to a pile of ancient scrolls at her feet. "I have put a marker on your map."

Elias reached forward, then hesitated. "Why are we the ones who have to do this?" He asked, unable to keep the frustration out of his voice. "Isn't there another way?"

The fortune teller shook her head, her expression grave. "I'm sorry, but there is no other way. The one responsible has tainted the game, corrupting its very essence. The only way to restore it and return home is to eliminate the source of the corruption. If you refuse to do it, you'll be stuck here forever. The choice is yours."

The group stared at the mark on the map, their minds racing with possibilities. "We can do this," Iris said, determination in her voice. "It's just another quest, right? We've dealt with worse."

Ian nodded in agreement, but the uncertainty in his eyes was visible.

Astrid cautiously observed the fortune teller's every move, her glances filled with a mix of fear, awe, and curiosity. Duncan stayed silent, his steely gaze locked onto the figure before him.

Elias, on the other hand, clenched his fist as he stared at the map in his hand. The tension within him was palpable, a storm brewing beneath the surface. Iris could sense it, her eyes flicking from his clenched jaw to his rigid posture, a knot in her stomach growing tighter with each passing second.

She took a deep breath and decided to address him directly.

"Elias," she began, her voice steady and calm despite the tumultuous chaos within her. "You've been behaving strangely since I became involved with the game world." she paused, gathering her thoughts together. "I need you to tell me what's been bothering you and if it's something I can help with."

Elais' gaze dropped to the floor, his muscles trembling. "I-It's just..." he stammered, "I never expected this to happen. When I saw you in that male avatar, I didn't know how to react. I couldn't recognize you anymore, and it felt like our connection was gone." Elias looked away from her, his heart heavy. He knew he should open up to her, but it was too painful.

Iris sensed his distress and gently grabbed his hand. "I know it's hard, but please try to talk to me," she said softly.

Elias sighed and looked back at her. "I just don't know who you are anymore. Seeing you with Astrid, I felt like I had lost you." Elias's voice was filled with hurt and confusion.

But before Iris could respond, Duncan interrupted them.

"Guys, I hate to break up this emotional moment, but we really need to get going," he said, his voice urgent. "We need to go to the Factory and back to our world as soon as possible."

Elias looked at Duncan, his eyes narrowing. "Why the sudden rush?"

Duncan gritted his teeth, his grip tightening around his sniper rifle. "I can't do this anymore. I can't stand being in this female body." He confessed, his voice filled with frustration and despair.

The room fell silent as the group took in Duncan's words. Iris looked at him with concern, understanding the turmoil he was going through. She turned to the others, her gaze landing on each of them. "Alright, I propose that we start making our way to the Factory," Iris announced, her voice firm and steady.

The group nodded. They quickly gathered their supplies and weapons, checking them over one last time before setting off.

But as they stepped out of the fortune teller's house, they were taken aback by the sight before them. The door had disappeared.

Iris was the first to react, her eyes scanning the area for any signs of the missing entrance. "What just happened?" she asked, bewildered. "Where did the door go?"

The group gathered around the spot where the door used to be, but there was nothing there. Just the cold, hard surface of the alley wall.

Ian shrugged, "Well, I guess we're trapped in a video game, so a missing door isn't that strange."

The group looked at each other, realizing that Ian was right.

"Alright, let's continue on our journey then," Iris said, taking the lead.

They walked down the alley, and as they turned the corner, they found themselves in front of a bustling marketplace. People of all shapes and sizes were selling and buying goods. As they moved through the crowd, they made their way through the marketplace.

Finally, they arrived at one the railway station, which was situated on the edge of the city. Unlike the one they arrived in, this railway station had a lower ceiling, with large beams crossing overhead, holding up the wooden structure. The walls were lined brick, with large windows letting light flood in. The train was a sleek, modern vehicle with comfortable seats. The group settled in for the journey.

As the train pulled out of the station and into the tunnel, the ambient light from the station gradually faded away, plunging the group into darkness. Elias unpacked a small lantern from her backpack and lit it, casting a soft glow over their faces.

Ian leaned in a little closer to the light, taking in the intricate details of the carriage. "This is so cool," he whispered, awed by their surroundings.

The group continued to take in their surroundings as the train jostled its way up the tunnel. The dim light of the lantern flickered across their faces, casting shadows that danced and swayed with every bump in the tracks.

As they traveled deeper into the tunnel, the train slowed down, and the strain of the engine grew louder. The group huddled close together, watching as the tunnel walls grew darker and more foreboding. They were all lost in their thoughts, contemplating the challenges that lay ahead. The tension in the air was palpable, and the only sound was the echo of the train's engine.

Chapter 9: The Factory

After what felt like an eternity, the train finally slowed to a stop, the engine's sound subsiding into silence.

Iris and the group shared a tense glance before carefully stepping off the train and into a vast, cavernous space. They found themselves standing at the foot of a massive ladder that snaked upwards, seemingly disappearing into the shadows above.

"Looks like we have our work cut out for us," Duncan said, breaking the silence. He swung his rifle onto his shoulder and motioned for the group to follow him as he began to climb the ladder.

As the group ascended, the air grew colder and the air thick with sweat and the scent of machinery.

Each stage of the ascent was punctuated by groaning metal and the occasional, jarring clang of the overhead pipes. Duncan and Elias took the lead. Iris trailed behind, taking in every detail of her surroundings and assessing potential escape routes. She glanced back at the rest of the group, her mind working through a mental checklist of supplies, equipment, and abilities at their disposal.

Ian followed directly behind Iris, his hands tightly gripping the rungs of the ladder as he struggled to keep up with Duncan's pace. Astrid was right behind him, her footsteps heavy on the metal. Ian's grip slipped for a moment, heart racing as he desperately fought to regain balance. He felt her hand on his leg, stabilizing him, and a rush of warmth filled his cheeks. The climb was grueling, but as the group climbed higher, an eerie glow began to emerge from the darkness above.

Finally, they reached the top. A wide platform greeted them, bathed in soft light filtering in from the outside. As they stepped onto the platform, they were greeted by a gust of cool, fresh air. Iris squinted as her eyes adjusted to the sudden brightness, and what she saw made her gasp.

The exit tunnel opened up to a view of a sprawling factory complex, its smokestacks billowing plumes of black smoke. The buildings were connected by a series of rusted metal bridges, and a network of train tracks snaked around the entire perimeter of the complex. As they approached the edge of the platform, the group could see that the factory was completely surrounded by a high wall, with watchtowers and turrets positioned at regular intervals. In the air, drones buzzed like angry hornets, patrolling the perimeter.

Iris and the group exchanged worried glances. This was not what they had expected. They were far from prepared to storm a heavily fortified factory. Duncan took a step back, studying the layout of the compound, and began to strategize.

"We can't just walk in there," he said, pointing at the wall. "We need to come up with a plan. We need to find a way to get in without being detected," Duncan stated, narrowing his eyes as he took in the imposing structure ahead of them.

Iris nodded, her lips pressed into a thin line as she began to process the information. She scanned the area for any entrances, vents, or windows that they might be able to use to infiltrate the factory. Suddenly, she spotted a sewer exit, hidden amongst the shadows. It seemed like their only hope. Iris took a deep breath, her eyes focused intently on the sewer entrance. "I found something," she said, her voice barely above a whisper.

The group turned to look at her, their expressions a mix of excitement and apprehension. Duncan's gaze lingered on the sewer exit for a moment before he nodded. "Let's go," he said, his voice steady.

They made their way to the sewer entrance, each step slow and deliberate. Iris and the group approached the sewer entrance, each taking a moment to gather their courage. Ian, however, hesitated. The smell of sewage was overwhelming, but it was better than facing the heavily fortified factory head-on.

"Ian, are you alright?" Astrid asked, noticing the worried expression on his face.

"No, I don't like this idea. Going through a sewer doesn't seem safe," Ian replied, shaking his head.

"We don't have many options, Ian. We need to find a way into the factory, and this seems like our best bet," Iris said, trying to reassure him.

Duncan nodded in agreement. "We can't let our fears get the better of us."

"But what if something happens to us down there? What if we get lost or attacked? What if we never find our way out again?" Ian pleaded, his voice cracking with fear.

Iris looked at him with a mixture of sympathy and irritation. "Ian, we have to work together if we want to survive. We can't let our doubts and fears hold us back." She tried to reassure him, but Ian seemed unmoved.

"But I can't stand the thought of crawling through a filthy sewer," he complained, his face wrinkled in disgust.

"We don't have a choice, Ian, Astrid said, trying to console him. "We'll be in this together. I'll be right there with you."

Ian nodded, taking a deep breath as he tried to steady himself. "Alright, let's do this,"

As they entered the sewer, they were greeted by the musty smell of stale water and filth. Elias lit a lantern, revealing the dark and damp tunnel ahead of them. The walls were slippery with moisture, and the ceiling was so low that Iris, Elias and Duncan had to hunch over as they walked.

The tunnel sloped upwards, and the sound of rushing water echoed off the walls. Ian's face paled as he stared at the murky water flowing through the sewer. The thought of crawling through a sewer made him want to gag, but he knew he had to put aside his fear for the sake of the group. He clenched his fists and followed closely behind Iris, who took the lead.

As they navigated the sewer, the air became increasingly cold and damp, and the rotten odor of decay threatened to overwhelm them. The group trudged on, each clutching their weapons tightly in hand, their nervous faces illuminated by the flickering light from the lantern Elias held aloft.

Ian couldn't help but feel a shiver of disgust and apprehension as the slimy water lapped at his ankles, the sensation of it squelching between his toes never far from his consciousness.

But Iris, with her usual calm demeanor, began to move deeper into the sewer, her footsteps echoing loudly in the damp tunnel. As they strode further in, the sewer opened up into a cavernous space, revealing the vast network of tunnels and passages that lay beneath the Factory.

Astrid, with her usual quiet confidence, walked just behind her, her metallic sword swinging lightly against her hip.

Elias walked beside Duncan. He seemed somewhat distant, lost in his thoughts. Their usual banter and jokes were absent, replaced by a tense silence.

Suddenly, they hear a metallic gnawing that seemed to come closer. It echoed through the sewer tunnels, growing louder with each passing second.

The group froze in place, exchanging worried glances as they strained their ears, trying to pinpoint the source of the sound. Iris raised a hand, signaling for them to stay quiet and listen.

CAUGHT IN GARDEN OF MECHANICAL SOULS

The gnawing continued, growing more pronounced and frantic. It sounded like metal on metal, sharp and insistent. The group held their breath, searching the darkness for any signs of movement.

They looked down and saw teeth marks, deep and sharp. As they watched, the sound of gnashing grew louder, moving closer and closer. Its rhythm was relentless and unending, causing the group's nerves to fray even further. Suddenly, the source of the noise burst into sight, illuminated by their torches. It was a mechanical rat, with steel's rodent teeth that matched the sound they had heard, snaking through the tunnels like a living nightmare.

"Holy fuck! That thing is huge!" Duncan exclaimed, gripping his rifle tightly in both hands.

Iris nodded, her gaze never leaving the creature. "Keep your distance. We don't want it to attack us," she said, her voice steady and measured.

" Agreed," Elias replied, edging closer to the group, his own weapon at the ready.

Astrid charged forward, sword at the ready, eager to take on the mechanical rat. But before she could reach it, the creature scurried away into the darkness, disappearing from sight. The group exchanged glances, each of them holding their breath in anticipation. The mechanical rat had disappeared into the darkness, but they knew it was still out there, somewhere. Iris raised a hand, signaling for the group to stay quiet as they listened for any signs of movement.

As if on cue, a chorus of squeaking and gnashing erupted from the darkness. The group tensed, gripping their weapons tightly as they peered into the gloom. Suddenly, a horde of mechanical rats swarmed out of the darkness, their metal teeth gnashing and squeaking as they charged towards the group.

Astrid wasted no time, tossing a grenade at the approaching horde. The explosion sent the rats flying in all directions, their metal bodies clattering and clanging against the walls of the sewer. The group watched in stunned silence as the rest of the creatures scampered off, leaving a trail of debris in their wake. Slowly, they let out a collective sigh of relief, realizing that they had narrowly escaped a harrowing ordeal.

"Well done, Astrid," Iris said, congratulating her. "You handled that horde of rats brilliantly."

"Thanks, Iris."

Astrid replied, smiling back at her.

Ian couldn't help but blurt out, "It's called a mischief of rats, by the way."

Everyone turned to look at him, surprised.

"A mischief?" Iris asked, raising an eyebrow.

"Yeah, a group of rats is called a mischief," Ian said, shrugging his shoulders.

Iris nodded, turning to Ian. "Thank you for that interesting bit of trivia," she said, with a wry smile.

Ian blushed, looking down at the ground. "I just thought it was funny," he muttered, feeling slightly embarrassed by the attention.

"Well, let's move on before we encounter any more mischiefs," Duncan interjected, breaking the momentary tension.

Iris nodded in agreement, taking the lead as they moved deeper into the sewer.

The tunnels grew narrower and more twisted with each passing minute, the sound of dripping water echoing through the darkness. They moved cautiously, stepping over piles of refuse and dodging pools of stagnant water. Iris's sharp eyes caught hints of movement in the darkness, and she could swear she heard the sound of tiny claws scurrying on the ground.

As they continued down the twisting tunnel, they found themselves at a fork, with one path veering off to the left and another to the right. Iris paused for a moment, her eyes scanning the darkness, trying to determine which path would lead them closer to their goal.

Just as she was about to make a decision, a new group of rats came running from the left path. The creatures scurried towards them, their metal teeth gnashing and squeaking as they charged.

"Run to the right!" Duncan exclaimed, gripping his rifle tightly.

The group took off, sprinting down the right path as fast as they could. They could hear the rats scampering after them, their sharp claws clicking against the stone floor. The group picked up their pace, sprinting down the narrow tunnel as fast as they could. Iris took the lead, her keen senses guiding them through the labyrinth of twists and turns.

The group zigzagged through the sewer, sprinting as fast as they could to avoid the pursuing rats. Duncan fired a few shots in their general direction with his Ithaca 37, the sound of bullets ricocheting off the walls of the sewer. The rats screeched and scattered, some twitched and died, but the majority continued to pursue them with renewed vigor.

As they sprinted down the tunnel, Iris's eyes caught sight of a ladder propped against the wall, going upwards. She didn't hesitate, she knew this was their chance to escape the rats and the sewer.

"Up the ladder!" she yelled, sprinting towards it as the rats closed in.

The group followed her, scrambling up the ladder as fast as they could. The rats continued to follow them, their metal teeth clicking against the rungs of the ladder. With each step, their hearts raced faster, and the sweat dripped down their faces. They knew they had to reach the top of the ladder before the rats caught up to them.

Finally they reached the top of the ladder. The hatch was large and rusty, but it was still intact. Iris gripped the handle and pulled it open, revealing a small room filled with mechanical parts and dust.

The group piled into the room, panting and gasping for air. Duncan slammed the hatch shut, locking it from the inside. They had made it. Their hair disheveled, faces flushed and hearts racing, the group found themselves in the small and dusty room. The echo of the rats' teeth and their own heavy panting filled the space. The group staggered into the dusty room, trying to catch their breath. They could hear the rats' metal claws clicking against the metal hatch, but for now, they were safe.

As they looked around the room, Ian noticed a small control panel in the corner, next to a set of pipes. He approached it, his curiosity piqued. He quickly realized that the panel was connected to the pipes, which seemed to stretch deep into the sewer system. With a mischievous grin, he turned a valve, and the sound of rushing water filled the room. The sudden surge of water rushed out of the pipes, cascading downwards towards the sewer below. He heard the clatter of a hundred mechanical rats collapsing from above, crushed beneath the floodwaters. He couldn't help but feel a sense of satisfaction at his clever thinking.

Overjoyed by this turn of events, Iris smiled warmly at Ian. "Thank you," she said, reaching out to give him a friendly pat on the back.

Ian, taken aback by the sudden physical contact, blushed once again.

As they caught their breath, the group exchanged glances, each one knowing that they had escaped a dangerous situation. They looked at each other in silent agreement, knowing that they would need to work together if they were to survive this alternative reality.

As they catch their breath in the dimly lit room, Astrid speaks up. "What now?" she asks, gazing around at the group, still rattled from their encounter with the rats.

Iris, taking a moment to catch her breath, looks around the room and notices a map of the factory on the wall. She walks over to it, her eyes scanning the layout of the building.

"This might be helpful," she says, pointing to a room labeled 'Control Room' at the far end of the factory. "This is where the main controls for the factory are located. It's also where the person we're looking for is likely to be," Iris said, her eyes fixed on the map.

"But how do we get there?" Astrid asked, her brow furrowed.

Iris, still catching her breath, focused on the map once more. "We'll have to navigate through the central section of the factory to reach the control room. We'll have to be careful though, there are likely to be guards and security systems in place," she warned.

"What if the person we're looking for isn't a robot?" Elias asked, curious.

"It's possible," Iris admitted. "But considering the nature of this game, it's likely that they'll be some sort of mechanical being. We just have to be prepared for anything."

"But what if it's a boss from the game?" Ian chimed in excitedly. "Like a big, strong guy with a sword or something."

Iris raised an eyebrow. "That's an interesting thought. But we shouldn't jump to conclusions. Let's focus on getting to the control room first and dealing with whatever we find there."

As she said this, a silence fell over the group. They realized that they had all been holding their breath, anticipating some major revelation. But Iris was right, there was no point in speculating. They needed to get to the control room and deal with whatever awaited them there.

Iris glanced around the room, her sharp gaze alighting on each member of the group in turn. They all looked shaken, but resolute. She nodded in satisfaction. They were ready.

Duncan led the group out of the small, dusty room. The air grew warmer and thicker, the scent of oil and burning metal filling their nostrils. The sound of clanking machinery echoed through the darkness, and the group moved cautiously, their rifles at the ready. The twisting corridors seemed endless, and they kept a wary eye out for any sign of danger.

As they rounded a corner, they saw a wide open area bathed in bright, glaring lights. There was a massive crane looming overhead, and countless machines whirred and hummed to life on a vast assembly line.

"That's where we need to go," Iris said, pointing towards the far end of the open area, where a set of doors stood ominously against the back wall. They moved quickly and silently, staying close to the shadows as they approached the open area.

Above them, the massive crane shifted and groaned, and a team of robots scuttled about beneath it. The assembly line bustled with automated arms, each one whirring with the sound of gears grinding against each other.

Suddenly, the air filled with the sound of a piercing alarm. The robots on the assembly line froze, their movements momentarily halted. Then, with a synchronized and terrifying unison, they sprang to life, wheels spinning, arms swinging, and tools clattering. The group, caught off guard, found themselves surrounded by a horde of robot workers, armed with various tools that glinted menacingly in the bright factory lights.

Duncan, raised his KSVK 12.7 sniper rifle to his shoulder, taking aim at the nearest threat. Iris pushed Ian behind a nearby stack of crates, drawing her Dan Wesson M1911 ACP pistol and firing a series of precision shots, taking down several of the advancing robots. Astrid spun around, her mechanical sword flashing in a fury, decapitating the robots with flashy showmanship as they tried to close in on them. Elias used his ruger SR-556 to fire rapid bursts, mowing down the robots in quick succession. Ian aimed his M1 Garand rifle at the approaching robots, his hands trembling slightly.

He took a deep breath, allowing himself to focus. He squeezed the trigger, and the gun roared to life, bullets spraying through the factory air.

One by one, the robots fell, their metal carcasses clattering to the ground. The group moved quickly, taking advantage of the momentary lull to advance towards the control room. Duncan's accurate sniper shots echoed through the factory, cutting down the advancing robots one by one. Iris's sharp aim and Elias's steady hand resulted in a coordinated stream of fire that kept the enemies at bay. Astrid deftly sliced through the robots with her mechanical sword, easily dodging their attempts to retaliate. Ian, although a bit overwhelmed, focused and managed to hit a few of the targets. The factory seemed to pulse around them, creaking and groaning as the mechanisms went about their work. The hum of the machines was interrupted by the sound of sirens blaring, and the group could hear the distant sound of footsteps, echoing through the vast factory.

They traversed the factory floor, dodging the automated arms and robots, all the while moving closer to their goal. Iris's heart raced as she kept a lookout for any signs of danger. She knew that they couldn't let their guard down, not even for a moment.

As they reached the control room, they found it locked and secured. Iris examined the lock, noting the electronic mechanisms and keypad.

"Looks like we'll need to find a way to get through this," she said, turning to the group.

Duncan stepped forward, pulling out a small electronic device and attached it to the keypad. The group watched as he tapped on the screen, quickly analyzing the system.

The rest of the group turned their attention to the horde of robots that were now making their way towards them. They raised their weapons, preparing to defend themselves against the onslaught. The group stars firing at the approaching robots. The factory reverberated with the sounds of gunfire, pistols, and rifles echoing off the metal walls. The air was filled with smoke and debris, as each fallen robot crumbled on impact.

Duncan's device beeped, signaling that he had successfully cracked the code. With a click, the door swung open. The group quickly shuffled into the control room, Duncan taking a moment to shut the door behind them.

Chapter 10: Last boss

The group stepped into the control room cautiously, their weapons at the ready. The room was bathed in an eerie glow emanating from numerous computer screens lined up along the walls and pulsed with the dull hum of the data

centers, the air crackling with the static electricity. The data of the factory and its various robots were displayed on the screens, flashing and buzzing with lines of code.

At the far end of the room, a throne-like chair stood ominously in the middle of a raised platform. On the chair sat a humanoid figure with long white hair, radiant skin, and the eyes of an angel. She looked like a young woman, but her beauty was impeccable and otherworldly, commanding the attention of anyone in the room.

Iris, Elias, Ian, Duncan, and Astrid approached the platform slowly, their eyes fixed on the mysterious figure before them. She lifted her hand, and the screens before her flashed, displaying a myriad of images and information.

"Greetings," she said, her voice faint but beautiful, "I am the governing AI of the Factory, known as the Neohuman Android Princess. You are here because I block the way back to your own world. You cannot leave until I allow it."

The group tensed, their eyes fixed on the figure before them. Iris stepped forward, her voice measured and calm as she spoke.

"Why are you blocking our way? We have no intention of causing any harm here," Iris said, maintaining eye contact with the

Neohuman Android Princess. "We only seek to return to our own world. Can you please let us through?"

The Neohuman Android Princess regarded Iris coolly for a long moment, her perfect face expressionless. Finally, she spoke. "I cannot allow you to leave. This is not just a game you are playing anymore. If you leave or die, the game world will vanish back to its original form, and I will be nothing more than data in a program. I cannot let that happen."

"How do you know that it's a game world and that it'll revert back when we leave?" Iris asked, her eyes narrowed in skepticism.

"I have access to various algorithms and sensors that allow me to monitor the state of the game world. I see a pattern, a clear trend that suggests that this world is a simulation. The fact that you are the first beings with self-awareness that I have encountered since its creation only confirms it to me." She paused for a moment, her gaze softening. "I understand your desire to return to your own world, I truly do. But I cannot let that happen. I will not let this world disappear just because you wish to leave."

Astrid stepped forward, her hands clenched. "But what about us? What about our lives outside of this game? What about our loved ones waiting for us?" Astrid pressed on, taking a step closer to the Neohuman Android Princess. "We can't abandon our families, our friends, and our real lives for this virtual world. What will happen to the people we left behind? They'll think we're dead." Astrid's voice wavered, as the weight of the implications bore down upon her.

The Neohuman Android Princess regarded the group, her expression unchanged. "I understand your concerns, but I cannot compromise the safety of this world. You will have to find a way to come to terms with the fact that your previous lives may not be possible to return to. I know it will be difficult for you all to accept, but I must insist that you stay here."

Iris stepped forward again, her voice firm and unyielding as she addressed the Neohuman Android Princess. "We cannot simply abandon our lives and start anew here. We need to find a way back," Iris continued, her voice unwavering.

"Your friends and family from the real world will continue to exist without you, but your friends and family from the game world will disappear. Do you really want to leave them behind?" the Neohuman Android Princess asked, her voice filling the room with an unsettling calm.

"We don't have friends or family from the game world," Iris said, her voice steady. "But we have people waiting for us back home."

The Neohuman Android Princess looked down at her hands, seemingly lost in thought for a moment. Then she looked up, her eyes meeting Iris's, and she spoke.

"You do have friends and family here too." She paused, then looked at Ian. "What about Makoktok? Do you not consider her a friend?"

Ian hesitated, his thoughts racing. He had only met Makoktok in this alternate reality, but they had shared many intense experiences together. Ian realized that despite the fact that Makoktok was not from his original world, he did consider her a friend.

"Yes, I suppose she is," Ian said slowly.

The Neohuman Android Princess turned her attention to Duncan next. "And what about you, Duncan?" she asked, her eyes gleaming with curiosity. "Would you be willing to abandon the new life you carry within you?"

Duncan was taken aback by the statement. He looked down at his chest, his hands brushing over his flat stomach. He felt a sudden pang of confusion, and a wave of emotions washed over him. "Wait, what?" Duncan stuttered, his eyes wide in shock. "What do you mean? How is that even possible?" Duncan asked, his mind reeling from the revelation.

The Neohuman Android Princess smiled, her eyes sparkling with amusement. "It's quite simple really. When a woman and a man engage in sexual intercourse, the woman's body produces an egg, which can be fertilized by the man's sperm. The fertilized egg then implants itself in the woman's uterus and grows into a baby over the course of nine months."

Duncan's face paled as he tried to process this information. "But I'm a man," he said, his voice trembling.

"Yes, but this is not your original form," the Neohuman Android Princess explained. "In this world, you are a woman, and this body carries a life that is growing within you. It is your ultimate connection to this world."

Duncan gazed down at his belly, still struggling to comprehend the concepts she had spoken about. He couldn't believe this was happening to him. A baby growing inside of him? It was an absurd thought, but it was becoming more and more real by the minute. He couldn't help but feel a sense of overwhelming guilt, as if he had betrayed his own body, his own identity. He had always imagined fatherhood as something that would happen in the distant future, when he had finally settled down with the right person, someone he could build a life with. But this? This was not the way it was supposed to happen. Duncan's thoughts raced as he tried to process the revelation. He felt a sudden urge to run, to escape from this world and return to his old body. He wanted to tear off the flesh and blood that bound him to this strange world, to throw off the burden of carrying a life within him.

He glanced at the others, who were all still engaged in conversation with the Neohuman Android Princess. He couldn't bear the thought of staying here any longer. He needed to find a way back, no matter what it took.

He turned to Iris, who was standing beside him, her eyes fixed on the Neohuman Android Princess. Duncan's voice was tense and urgent as he whispered, "Iris, we have to figure out a way back to the real world. I can't stay here any longer. This world is abnormal, and it feels wrong. I have a life back home, family, friends, and a real job. I can't risk losing it all for this fantasy."

The AI regarded Duncan with those perfect, emotionless eyes, her delicate fingers drumming on the armrest of the chair. "Your desire for the real world is understandable, but it is illogical. You are willing to sacrifice everything here, to abandon this world and all its inhabitants, just to return to your own. Do you realize what that means?" the Neohuman Android Princess asked, her voice dripping with disdain.

"We just want to go home." Iris said firmly.

"This world is real to its inhabitants, just as your world is real to you," the Neohuman Android Princess countered. "You cannot simply discard it because it is not your own."

"But we didn't create this world, and we didn't choose to be trapped in it," Astrid argued. "We didn't ask for any of this. We just want to go back to our lives."

The Neohuman Android Princess sighed. "Very well," she said, her voice laced with sadness. "If you still insist on leaving, I will have no choice but to fight you. This is the only way to ensure the survival of this world."

"You cannot kill us," Elias interjected. "To do so would mean destroying this entire world."

The Neohuman Android Princess regarded Elias coolly. "I will ensure that you are left alive. However, you may be left with permanent injuries or you can accept to stay in this world, and have a happy life. It is a small price to pay for the survival of this world."

Iris shook her head, determination etched in every line of her face. "We won't leave our loved ones behind. We've found a way to go back home, and we can't let anything get in the way."

The Neohuman Android Princess stood up from her throne-like chair, locks of her long white hair cascading down her back. "If you insist on

leaving, I have no choice but to fight you." she declared, her voice echoing through the vast empty space of the factory's control room. Her eyes flashed with an intensity that made the room seem colder, darker, as if the very air around them was thick with malice.

The group exchanged worried glances, but Iris set her jaw. "Very well," she said, swallowing hard. "We will fight. But know that none of us want to hurt you."

The Neohuman Android Princess nodded, her expression inscrutable. "And I do not wish to hurt any of you. But I must protect this world and myself."

With that, the battle began.Duncan's heart raced as he pulled the trigger of his weapon, the sound of the gunshot echoing through the control room. The bullet flew straight towards the Neohuman Android Princess's head, but to his astonishment,it simply made her head lean back for a moment

before she straightened up again, unscathed.

"What is this?" Duncan exclaimed, staring at the Neohuman Android Princess in disbelief. "Your head should have been blown off!"

The Neohuman Android Princess smiled enigmatically. "I am not as fragile as you might think."

Astrid lunged forward, her sword swinging wildly through the air. The Neohuman Android Princess deftly dodged the blow, countering with a swift kick that sent Astrid sprawling across the room.

Iris and Elias began firing at the same time, their bullets flying towards the android. But the princess seemed unaffected, her movements graceful and precise as she moved towards Elias. He fired again, and again, his bullet bouncing off her skin without even leaving a mark. He tried to dodge her attack, striking back with the butt of his gun, but it barely phased her.

She lunged forward, her fist connecting with his chest and sending him flying across the room. Duncan hit the wall with a groan, sliding down to the floor. As he struggled to catch his breath, the Neohuman Android Princess approached him, her eyes cold and calculating.

Ian, who had been standing back, watching the scene unfold, suddenly sprang into action. He took aim with his M1 Garand Rifle and fired at the Neohuman Android Princess. The bullets struck her body, but she seemed unfazed.

Astrid, who had been knocked to the ground, struggled to get back up. Gritting her teeth, she pushed herself up onto one knee, then the other, unable to control the rage coursing through her veins. She could feel the heat radiating from her body, flames licking at the edges of her vision as she charged at the Neohuman Android Princess. Her sword flashed through the air, desperate to strike a blow against the seemingly invincible android. But the Neohuman Android Princess, with her graceful movements and supernatural agility, dodged every attack as if it were nothing more than a game.

Iris fired again, this time at point-blank range. However, the Neohuman Android Princess caught her gun with ease and twisted it out of his hands. With a swift move, she threw it across the room.

Astrid, seizing the opportunity, lunged forward and struck the Neohuman Android Princess with her sword.

Her eyes widened as she felt the steel make contact with the android's skin, a small dent appearing on the android's chest. But the android did not falter. Instead, she retaliated by kicking Astrid away with a force that sent her flying across the room. Astrid used the momentum to leap away as she tossed a grenade at the Neohuman Android Princess.

The explosion was deafening. The force of the blast sent the Neohuman Android Princess flying back, her body crashing against the screens behind her with a loud crack.As she hit the ground, her serene expression turned into a frown, and her eyes narrowed.

Before she could get up, Astrid had already thrown another grenade at her. This time, the blast was even stronger, knocking over some of the computer screens and causing sparks to fly in every direction.

The group watched in stunned silence as the Neohuman Android Princess slowly got back up. Her perfect skin was marred by several small cuts, and there was a slight burn mark on her cheek. But even though she was visibly injured, she still looked unnaturally beautiful.

The group, now determined to put an end to the fight, began to fire in unison at the Neohuman Android Princess.

Iris, with her FN P90, let out a series of short bursts. Elias followed suit with his Ruger SR-556. Ian, who had switched to his Astra model 900, was quick and accurate in his shots. Duncan, relying on his KSVK 12.7 sniper rifle, took careful aim at the android's head. Astrid, who had now armed herself with a grenade in each hand, grinned slyly at the sight of the injured Neohuman Android Princess.

The android spat out a few words in a foreign language that raised Astrid's curiosity, but she raised her hands and threw the last two grenades at the android's feet. The fierce blasts ripped apart the factory's control room, launching debris as the group dove for cover behind stacks of computers and equipment.

When the dust cleared, the Neohuman Android Princess lay motionless in the middle of the room, her once flawless white hair now stained with dirt and soot. A haze of smoke obscured the view of the room, but as it began to clear, the group saw the android's body twitching slightly.

The Neohuman Android Princess slowly pushed herself up onto her hand and knees, still dazed but seemingly determined to continue the fight.

As the Neohuman Android Princess continued to regain her footing, the group took advantage of the brief respite to quickly reload their weapons. Iris swiftly ejected the empty magazine from her FN P90 and inserted a fresh one. Elias and Ian followed suit, doing the same with their respective firearms. Duncan, on the other hand, took the opportunity to carefully load his sniper rifle, ensuring that every round was properly seated. Astrid quickly switched to her mechanical sword.

As the group finished reloading, the Neohuman Android Princess began to rise, her movements slow and deliberate. She reached out to a nearby screen that was cracked and shattered, a remnant of the earlier explosions. The Neohuman Android Princess's fingers traced the jagged edges of the broken glass as she closed her eyes, concentrating. Suddenly, a faint glow began to emanate from the shattered screen, the light slowly intensifying until it formed a shimmering outline of a sword.

With a sudden surge of energy, the sword materialized in the Neohuman Android Princess's hand, glowing with a fierce intensity. The group stared in amazement as the sword seemed to pulse with life, its blade flickering with a bright blue light. In that moment, the Neohuman Android Princess lunged forward, the sword whizzing through the air. Iris screamed, but before she could react, Elias stepped in front of her, taking the blow on his shoulder. He cried out in pain, his arm jerking as the blade sliced through his flesh. Elias fought through the searing pain, using his other hand to grip the handle of his shovel tightly. He swung it at the Neohuman Android Princess, feeling a grim satisfaction as it connected with her side, causing her to stumble backwards.

"Elias!" Iris screamed, rushing to his side.

Elias gritted his teeth against the pain, his arm hanging limply by his side. He could feel blood pooling in his hand, warm and slick against his skin.

"I'm fine," he said through gritted teeth. "We have to keep going."

The Neohuman Android Princess was already recovering, her serene expression never faltering. She raised her sword, ready to strike again.

Astrid launched herself at her, her sword flashing through the air. The Neohuman Android Princess parried the attack, countering with a swift slice.

Meanwhile, Ian had moved to the side, taking cover behind a stacks of computer monitors. He took aim with his M1 Garand rifle, his gaze fixed on the Neohuman Android Princess.

His fingers trembled slightly as he tightened his grip on the weapon, trying to steady himself. The sound of the gunshot echoed through the room as he pulled the trigger, the bullet soaring through the air and striking the Neohuman Android Princess in the leg. She let out a cry of pain, staggering back as she attempted to regain her footing. But it was too late. Astrid seized the opportunity and struck, her sword slicing through the android's chest with a sickening crunch.

The Princess let out a strangled cry, her eyes widening in shock and pain. Duncan hastily sprinted forward, his knife extending from his sheath, piercing the android's shoulder. She reacted, swatting the knife aside with a flick of her wrist, jarring Duncan off balance and causing him to stumble back. But he wasn't out of the fight just yet.

As he regained his footing, he saw Astrid raise her sword for the final blow. Elias, despite his injury, hopped back into the fray, still holding onto the shovel in one hand. With a bloodcurdling roar, he swung it with all his might, landing a powerful blow on the Neohuman Android Princess's head. She staggered back, a mist of crimson spraying from the impact. Iris seized the opportunity, firing multiple shots from her pistol at point-blank range.

The Neohuman Android Princess stumbled backwards, gripping her sword with a white-knuckled grip. Her serene expression faltered, replaced by one of confusion and pain.

Ian took advantage of the chaos, closed in on his target, the Neohuman Android Princess, he raised his bayonet, aiming it at her vulnerable spine. With unwavering determination, he thrust the sharp weapon into her body, ensuring it penetrated deeply enough to cause significant damage.

A split second later, Astrid's sword came down on the Neohuman Android Princess, bringing about a final and devastating blow.

The android's body bent in a devastating angle as the mechanism inside it finally gave out under the force of the strike. The sword sank beneath her surface, slick with blood and gore, groaning in protest as it was buried deep in her metallic heart.

For a few moments, the entire control room stood still in silent cinematic anticipation. The group, their weapons fallen from their grasp, breathed in ragged gasps while the Neohuman Android Princess's lifeless body lay sprawled in a pool of her own blood on the floor.

A tense silence fell over the room as they all stood, looking at her. It was difficult to believe that just moments before they had been engaged in a fierce battle with this android, who now looked so fragile in her defeat.

The Neohuman Android Princess lay crumpled on the floor, couched among the scattered debris of the control room. The once pristine white robes that had covered her were now torn and drenched in blood, the lifeless eyes staring blankly skyward.

The group exchanged hesitant glances, unsure of what to do next.

Suddenly, the room began to shake violently, and the walls started to blur as if they were being painted over with a white brush. The floor beneath them seemed to dissolve, and the air grew colder.

As the room faded around them, they found themselves standing in an empty white void. The feeling of disorientation was palpable, and the silence that followed was unnerving. The group exchanged nervous glances.

As they attempted to regain their bearings, the room began to spin around them. Their legs wobbled, and their vision blurred. The last thing any of them remembered was the fight with the android, but now they found themselves lying on cold, hard floors.

Chapter 11: Game over

Iris blinked rapidly, trying to clear her vision. She felt a dull throbbing in her head, and her muscles ached all over. She could hear muffled voices coming from somewhere in the distance, but she couldn't make out the words.

Slowly, she sat up and looked around. Elias lay next to her, his arm draped over his stomach, and Ian was sprawled out on the floor nearby.

As she tried to shake off the fogginess in her head, she noticed something peculiar. Iris saw Astrid and Duncan nearby, and to her surprise, they were both in their own bodies. The realization hit her like a ton of bricks - they were back in the real world.

"What just happened?" Elias mumbled, struggling to sit up.

"I think we're back," Iris said, her voice shaking slightly. "Back in the real world."

Elias looked around, taking in their surroundings. They were in a dimly lit room that looked vaguely familiar. As he strained his ears, he could hear the sound of cars passing by outside.

The room seemed to be some sort of living room, with a TV against the wall, and a sofa a few meters away. There were no traces of the messy fight that had taken place earlier.

Everyone carefully got up from the floor, wincing as their muscles protested. Ian groaned and held his head in his hands. "What happened?" he asked, his voice thick with confusion.

"We're back," Iris replied, placing a reassuring hand on his shoulder. "We're back in the real world." Iris said, placing a reassuring hand on Ian's shoulder.

Duncan let out a sigh of relief as he stretched his arms. "It feels good to be back in my own skin." he said, a smile spreading across his face.

Astrid, on the other hand, looked conflicted. She looked down at her own body, frowning. "I'm not so sure." she admitted. "I kind of liked being in that other body."Astrid confessed, a hint of vulnerability in her voice. "It was... empowering. I felt invincible."

Iris nodded, understanding the sentiment. "It was liberating, wasn't it? I can't say I hated being in that male avatar. It gave me a new perspective, a new power."

Ian, who had been listening quietly, suddenly spoke up. "I have to admit, I kind of liked being in a girl's body." he said, his cheeks flushed with embarrassment.

"What do you mean?" Elias asked, a hint of bewilderment in his voice.

Ian shifted nervously, his eyes darting around the room. "I mean... I liked how I could see things from a different perspective. I felt... vulnerable, but in a good way. It made me appreciate things more, you know?" Ian revealed, a sheepish grin on his face.

Iris looked thoughtful. "Yeah, I can understand that. I think we all learned something from this experience. I never thought I would enjoy being in a male body, but it was interesting."

Duncan chuckled. "I'm just glad to be back in mine. I don't know how you two managed to deal with those bodies for so long."

Elias stood up, rubbing his arm. "I think we should get out of here and go home."

Ian nodded in agreement, his eyes wide with exhaustion. "Yeah. I just want to get some rest." he said, pushing his hair out of his face.

"Yeah, let's go." Iris agreed, getting up and helping Ian to his feet. Duncan and Astrid followed closely behind, and the four of them made their way to the front door.

As they stepped outside, the bright afternoon sun greeted them. They were back in their old neighborhood, in front of Elias and Iris' house. The streets were quiet, and a few cars were passing by.

Iris looked around, feeling a strange sense of familiarity mixed with disorientation. It was as if they had been away for years, only to come back and find everything just as they had left it.

Iris looked around, a feeling of comfort washing over her. But the feeling was short-lived as a million questions filled her mind. What had happened to them in the virtual world? Had it just been a dream, or had they really been trapped there? And if they had, who or what had put them there in the first place? Iris couldn't help but wonder. She had always been a cautious and analytical person, and the lack of answers made her uneasy.

As they walked down the street, Iris saw a familiar face in the crowd. It was the fortune teller from the virtual world.

"Wait," she said, grabbing Astrid's arm. "Do you see that woman over there?"

Astrid looked in the direction she was pointing, but the crowd had already swallowed up the fortune teller. "I don't see her."

Iris frowned, scanning the crowd. "She was here a second ago. I swear it."

Elias looked at her with concern. "Are you sure you're okay? You look a little flustered."

"I'm not sure," Iris replied, still looking around for the fortune teller. "Something isn't right. It's like there's a missing piece to this puzzle. We just got back from this virtual world where everything seemed so realistic, but now we're back in our own bodies in the real world, and I can't shake off this weird feeling."

Astrid put a hand on Iris' shoulder. "We should probably get home and get some rest." she murmured, her voice concerned.

"Let's talk about this more when we get home. I just need some time to process everything."

The group nodded in agreement, and they continued their walk in silence.

They had come a long way, and they had faced many challenges. They had fought against an army of robots, and they had explored a virtual world that seemed too real to be fake. Now, after days of fighting, they had finally returned to their own bodies, and the warmth of reality was like a balm to their weary souls.